THE CRYMAN

ISBN 978-1-64456-633-6 [Hardcover]
ISBN 978-1-64456-634-3 [Paperback]
ISBN 978-1-64456-635-0 [Mobi]
ISBN 978-1-64456-636-7 [ePub]

Library of Congress Control Number: 2023943096

INDIES UNITED PUBLISHING HOUSE, LLC
P.O. BOX 3071
QUINCY, IL 62305-3071
indiesunited.net

THE
CRYMAN

D. KRAUSS

INDIES UNITED PUBLISHING HOUSE, LLC

Chapter 1

"That's one small step for man..."

Aaron held his breath.

"...and one giant leap for mankind."

Aaron exhaled with sheer joy, sheer ecstasy, and some puzzlement. What's the difference between man and mankind?

Who cares! They're on the moon!

He leaped from the floor – in one surprisingly coordinated movement –and danced before the smoky images of Neil Armstrong's oddly canted leg (made so by the angle of the landing gear camera) feeling around the solid gray surface. "Oh, my God!" Aaron crowed. "We're on the moon! We're on the moon!

A simultaneous "Don't you blaspheme!" from Mom and "Get the HELL OUDDA DA WAY, boy!" from Dad followed by an immediate, "So what? It's just the moon!" from Kathy. Nothing from Darrell, who was, inexplicably, asleep. Little twerp.

"Just the moon?" Aaron gaped at Kathy's petulant little moué as he, wisely, danced the hell oudda Dad's way. "Just the moon?" expressed again as he danced out of the living room, through the kitchen, and out of the door, Dad's, "Boy! You get your butt back in here!" having no effect, no effect.

Because this was a night of pure magic. No, pure science. And triumph.

And fog. Steamy fog at that, here in the middle-of-nowhere, swamp-laden, pine-tree'd hotter-than-heck werewolf-haven, deep deep south Alabama.

The mist gathered at the usual spots around the house, camouflaging zombies and vampires and Frankensteins as they stole closer, eyes bright with hunger, but Aaron, invulnerable because science was ward and cloaked him like Dr. Strange's Robe of Levitation... well, that was magic, but the principle remained the same. The backyard pole light reflected off the fog into his eyes, ruining his night vision, but that didn't matter, either, because up there, all white and clean and wonderful...

...the moon.

Our moon. America's moon.

Aaron danced up to the telescope, the one Dad had bought from Sears and Roebuck for Aaron's birthday a year ago, surprise, because Dad thought it a toy and all toys were for babies. "Why don't you want a football or a basketball or somethin' like that?"

Because, Dad, if you really, really wanted to see the most unathletic kid in Alabama — heck, the country — at his most babyish, Dad, then just watch me try to dribble a basketball while running down Damascus Elementary School's warped floorboard court. That's how I earned the nickname, "Spaz."

But Aaron wasn't a spaz with the telescope.

Aaron centered the spotter scope dead in the middle of the moon, set the screws down, and took a preliminary glance through the lens. The blast of white light blew his eye apart and he blinked, stepping back to rub out the afterimages. Be nice to have a moon filter, or a more professional scope, but asking Dad for either was pointless. On this subject, he and Dad agreed — Aaron's telescope was a toy. But a useful one.

Aaron braced and went back to the lens. Gently, now, take your time. His eyes teared but he held steady and... there. There.

The moon. My moon.

Craters and rays and seas whirled, and at any other time, Aaron would be entranced, risking permanent blindness while trying to memorize details, but he wasn't looking for the usual stuff tonight. Oh no. He focused on the Sea of Tranquility and knew, just knew, if he looked hard enough, he'd see it.

The Lunar Command Module. The Eagle.

Aaron squinted, holding his breath. Had to be there, had to be. The only man-made item on the moon... well, okay, there was the Orbiter, but that should be on the other side, out of view, and some Soviet stuff, but he wasn't about to waste his time with Commie crap. So, concentrate.

The image swam and he blinked, and then his eyes swam, so he blinked again, and things wavered and blurred, but he stayed with it, and there. There! Clarity. He held his breath, staring at the deep gray surface, looking for a reflection, anything, even a flash from the orbiting Command Module...

"*AaaAAuh!*"

Gasping, Aaron shot straight up, knocking the scope off target. He stared hard at the fog-shrouded edge of the woods. What the heck was that?

Silence, and that made him even more nervous. This place, this barely livable swamp, was full of strange, degenerated creatures (like his 8th-grade class, giggle) that called and crowed and cackled in weird, unearthly pitches twenty-four hours a day, raising Aaron's neck hairs. But he'd never heard anything like THAT sound before. And worse, all the other calls and crows and cackles had stopped. Dead.

Intent, Aaron peered past the pole light.

Nothing. The fog swirled, occasionally revealing a patch of that weird Spanish moss hanging from the trees here and there. Aaron caught his breath because Spanish moss was alive. It was. On moonlit nights, it flowed off the trees and wound about the yard like a gray boa constrictor, looking for children to smother. How many times had he heard its brittle fingers scraping at the den window while he tried to sleep?

On moonlit nights...

The terror fell on him like an avalanche, freezing his breath, locking his legs to the ground. He was sure — *sure!* — that gray tendrils crept along the ground seeking to cocoon his body, then drag him into the woods and suspend him from a tree branch, and slowly drain him of fluids. A little whimper escaped him.

Snap!

Aaron should have collapsed in sheer fright, but terror held him rigid. Something walked along the edge of the woods behind the chicken coop! Barely able to breathe, he stared hard at the darkness.

A fox?

Had to be, and Aaron almost did fall, this time from sheer relief. Of course. It was looking for a chicken dinner. A somewhat clumsy fox at that, breaking branches here and there.

Hmm.

Foxes weren't generally so obvious. Was it rabid? Aaron chilled anew.

5

An odor wafted about him. Aaron sniffed, trying to identify it, and wrinkled his nose in disgust. Repellent, like old leather left wet in a closet for a couple of years: mold and age and dank, with an underlying tang of dried sweat and manure. Good Lord (sorry, Mom), what's this fox been doing – living in an abandoned sewer?

The smell expanded, filling Aaron's nostrils to the point of dizziness, as the creature approached... Oh no. Holding his nose, Aaron peered hard at the woods behind the coop, trying to spot it...

The night moved.

A giant black shadow crept along the trees, massive, dark upon dark, and dripping malevolence. Aaron's heart stopped. Paralyzed, helpless, in the thrall of the ogre or troll stalking him under the bright, exposing moon: a monster with the gaze of a basilisk, about to stride across the yard, remove Aaron's head, and suck out his innards through his newly exposed neck hole.

As if it heard his thoughts, the thing stopped on the edge of the woods, cocked its tree-shadowed head to one side, and smiled.

A trick of moonlight caught perfectly the red-encrusted, filed parasymphyseal spikes that substituted for teeth. Reminded him of a shark, but an evil, gloating, lustful one, the joy of murdering Aaron clear on its face. So frightened was he, Aaron couldn't even wet his pants. He was about to die, and rather horribly, here, in his own backyard, eaten by a nightmare while Neil Armstrong cavorted on the moon above—

"Boy!"

Dad's yell cut through the night, breaking the spell like a battle between two dark wizards. Aaron sagged as if cut from binding ropes and fell to his knees, immediately yanked to his feet by his shirt lapels. "Now just what in the HELL are you doing out here?" Dad, roaring in his face, another monster.

"I... ah!" Aaron was split between two tasks, keeping Dad from murdering him and trying to point at the monster in the woods so Dad could get his shotgun and murder it, instead. Or at least try to. Aaron wasn't sure if something so evil could be killed with mortal weapons.

"You WHAT?" Dad hauled him off his feet one-handed, straight into the air, further proof that Dad was the strongest man in the world. As if the disciplines he administered with the short Mexican bullwhip he'd bought during one family trip to El Paso weren't enough proof.

The rebellious part of Aaron was profoundly annoyed by this. A monster bore down on them and Dad was more concerned about some private violation of his ever-changing rules of decorum? Like, really, what's the problem here? It's a night of Magic and Science, and Aaron's in his own backyard bothering no one, participating in a world event in his own small way, and there's no school because it's summer and nothing really he had to do tomorrow, so what the hell is the problem?

Oh, and Dad, there's a monster bearing down on us.

"Dad!" Aaron managed the whole word, despite being choked to death, "Look!" and he managed a frantic hand point at where the monster was.

Was.

Gone. Just gone.

"What?" Dad, suspicious but still dangling Aaron, followed the point because he never ignored a warning. Must be those years he spent in France as a scout for Patton. But there was nothing there for Dad to see.

"A monster!" Aaron choked around Dad's vise hand, "There was a monster by the chicken coop." Too late, Aaron realized that, without supporting evidence, this wouldn't be well received.

It wasn't.

"A mon..." Dad paused just long enough to gather strength and, mini-seconds later, Aaron flew through the air and crashed into the side of the washhouse, catching the foot of the tripod on the way and spilling the telescope. He hoped that sound of breaking glass wasn't a lens.

"I'll monster you!" Dad roared, reached down, and, this time, flung Aaron towards the house. "Get your ass inside, boy!"

As he scrambled up the steps, Aaron was oddly grateful for Dad's rage. One monster had vanquished the other.

Chapter 2

"I saw a monster last night."

Aaron watched for Kathy's usual reaction, a mixture of scorn and intrigue that, depending on her mood, earned him a laugh right in the face or a raised eyebrow of further inquiry. But her expression remained neutral as she considered it. "Where?" she finally asked.

So, it is to be further inquiry, eh, Holmes? "There," he pointed towards the chicken coop. "In the woods."

The two of them stood in the back shade of the washhouse, which gave them a view of the tool shed, the chicken coop, and the edge of the very place where Aaron had seen the monster. It was already noon, and the sun was beating them in waves of Alabama hot, but, also, purifying the area of any lingering evil. Aaron felt safe. Having Kathy nearby made him safer.

This was the first chance he'd had to tell her about last night. Last night. He shuddered, whether from the memory of shark teeth or Dad's quasi-murderous strapping, he couldn't tell. A combination of both, he supposed. He'd huddled under the sheets of the fold-out couch for most of the night's remainder, sure the monster would come through the open window or Dad would come back to finish the job. Darrell snored away on the other side, as oblivious to the mortal danger as the little twerp was to most things.

Aaron had finally fallen asleep as the dark became gray, only to be rudely awakened by Dad's, "Get your ass up, boy!" and shoved out of the door to feed the chickens and find eggs. He'd weighed death-by-monster against death-by-Dad and concluded Dad was the more immediate danger, so he'd entered the chicken yard warily and made an egg search. There'd been none, and Dad blamed Aaron's late night telescoping for that. Aaron knew it was the monster's fault: what self-respecting hen would lay an egg when death slavered a mere ten feet away? Empty-handed, he detoured around the washhouse and gingerly reset the telescope on its tripod and, yep, the big lens was broken. So much for further moon scrutiny.

Kathy examined the direction of his point, a look of doubt creasing her face. Not that he could blame her; he was asking for more support than he, by rights, deserved. She'd already saved him from another strapping this morning, after he'd reported the telescope's damage, rolling her eyes and frowning at Dad as he railed at Aaron because stupid kids didn't know how to take care of or appreciate what Dad's hard-earned money bought – a conclusion Aaron found shockingly unfair because, after all, who had pushed him into the tripod, huh, Dad? – until, muttering, Dad had pushed away from the table and stalked off to get ready for work.

Aaron didn't understand her power over Dad, which was far greater than Mom's, who stood at the stove frowning at bacon and biscuits, pretending not to notice anything.

"Let's go see," Kathy commanded and launched off the washhouse wall, heading towards the woods. Surprised but pleased, Aaron fell into her shadow. She usually regarded him as a helpless uber-geek, but from time to time, she'd be up for one of his adventures. Which was cool.

Cool. Kathy was cool. Aaron wanted to be cool. Like the kids on Bandstand and the disc jockeys on WBAM (the Big Bam!) playing the Shondells, who were shooting down and turning around and come on, Moany! and Fifth Dimension (Florence Larue, I love you). But the concept evaded him, even when Kathy's boyfriend, Sawyer, illegally over at the house one night when Dad was gone, told Aaron to "Be cool."

Yeah, he meant for Aaron to keep his mouth shut, but Sawyer, guitar player, locator of the best swimming holes, possessor of a beat-up junker pickup truck (even though he still had a year before he could get a license), and lore of All Things Swamp, was the word's epitome. Aaron wanted to be Sawyer. Then he'd be cool.

But coolness was a combination of the right genes and capability, neither of which Aaron had. Good looks, as in both Kathy and Sawyer's cases, and social adroitness, which even Darrell displayed on occasion, had bypassed him. Coolness couldn't be faked either, something he'd discovered last spring when he'd worn a Nehru shirt and love beads to school. "Wot the hail ar yew s'posed ta be?" Gar Avis, king of the peanut-farmer kids, had grabbed Aaron's front and yanked him out of his seat – for the skinniest kid in America, Gar sure was strong – "Some kinda California queer?"

By lunch, the beads lay scattered up and down the hallway with at least two Doctor Pepper's poured over him. The shirt was now a gun-cleaning rag.

Nerd you are. Nerd you shall be.

"Where?" Kathy asked as they broke the plane of the woods.

"Right about where we're standing." Aaron looked nervously around. The woods provided enough cover for the monster to sneak up.

"Tell me what it looked like."

So Aaron did, watching with satisfaction as her eyes rounded and brows rose. She turned and peered deep into the woods, intent and frowning. "What's that?" She snapped up straight, her finger pointing.

Aaron followed her point, breath held, eyes wide, chills of fear breaking the heat. Oh my God! "Where? Where?" he gasped, squatting to get a better look through the brake, sure the monster was there, grinning at them.

"Here!" she roared in her best Boris Karloff as she grabbed his arm.

Aaron shrieked, a little girl shriek, and almost fell over. Kathy *did* fall over, laughing so hard she sat down, helpless, on the pine carpet. "You should see your face!" she wheezed between gales.

"That's not funny," Aaron said, but all that did was fuel more laughter until she rolled over, clutching her stomach. "Stop!" he insisted, the flush of embarrassment coursing through his body.

"Oh, you're sooo gullible!" she jumped up, pushed him, and took off like a rocket through the woods.

"Hey!" he called, recovering his balance, in pursuit, monster forgotten. Her course blasted through devil's claw and muscadine and great gobs of Spanish moss, hanging like curtains from the pines. All these were great monster ambush sites, but Aaron counted on the purifying power of the sun to keep evil at bay and raced after her. "Wait up!" he called and got a mocking laugh in response.

They sped across the back part of the property, dipping into the small valley that followed the swamp creek, and Aaron immediately knew where she was going. He veered onto a straighter but harder course, thorn bushes tearing at his shirt and kudzu vines tripping him, but still arrived at the same time she did at the Magic Sawdust Pile.

It was magic because it was inexplicable: a ten-foot-tall giant mass of crusted old sawdust, smack in the middle of a swamp clearing. There simply was no reason for it to be there; the creek too shallow and slow to power a mill, and no buildings of any kind nearby. But, there it was, spongy and soft and inviting.

"Geeeeeronimo!" Aaron launched off his last step and flew into the pile chest first, immediately buried by an avalanche of top dust. The pile shuddered as Kathy soared past him and landed about three feet up, immediately tumbling down the face. Laughing, they air-assaulted the Magic Pile, running up its still cohesive surface and flying over the other side, sweeping back up as soon as they regained balance. The air was cooler here, and they jumped and pushed each other and raced around and over the pile and it was all summer in a day and they were free and crazy and transported off this world, wrapped in sorcery.

They wore themselves out after a hundred or so more jumps and rested on top of the pile, the sawdust itching but not unpleasantly, an odd breeze drying their sweat, an even odder opening in the canopy giving them a white sky. "Hey, look!" Aaron said, pointing at a small moving dot. Airplane. Rare occurrence in these remote parts.

Kathy followed his point. "Wonder where it's going?"

"Pensacola," Aaron decided. "It's a Navy plane." The dot was featureless and could have been a Russian jet for all Aaron knew, but the only aircraft in the area were military ones hangered at Ft. Rucker north of them, and this one was heading south, so had to be.

"Paris," Kathy brushed her blonde-red hair out, "It's going to Paris."

Aaron snorted. "Paris isn't that way."

"Paris," she insisted, "and all the people on the plane live in castles and eat long bread and cakes and speak French to each other."

Aaron picked up the game. "And they wear funny Napoleon hats and yell "*Sacre Bleu*!" at the cars and each day they climb the Eiffel Tower."

"Then they'll go to London and curtsey to the queen," and they were off, the passengers performing Shakespeare plays before dukes, going to the North Pole to feed polar bears and then to Canada to find gold and Mounties and the little airplane dot was out of sight, heading towards its world adventures.

Kathy stared after it. "I wish I was going with them."

Aaron blinked at her, because the tone was different, not a child's wish, but a plaintive song for rescue. "Why?" Aaron felt a little hurt. Maybe she wanted rescuing from him.

Her expression was unreadable. "Because there's a better world out there."

"French people aren't better."

She sighed, "God, you can be such a nerd." She fumbled at the sawdust with nervous fingers. "You think this is a great place?" Her nod took in the swamp.

"Well, no. Oklahoma was better."

"Oklahoma." She was dismissive. "It wasn't better. We were just younger. We didn't know what was going on."

That stung, because Aaron loved Oklahoma, their little brick house on a little side street in Lawton, Dad flying helicopters on Ft. Sill, Aaron's best friend living right next door and there were X-Men comics and baseball games and riding bikes way past dark chasing bats and the school was only three blocks away and Gayla, Aaron's sort-of girlfriend... and then Dad got another job flying helicopters at Ft. Rucker, and here they were.

"So what was going on?" he asked.

Silence. Aaron looked at her. Her face closed, storm clouds on her brow. "Bad things," she whispered.

A twig snapped.

Their eyes widened simultaneously and both sat up, heads turning to the source. The swamp went silent; the wood thrushes ceased their battering of the undergrowth, the caws and twitterings and rustlings and the thousand and one other voices of the swamp ceased, like someone lifted the needle off a phonograph. From their sawdust perch, Aaron and Kathy quartered the surroundings, searching for what moved, what presence was so terrifying it shut down nature, and Aaron knew it was the monster. And they were both dead.

"What's that?" Kathy whipped a finger at shadows swaying in the undergrowth.

"The mon—!" Aaron began his shriek, feet gathering underneath to bolt from those shark teeth, but it was too late.

"*YAAAAAAAAA*!" Three bellows of attack as three forms burst from the scrub in a somewhat coordinated assault on the pile and it wasn't the monster. No, thank God, it was Gary and Stan and Cindy, and Aaron's "Monster!" scream died on his lips, thank God, or he would never hear the end of it, and now, suddenly, they had a real game of King of the Hill going.

Which Kathy won handily, since she was bigger than Gary and Cindy, and Stan was too much of a gentleman to push her and Aaron, well, he could never beat Kathy at anything. But who cared?

Ten minutes later, exhausted, laughing, brushing sawdust out of their hair, they flopped about the pile acquiring more sawdust. "You guys here for the weekend?" Aaron asked, digging a fist deep into the cool pile.

Gary snorted, "Weekend's over. It's Monday, doofus."

"You know what I mean." But that hurt. Gary was good at finding, and needling, Aaron's weaknesses.

Stan rescued him. "We're here until school starts," he said. Stan always rescued him. He was the oldest of the three, a dark-haired chisel-chinned athlete going into high school next year, open, calm, quite a contrast to yellow-haired and volatile Gary, who smoldered and challenged and looked at the world as a collective enemy.

"We're staying with Gramma," Cindy, dark-haired and still waters, offered in unnecessary explanation, but Aaron warmed anyway. So, extra playmates until at least the last part of August, when the Alabama schools opened their doors and the hot hallways, coated with melting shellac, sucked the sneakers right off his feet and hot, unmoving classroom air and frowning bun-haired old lady teachers sucked the living soul right out of his mouth. Gary, Stan, and Cindy lived far away, in Dothan, lower Alabama's only approximation of a city, and Aaron looked forward to their frequent visits to the grandparents, who lived across the road. Even Gary, when they weren't mad at each other.

Kathy said nothing, nodded coolly, and Aaron saw Stan's eyes lighten and warm as he looked at her. Forget it, Stan, you're no match for Sawyer. "Did you see the moon landing last night?" Aaron asked.

Stan grinned, "Yep. Had to sneak, though. Gramps and Gram go to bed with the cows," and he eye-rolled and Aaron laughed. Their grandparents' country customs were a constant source of amusement.

"Moon landing," Gary snorted, "What a waste. Bet they didn't even go. Bet it's fake."

"What?" Aaron was scandalized. "Are you crazy? They didn't fake it!"

"How do you know?"

And they were off, arguing as they always did, Gary more and more belligerent and Aaron more and more bewildered as Stan laughed and Kathy looked at them as if they were both idiots. Which Gary was.

"You just can't FAKE something like that!" Man, Gary was so stupid!

"Sure they can! They can fake anything! What, you in love with the astronauts or something?" and he made kissy noises at Aaron.

Aaron's jaw dropped because that was so silly! He gathered breath for a hot denial when Cindy quietly said, "I thought it was wonderful."

Gary snorted but said nothing. Aaron blinked at her, surprised that someone else, a girl at that, held his same view. Cindy stared back at him and Aaron saw a swirl in her eyes and something stirred within him...

"Hey!" a squeaky, annoying little voice from the edge of the clearing cut through them all.

Great. Darrell had found them.

The little asthmatic butterball twerp vibrated into the clearing, "You're gonna be in so much trouble!" he chortled at Aaron and Kathy, referencing the sawdust mess.

They looked at each other. "Pile pitch," Kathy said and, as one, the two of them leaped off the sawdust and tackled Darrell before he had a chance to escape, grabbing feet and hands and dead-man-walked the little jerk up to the edge. "One... two..." they began swinging him in rhythm as the other three scrambled, laughing, out of the way while Darrell screamed, "Stop! Stop!"

"...three!" and they let go at the top of the swing. Darrell sailed cockeyed into the pile because Aaron wasn't as strong as Kathy, instantly swallowed by sawdust and emerged seconds later, spluttering, "Do it again!"

So they did. And so did all the others, everyone changing positions from thrower to throwee, sometimes four assisting depending on the size of the victim, until they were all sawdust covered and choking and laughing and collapsed on the still mysteriously intact pile, baking in the now apexed sun.

"Waddya want to do now?" Gary finger-poked the pile.

"I'm thirsty," Darrell complained.

Aaron kicked at him half-heartedly but the little twerp was right. It was hot and their collective throats were covered in dust.

"Gramma made lemonade," Cindy said and they all looked at each other, mutual decision instantly reached, and were off, down the pile and winding along the little trail that followed the miasmic creek through the swamp and back to the road. They paired, Kathy and Stan leading, Darrell and Gary in an appropriate match-up right behind, squalling at something or other, and Cindy and he bringing up the rear.

"Did you see when Neil Armstrong stepped off the ladder?" Aaron looked at her, not sure if the magic was truly shared.

"Oh, yes!" her eyes shone, "And when they showed the footprint in the dust!"

There was a rapture like his own on her face and he stumbled over a root, so taken was he. "I know!" he gushed, "I ran right outside to look through the telescope at them!"

"You did?" she giggled, pleased, "What did you see?"

"I saw..." he hesitated, unsure if he could tell her, but she was so open, so in tune, "I saw a monster."

She stopped, brow furrowing, "On the moon?"

"No, no," he said hastily, "In the backyard. It was big, had big shark teeth."

Her mouth dropped open, her eyes widening in fright. "The Cryman!" she gasped.

D. KRAUSS

Chapter 3

"You seen the devil, that you have," Gramma Eckhart nodded in vicarious terror as she poured out the last of the lemonade into Aaron's glass. He stared at her, half-scared, half-doubtful.

Gary was all doubtful, "Yeah, right!" he snorted and held up two fingers behind his head like devil horns, "*Rrrowr!*" he growled at Darrell, who giggled but shrank back.

"Now don't you be mocking, Gary Talley!" Gramma Eckhart's Baptist frown stopped him cold. "You call him down on you. The Cryman only goes to trouble."

Gary rolled his eyes so hard they might explode. "Oh, not THIS story again!"

Yeah, this story again. Gramma Eckhart had warned them about the Cryman on the million or so occasions they'd headed to its alleged lair behind the bull pasture, but that was just to keep them out of there. Which had never worked. The silly name had only made them laugh, and with several dismissive waves of hands, they had skipped away from her fuming attempts to regale them with silly old farmer-housewife scary tales. Which had not scared them.

But now Aaron had seen it. Now, Aaron was scared. "What kind of trouble?" he asked.

"The kind a devil likes. It eats the trouble in your soul." Gramma Eckhart nodded solemnly and turned back to pour a fresh pitcher of lemonade.

Aaron looked across the red-checked plastic tablecloth, an Aunt Jemima cookie jar in the middle holding everything down, chintz sheers in the two windows limp in the no-breeze. Gary was still deviling a still-giggling Darrell; Stan was blinking out of the windows, probably wishing they were outside, but Cindy shared Aaron's wide-eyed concern while Kathy... well, she was downright fascinated. "How does it know the trouble?" she asked.

"Can smell it," Gramma Eckhart nodded as she refilled glasses. "Like rotten meat on the breeze. He spends all day and all night crying for it. You listen sometimes you can hear him. And when he smells it, he's so happy. He comes outta his hidey-hole over there in the

26

Gulches," a gesture of her head towards the back of the house, "which is why I tell you children not to go back there."

The Gulches. Almost to a man, they stared in the direction of the far ridgeline and subsequent landfall back through woods and bramble, where the little swamp creek had carved the red clay lands of southern Alabama into a series of deep switchbacks and gullies that ran for a couple of miles, before hitting the rise near the southern edge of Damascus. It was an eerie, mist-filled, Spanish-moss-laden dragon hole, a baffling series of high-walled red canyons. They'd all been down there on one pretext or another, but rarely went past the first turn of the leading gully. Lots of snakes and spiders back there.

And, allegedly, the Cryman's hole.

Gary wasn't buying it. "I thought you told us not to go 'cause we'd get lost."

"Well, you would, but with the Cryman outta his hole, you'd get eaten, too," she leaned over the pitcher and stared Gary in the face. "'specially a troubled soul like you."

Gary's eyes widened, the scorn changing to uncertainty as he searched Gramma's face. She timed it perfectly, keeping her expression grave for the requisite seconds until breaking into a wide grin. "Gotcha!"

"I knew it!" Gary yelped over the subsequent laughter, "I knew you were funnin' us!"

"Well, some of it is funnin'," Grandma,

chuckling, refilled glasses. "But there is sumpin' living back there, sumpin' not right. So y'all stay out," she emphasized that last with an emphatic shake of her head.

"Stay outta whare?" Grampaw Eckhart stomped in right at that moment, his peevish voice cutting into the middle of them like a rusty razor. He was a short, acerbic, brown-leathery man with little tolerance of children, the perfume of outdoor work and tobacco chew hanging on him.

"The Gulches," Grandma answered without missing a beat. "Especially now that the Cryman's out."

"The Cryman?" Grampaw raised an eyebrow, "Whicha you kids is causing trouble?"

"All of 'em," Grandma snorted good naturedly and turned instantly to fixing her husband's lunch.

"Well," Grampaw eyed them balefully, "maybe a good day's work will fix that. I got some baling to do, and who's gonna help me with the cows?"

They cleared the kitchen in seconds, like someone had yelled, "Fire!" Moments later, they were trooping down the dirt trail that led past the corrals, the gigantic black bull there contained behind barbed wire, eyeing them even more balefully than Grampaw did. Aaron watched it nervously. The bull was bad-tempered and murderous, and he did not see how a thin strand of wire could hold it back. "Let's go before your grandfather catches us," he urged the others, disguising his real fear, and they all broke into a run.

Moments later, they plopped down among the pines covering the top of the ridge. "That was close," Stan said. He meant Grampaw, of course, but Aaron expanded the sentiment to include death by charging bull.

The breeze moved here, always did, no matter how hot the summer day. Aaron savored it, nose rising involuntarily to pine scent and distant animals and the several feet of untouched humus beneath them. He was lemonade-sated, content, the eternal days of summer stretching into infinity until he woke one morning to find summer dead and the yellow bus blowing its horn at the bottom of the driveway, a prisoner of Damascus School once more. But not for much longer: this was his last year at Damascus; a 9th grader now, top o' the heap in a school so small it numbered barely 200 students all the way from 1st through 9th grades, only twelve kids in Aaron's class and one of them was Kathy. Next year he was off to the closest actual high school, located in the closest actual town of Enterprise, a place so hick it raised monuments to boll weevils and thought only of football and drag racing and George Wallace, but which collectively regarded the residents of Damascus as even more hick than them. He shuddered. Next year would be bad.

But so was this year.

Face it, Aaron, even in a class of twelve, you remain an outsider, nerd, strange, unconnected. His only real friend all this time was the preacher kid, Connor, who was even more spastic and weird than Aaron, creating a natural affinity between them that Aaron regretted daily. But there was nothing he could do about it; the unspoken hierarchy of school social class had relegated the two of them as outcasts, the butt of ridicule and jokes by the farmer boys and avoidance by the pretty girls.

All three of them.

Aaron chuckled at that. In a class of twelve, seven boys and five girls, there wasn't a lot of choosing. And of those five girls, two were eliminated because one was fat and unattractive, the other, his sister. The remaining three – Linda Akins, Becky Dons, and Marla Bonoir – had, over the past few grades, more than communicated their disregard for him and Connor while lavishing it on Gar and his Neanderthal buddies, Cory and Steven.

And here he was, in love with Linda Akins.

"Waddya wanna do now?" Gary interrupted the reverie.

Aaron sat up, a half-formed daydream about finding Linda alone in the coat closet dissipating – which was a good thing because he really had no idea what he should do in that situation – "Hill slide?" he offered.

Immediate group acquiescence, and they

all trooped down the slope and grabbed the cardboard sheets they kept stored against the side of a particularly twisted pine tree, and then trooped back. Generations of pine needles covered the slope all the way down to an unfortunately placed ditch that wound from the base of the ridge around the entire pasture. The needle carpet was as slick as any ski slope, and cardboard was the perfect vehicle to take advantage of that.

"Geronimo!" Aaron called as he leaped onto the sheet, immediately propelled down the hill at almost highway speeds, barely missing the pine trees on the way because a cardboard sheet was not steerable, and it was luck more than skill that prevented collision. At about five feet from the edge of the ditch, he rolled off, the sheet continuing on and over, smashing into the opposite lip at leg-breaking velocity, hence the need to abandon ship.

They went through a lot of cardboard sheets in the course of a summer.

"*Eee-HAAAA!*" dopplered past him as Gary whizzed by, waiting until the last possible second before rolling off to avoid sudden death. Three more cardboard tornados descended, their riders escaping, followed by the slower ride of Darrell's sheet, dragged down by his butterball figure. He didn't have to jump; his sheet ground to a halt well before the ditch lip.

Laughing, they retrieved their sheets and ran back up the hill and re-launched and it was now an afternoon of speed and daredeviltry as they all tried to squeeze in as many rides as the heat and dwindling day would allow. It ended, as did most of these things, with Darrell plowing headlong into a tree, his weight-reduced speed preventing mortal injury, but scratching him up all the same. They all stood around as Darrell shrieked and cried as if the injuries were, indeed, mortal. But Darrell had long ago proved himself a mere crybaby and they silently endured his wails until he finally realized he would not get any sympathy.

Tree Vaulting next. They spread out, calling when a candidate pine was located, then all rushing to the spot and helping to pull the young and very tall, but still very flexible, tree to the ground. One of them grasped the top and the others let go, the tree throwing the rider like a catapult across the tree's arc. Several permanently bent trees in the area were testament to how popular this was.

Soon the heat and the ten thousand layers of pine sap coating their hands put an end to this and they rested under the bent shade of their latest victim.

"Man," Stan said, "could use some more of that lemonade."

"Yeah, it's hot," Aaron commented unnecessarily.

"Should we go back?" Cindy asked, shading her eyes and looking off towards the house.

"Nah," Gary tossed a pine needle like a spear, "I've got a better idea." He paused for dramatic effect. "Let's go find the Cryman."

Stunned silence, immediately broken by Aaron, "Are you crazy?"

"No, I'm not crazy," he threw a needle spear at Aaron. "Let's go find him."

"I'm not going!" Darrell, wide-eyed and already terrified, shook his head.

"You're not invited, twerp," Gary snarled at him and launched another needle spear which Aaron had to duck, "So, let's go."

Stan blinked at him. "Right now?"

"Yeah, why not?" and Gary rocked to his feet, dusting the remaining needles out of his hand and focusing on Aaron. "You coming?"

Aaron held up a stopping palm. "No way."

"What?" Gary sneered, "You scared?"

This, of course, was the ultimate kid put-down — to accuse another of fear. It was like kryptonite to Superman, or worse, a Professor X mind-control attack. Helpless before it, kids climbed unclimbable trees, walked flimsy boards laid between building roofs, or jumped into raging rivers because of it.

Or went looking for monsters.

Except, Aaron had a cross to ward this vampire. "Yep! I've SEEN that thing!"

"Yeah, sure you did," Gary said, "So, that's one chicken. How 'bout the rest of you?" And he looked around the group.

Aaron got hot. To be called a liar and a coward in one breath! Yeah, he was scared, but that's because he wasn't a liar; the Cryman was real. He jumped to his feet, ready for combat, when Stan broke the mood by saying, "I'll go."

Gary was probably more surprised than Butch since Stan was usually cautious, especially over actions that obviously led to their deaths. "You will?" Gary, suspicious, sought confirmation.

Stan nodded. "Yes. But not today. We need to plan this out."

"Plan?" Gary was incredulous, "That's stupid! Let's just go!" and he turned like he was already gone.

"No," Stan said. "It's too hot. We need supplies. Water, food." He paused. "Weapons." He let that sink in. "So, we'll go tomorrow morning."

"*Bockbockbock*!" Gary made chicken noises and did the chicken-wing dance, but it was mere face-saving. Even he saw the sense of it.

Which was why Stan ignored him and looked at Aaron. "You in?"

Aaron blinked. No, he wasn't. "See you in the morning," he said.

Chapter 4

"We'll need to get canteens," Kathy whispered. They were in her bedroom, sitting on her Princess canopy bed, which was a study in pink ruffles and colors. Bobby Sherman and David Cassidy posters graced the walls, and random stacks of *Tiger Beat* overflowed her nightstand. One wall shelf was crammed with her old Barbie gear, rarely touched anymore, another with Partridge Family and Monkees albums.

"Check," Aaron whispered back and added it to the list he'd started, right after the entry for "snacks." Twinkies, if they could sneak them out, but he'd settle for Mom-made peanut butter and jelly sandwiches. If he asked, she'd make them with little fuss because there's no harm in the kids going on a picnic. 'Course, if she knew they were on a monster hunt, she'd put the kibosh on the whole thing. Dad would shut it down on the principle that no kid should have fun until they had broken their backs in some category of hard labor for 12-15 hours first. Hence the need for discretion.

Aaron stared at his list and shook his head. This whole thing was taking on the complications of the Normandy invasion. First, they had to placate Darrell who, as soon as they got home, threatened immediate disclosure to Dad. Kathy and Aaron threatened immediate dismemberment if he did so, but that was an insufficient counter to a possible monster that Darrell didn't want to roust from its hiding place, much less face.

Aaron had, finally, promised access to a representative cross-section of his precious collection of Marvel comics: any *Two-Gun Kid*, but only those *X-Men* and *Fantastic Four* and *Sergeant Fury that were at least two years old*. That mollified the little jerk and Aaron had curated the collection and handed over the candidates; Darrell was in the den right now, gleefully leafing through them and probably tearing the pages while smearing them with remnants of chicken dinner. Aaron winced.

Selling out his comics for the chance to get eaten by a monster. How stupid was that?

Kathy's transistor radio, sitting next to

her bed, was tuned to WBAM. An old Four Tops song was playing, and Aaron hummed along with it. "Sugar Pie Honey Butt," he sang at the chorus.

She giggled. "Bunch, not butt!"

"I know," Aaron said and sang it anyway.

They were both giggling by the end of it. "Let's take that, too," he said, adding 'radio' to his list.

"You want the Cryman to hear us?"

Good point, but it would be great to have some music along. Zager and Evans, the Archies, the Supremes. Good stuff. "We'll turn it on when we're eating."

"Are we doing that before we go in the Gulch?"

Aaron considered. If they ate before, then they'd have energy to run. But they'd also be a tastier treat for the Cryman. "Before," he said. If they had the energy to outrun it, then they couldn't be a Cryman snack.

"Okay," she said, "So, the last thing is a weapon."

Took Aaron about a second. "I'll take Dad's Luger." The one Dad'd taken off a dead Kraut after the Battle of the Bulge.

She frowned at him. "You sure?"

"Yeah." He made another entry. "He won't even know I've got it." Aaron had already taken it into the woods several times without Dad knowing. Should be even easier tomorrow because Dad was working.

"So, are we good?"

"Think so," and he held up the list for her to read.

"Looks like it. Don't forget to add knapsacks." She tapped the paper.

"Well, yeah," he said, "That's so obvious I didn't have to add it."

"You better. You're such a dweeb, you'll forget them," and she laughed.

Aaron's face flamed. "I am not a dweeb!"

"You're the King of Dweebs. Or, maybe the Prince. Connor is the King."

"We're not dweebs!" Aaron shouted.

"Pipe down in there!" Dad yelled from somewhere up the hall.

That hushed them as they held respective breaths, waiting for Dad to storm the room and administer just punishment for disturbing Walter Cronkite or whatever stupid news show he was watching. When no giant steps pounded in their direction, they breathed again. "Dweeb," she whispered.

"Well, if I'm such a dweeb, why are you going, then?" he whispered heatedly.

She cocked her head, considering. "Because, it'll be fun."

Aaron looked at her. She was hot and cold these days; on any given morning, the little girl who lived in a pink room and loved the Monkees, by that evening she'd be scorning Susan Dey and playing her Stones albums. Donna Reed in the morning, Grace Slick in the afternoon. Play jacks or hopscotch and then sneak off with Sawyer, all in the same day. He wasn't sure who she was anymore. But he *was* sure that he was losing her.

And if she thought it was fun right now, there was a good chance she would change her mind and think it stupid by morning. "You sure it's not just kid stuff?" he asked.

"Of course it's kid stuff," she snorted, "but it's fun kid stuff."

Okay. All bases covered. Aaron relaxed.

Speaking of the Stones... the cowbell started and Mick Jagger sneered tinnily through the speaker, "I met a covered Barsoom queen in Memphis..." at least that's how Aaron deciphered the lyrics, thinking it was a John Carter of Mars reference. "DO DA DOO!" he immediately picked up the guitar.

"She tried to take me outside for a ride!" Kathy added her interpretation of the next line and before they knew it, both were bellowing, "HOOOOOOWOOOOOOWOWOWONKYTONK WOMEN!"

"Deedeedeedeedeedeedeeeee!" Aaron added the guitar part...

"Shut up in there!" Dad roared from his stupid news program and they were immediately silent but giggling, watching the door for the expected Dad attack. No creak of his easy chair descending, no stomp of big feet, no *whoosh* of the bullwhip taken off the wall.

Safe.

"You know what that song's about, right?" Kathy asked.

He snorted, "Of course!" but was uneasy.

It was one of those songs filled with winks and nudges, like "Hanky Panky" and "Louie Louie" and Aaron was not quite sure why. Sex, of course, but he wasn't all that sure what sex, exactly, was.

"Yeah?" Kathy, in character with the topic, leered at him. "What, then?"

Caught. Aaron knew he was bound to say the wrong thing. Yeah, sure, he knew the basics of sex, courtesy of an equally leering brief by drunk Dad one night about two years ago, but he did not have the nuanced understanding that, apparently, every other person in a 50-mile radius did, especially the peanut farmers at Damascus School, who chortled and sniggered and named and described acts Aaron either did not know or could not imagine. So, retreat, and give a safe answer. "Women in a honky tonk! *Sheesh!*"

She leaned closer, "Whores!" she breathed.

Aaron blinked. He knew that word — it was the label for any girl who would have sex with any boy under any circumstances, which was dirty and sordid and animal.

And exciting.

Aaron felt a deep stirring. He wanted to know some whores, like Kathy's friend Marla, the ice-blonde teaser in their class walking the hallway, arms linked with Gar Avis, his meaty, clay-red paw on the top of her butt, an act that sent quivers through Aaron's stomach as he watched. And here was Mick Jagger singing about that? How could the radio people allow it?

"Is not!" he scorned.

"Is!"

"Is not. It's about honky tonks."

"And what do you think honky tonks are?" She stared at him cross-eyed, disbelief on her face.

Aaron knew, despite his best efforts, that he had stepped right in it, and was about to reveal, once again, his naivety. "Bars?" he furrowed his brow.

She laughed, somewhat ridiculing, but gently, and Aaron was relieved because at least he was on the right track. "Yeah, there's bars in them, but they're whorehouses!"

"Whorehouses!" Butch exclaimed, incautiously.

And, unfortunately, too loudly.

"Boy!" Dad burst through the shuttered door with so much force that Aaron was sure it broke. "What the HELL are you talking about?"

The violence of the entry shocked Aaron into paralysis, even more so by Dad's raving, saliva-flecked, demon face hovering six inches from his own. Kathy had retreated across the bed to a far corner, hoping sheets and pillows provided safety, but they didn't. They never did.

Dad seized Aaron's collar in his vice-like demon grip and yanked him roofward. "I asked you a question!"

His throat closing, Aaron had seconds to answer before his neck snapped and Dad tore his heart out and ate it. But if he told the truth, fractured neck and eaten heart would be the mildest of the injuries inflicted; Dad would also pull Aaron's intestines out through his belly button and then burn his carcass on the front lawn as an example to others. "I..." he gasped.

"What?"

Dad's flaming eyes seared him as his fingers tightened, turning Aaron's collar into a hangman's noose. Milliseconds left to live, so do something! "More houses!" Aaron choked.

Dad blinked, the answer so baffling, it extinguished the flame. "What?" This time it was a real question, not a rhetorical one to justify dismemberment.

Aaron leaned back enough to relieve the pressure on his throat, "I was sayin'..." he thought furiously because this line of crap needed support. "...that we needed some more houses. You know, one for me, one for Kathy, one for Darrell."

Dad, thoroughly confused by this, released him and stood up, staring at Aaron like he'd lost his mind. "Boy? Are you crazy or something?"

Go with it. "Well, just thought it would be nice."

Dad blinked again, then storm-eyed Kathy, who nodded vigorously in confirmation. Dad looked back at Aaron, then, miraculously, started laughing.

Whew.

"Boy, I don't know where you come up with stuff like this," Dad was actually wiping his eyes with mirth. Good. Keep the hands occupied, "You must think I'm made of money or something. And you don't take good care o' this place, so how would you do with your own?"

I'd do great, Aaron thought, because I'd be away from you. But he was smart enough not to voice that. "Yeah, I guess," said in his best Uriah Heep.

Dad stood straight, the demon gone, shook his head at the burden of such a stupid son, and then stared full at Kathy. Something flickered in his eyes, a touch of the demon, and Aaron felt Kathy stiffen behind him.

Uh oh. Was Dad going after her now, some offensive blanket on the bed or one of the wall posters sufficiently out of alignment to justify punishment?

The moment froze and Aaron felt the beginnings of panic rise in him. If Dad came after her, then Aaron would have to admit fault, and end up the smoking pile of meat on the front yard, after all. But Dad only stared a moment longer, then wheeled. "Keep it down in here," he grumbled, and walked out.

Aaron held his breath to ensure this wasn't a trick, but the creak of Dad re-engaging his overstuffed chair in the living room signaled safety. "*Whew*!" He looked at Kathy, whose stricken face revealed how afraid she'd been. Why, Aaron didn't know; he'd been the

43

immediate target of dadwrath, not her. Although, in her defense, that focus was far-ranging.

She held her breath for longer than Aaron, her look more fearful, even after the chair squeak provided the all-clear. Aaron furrowed his brow. What's the problem?

A moment longer in fear mode, and she relaxed. She looked at him. "More houses?"

He shrugged. "Worked, didn't it?"

Chapter 5

Midnight. Had to be. Still pitch black outside, Darrell flopped all over Aaron, snoring and drooling the way he always did in a midnight-generated deep sleep. Aaron should gather his knees and push the little twerp off the other side of the fold-out couch and crash him to the floor, but then he'd start howling.

The last thing Aaron wanted was to call attention to himself.

Because something was moving around.

Aaron shouldn't know that: the attic fan squeaked at sound levels fairly close to incoming artillery as it pulled humid air through the window at hurricane speeds, providing some measure of relief from these godawful hot Alabama nights, the squeaks regular and actually soothing – he fell asleep to them. It took a startling and rather loud sound to break through that rhythm and wake him. Usually, that was Darrell running to the bathroom, an activity Aaron encouraged because he wasn't convinced of Darrell's continence. But Darrell was right here, slobbering all over him, so that wasn't it. No, something else was shuffling around loud enough to alert Aaron's night radar. What could it be?

The Cryman.

Aaron hastily pulled the sheet up to his nose, aware it was scant protection. He should get up, run over, and close the window, putting another layer of protection between him and the monster, but no. That would alert the Cryman, giving it the precise location of a tasty Aaron. Stay here. Maybe it'll go away.

Clunk.

Aaron jumped. That didn't come from outside; it was over by the bathroom.

The Cryman was inside the house!

Aaron, terrified, pulled the sheet hard against his lips, straining to make out the massive form of the Cryman looming out of the dark down the hall, its shark teeth bared, ready to tear Aaron's stomach out...

Wait. Massive form? How'd it get in?

Aaron blinked. The thing was too big to crawl through one of the open windows, not without tearing the screens. It couldn't even get through a door without breaking it down. Dad would have heard that and come out shooting, asking questions later – which was another good reason to stay in bed. Did it teleport? Aaron frowned. Gramma Eckhart never mentioned that, which was a rather glaring omission on her part. That meant it was a ghost, right? Aaron dismissed the thought. The Cryman was too solid, too present, to be spirit.

Shuffling foot sounds from down the hall now, and oh, okay – *whew!* – not some monster but another family member relieving themselves. Aaron concentrated, striving to identify the culprit, Mom or Dad or Kathy. If it was the first two, Aaron remained in peril. Adults, for some reason, regarded wakefulness as a felony.

Snick!

Relief flooded through him. Ah, it was Kathy; that was her door opening. "Hey!" he half-called out, careful not to wake Darrell. Or Dad.

Not careful enough. "Shut up, boy!" Dad hissed from the hallway, "Go back to sleep!"

Aaron buried himself as deep in the sheets as possible, the Cryman forgotten. Dad was a present danger which must be dealt with first, so feign sleep...

Wait a minute.

That wasn't the bathroom door. That had been Kathy's door.

Confused. Aaron strained his ears. Did she get up at the same time and run into Dad?

Aaron waited to hear them sort out who was going in first.

Dad. Hands down – but it was silent.

Aaron gathered breath to call out and ask what they were doing, but that constituted proof he had disobeyed Dad's order, which would prompt Dad to rush over, grab Aaron, drag him outside, chop off his arms and legs, and feed them to the Cryman – hey, waddya call a kid with no arms and legs?

First base!

A snort of laughter bubbled up his throat, which he hastily swallowed because it was further proof of his wakefulness, which not only meant amputation but dividing his remains into enough pieces he could also serve as second base. He stifled and listened.

Odd sounds. Creaks and rustlings, an occasional bump. But no yells, no slaps as Dad threw Kathy back into her bedroom and took over the toilet, no click of the bathroom light. No light at all, so Dad must be relying on his night sense for toilet aim.

Eww. Please don't miss.

Wait... Kathy's crying very quietly... evidence of the expected Dad attack, but, man, it must have been delivered with a feather touch. Rather uncharacteristic. Guess Dad didn't want Kathy's screams to wake up Mom and Darrell. Aaron being awake was crime enough. Should remedy that.

He squirmed into the sheets, causing the bed to *sproing* and he braced for the Dad dragon to roar down on him and punish the dual crimes of being awake and staying awake. But that didn't happen.

And then Kathy's doorknob turned again.

Huh? Kathy was going to the bathroom now? So, Dad had entered and used the bathroom and went back to bed without making a single sound, not even a toilet flush? Wow. He must have been an excellent scout.

Moments passed, and then Aaron heard the distinct sound of Dad's mattress sighing. He blinked. If he had identified his doorknobs and their timings correctly, Kathy should have run into Dad coming out of the bathroom, as she had run into him going in, but note, no sounds of such a meeting in evidence. What the heck? Had they silently passed bathroom possession to each other?

Aaron listened for a while but nothing else, not even Kathy returning to her bedroom. Could make neither heads nor tails of it. Oh well. At least it wasn't the Cryman. He rolled over and fell asleep.

Chapter 6

"Ready?"

No response, and Aaron stared at Kathy because, man, was she distracted. The two of them were leaning against the back of the washhouse again, the best place from which to launch a monster hunt. But if she didn't wake up, they weren't launching anything.

Long after Dad left for work, she'd shuffled into the kitchen, bleary and sulking and looking very much as though all she wanted to do was go straight back to bed. Alarmed, Aaron had sidled up to her and whispered, "We still going?" She'd nodded as Mom dropped some old toast on Kathy's plate and then disappeared into the living room for the morning news shows.

Ugh.

While Kathy ate, Aaron surreptitiously gathered supplies — a box of Twinkies filched from the pantry – ix-nay the PB&Js, since disturbing Mom right now may lead to a trip veto – Kathy's radio from the shelf next to her sheet-tossed bed and the canteens from the garage, filling them at the well tap.

Oh, and the Luger.

A quick dash into the bedroom and a shuffle through Dad's nightstand, easier than he thought because Mom was absorbed in the game shows that followed the news.

All set. That is, if Kathy will get with it.

"Ready?" he asked again.

She didn't even look at him. "Yeah," and pushed off, grabbing the Twinkies knapsack, leaving Aaron the heavier things. She moved like a zombie towards the creek trail, not even bothering to shield herself from the house. Aaron was sure they'd be caught, but nope, no Mom on the porch yelling hysterically, or, even more terrifying, Dad unexpectedly pulling into the driveway, jumping out of the truck, and raging after them.

Her carelessness was annoying. "Do you even want to go?" he asked, irritably.

She stopped, turned, and gazed at the house. "Oh, yes," then resumed her zombie stroll down the trail. Aaron shook his head and fell in behind.

It took longer than it should to reach the

road. A couple of times, Aaron had pulled ahead to urge her on but got no response, just the same plodding walk, so Aaron was fuming by the time they climbed the steep bank and reached the shoulder, sure that Gary and the others had started without them.

The sun cleared the ridge across the street and lit the world like a lava searchlight, stabbing his eyes with brightness and heat. He rubbed them back into shape and then peered in both directions. Vapor ghosts danced all over the road, the souls of run-over kids.

At least, that's what Kathy said they were, crying and begging for help. Aaron squinted, mentally cursing them. Get out of the way! Otherwise, he might step in front of some peanut farmer's speeding heap and end up a vapor ghost himself.

Maybe that's what they want.

That prompted an even more intense scrutiny. The road was clear all the way to Ochs' Store up there on the hill marking the way to Enterprise, and in the opposite direction, over the long stretch of falls and rises that ended at the Opp crossroads, but all of the miles danced in vapor. The ghosts were making strenuous efforts to trick him. Aaron wasn't falling for it, though, and checked again. Yes, there, about the fourth rise this side of the crossroads — a pickup truck. It was still far enough away to pose no threat and he said, "Let's go," and then sauntered across to the opposite shoulder. It was too hot to run.

Boy, was it! Aaron wiped at the sweat beads popping on his forehead and shaded his eyes at the ridge. Jeez, they'd all melt long before they reached the Cryman's lair. He slapped the canteen. "Good thing we brought these," he said to Kathy...

...who was not there.

Huh? He looked wildly right then left, but still no Kathy, and then whirled, fearful the vapor kids had grabbed her. But no, there she was, still across the road on the creek side. "C'mon!" he called and frantically waved her over.

Wake up!

She didn't move, just glanced at him and then back down the road, half-smiling. Aaron frowned. What, she didn't think she could outrun the truck? He looked but it was out of sight, below the second ridge back, which was still far enough away, although Aaron heard the roar of a missing muffler. "C'mon!" he yelled and waved again, "You can make it!"

She ignored him, still half-smiling, her eyes still down the road. Aaron tsked.

Oh, please, you can't beat that truck? Aaron could *crawl* back and forth before it reached them. Twice!

"Will you just cross?" he yelled, exasperated.

The resulting expression on her face was strange, dismissive. He steamed.

She's just gonna stand there being all safe and responsible and proper about crossing the street, huh?

Disgusted, he looked back down the road, waiting for the truck to pass and Miss Goody Goody Primpuss to come over without stubbing a toe or something. The truck popped over the last ridge just past the Eckhart's...

...and it all came clear.

Sawyer.

Jaw dropped, Aaron watched Sawyer's illegal duct-taped wonder-how-it's-still-running 400-year-old shockless rust-bucket Chevy, its brakes nothing more than metal on metal and tires so bald he could see through them, bounce and sway towards them at about 90 miles an hour, which was Sawyer's minimum speed. Fishtailing, Sawyer yanked over to the opposite lane and made a screeching halt between Aaron and Kathy. How he managed to avoid killing either – or both – of them, Aaron couldn't figure. Sawyer leaned out on the driver's side towards Kathy, only the back of his straw-colored DA haircut and sleeve-torn-out white T-shirt – the standard uniform of the American Redneck – visible. Kathy flounced around the front of the truck, the same strange look on her face, and Aaron looked nervously around to see if (a) other cars were coming and/or (b) Dad appeared out of the woods. Nope, and nope.

Kathy yanked the barely attached passenger door open and climbed in, Sawyer following her progress with approval. As she settled in, he leaned forward, his eyes blazing like sapphires, the corn-shock hair unruly in his eyes, a cigarette dangling from his lips, peering at the jaw-dropped Aaron. "Later, man," he said, then smiled and peeled out; well, as much as the tires allowed.

It was only after they had disappeared over the Ochs' Store hill that Aaron realized she had taken the Twinkies with her.

Chapter 7

"Took you long enough," Gary finished the sneer with a dismissive wave of the hand.

He, Stan, and Cindy lay sprawled under the shade of a catalpa tree covering the big gate of the bull's paddock. Aaron flopped down next to them. "Shut up," he said. He was too mad to put up with Gary.

"Where's Kathy?" Stan asked.

Aaron made his own dismissive wave. "She went with Sawyer."

Stan blinked, looking somewhat hurt. "Oh," was all he said. Stan knew Sawyer. Everyone did; the guy was just too cool not to be known by every kid within a thirty-mile radius.

Cindy sat up and looked at them all. "So I'm going to be the only girl?"

Gary was amused. "Looks that way," he almost sang it. "You gonna quit?"

"No." She crossed her arms, not happy.

"Maybe you should," Gary argued, "There's gonna be spiders and snakes and you won't be able to keep up."

Which was a lie; Cindy often outpaced them and had no more fear of snakes than Aaron did (which was 'some,' but not enough to keep him from running around the woods). She was completely intolerant of Gary in one of his moods, though. She glared, her unhappiness reaching nuclear levels, stood up, grabbed her bag, and flounced off.

Stan glowered at Gary. "Good move."

"More for us," Gary chuckled and grabbed Aaron's knapsack, which he'd discarded under the tree. "Let's see what you got." He looked inside and then frowned. "What, no food?"

"Kathy took it," Aaron groused as Gary pawed around.

"Well, you ain't gettin' any of ours... hey!" Gary's face brightened and he pulled out the Luger. "Cool!" He waved it around, feeling the heft. "Is it loaded?"

"Yeah, so be careful," Aaron said, wondering what he was going to do for food. Maybe he could shoot a squirrel with the Luger and cook it. But he didn't bring any matches. Dang. Maybe rub two sticks together?

"*Pew*! *Pew*!" Gary had leveled the Luger at the distant bull, which regarded them balefully. Aaron doubted the pistol could stop the bull from charging; if anything, it would give the creature greater impetus to drive straight through the fence, goring and stomping them all to death. Nervously, he looked at Gary, who was grinning.

"Put it back," Stan ordered and, after a few more *pews*! Gary did so. "Let's go before it gets any hotter." Still obviously disappointed, Stan rolled to his feet and grabbed his pack.

Good idea, Aaron thought, even though most of the fun was already gone from this expedition. No Kathy, no Cindy, and no food. Maybe he should go home, too. But, then Gary would start that *bock*! *bock*! *bock*! crap again and continue it throughout the rest of the summer, so why create an opening? Aaron stood, slung the knapsack onto his shoulder, the Luger slapping him painfully in the back, and lurched after Stan. They'd better find the Cryman, or this day was an entire waste.

The breezes had turned into hot exhaust by the time they wound their wary way past the bull, which eyed them with murderous intent until they got out of its range. They were sweating through their clothes at that point, and Aaron looked up at the merciless ball of fire, laughing at them from up high. If anything put a halt to this, it would be heat, not lack of food. He paused to take a big swig of water.

"Already?" Gary shook his head and

pushed past.

"Yeah, already!" Aaron mocked him. "It's hot out here!"

"Better save it," Stan said, taking a much smaller swig from his own canteen. "We've got a ways to go."

"And you might need all your strength to run away from the Cryman," Gary chortled and hupped the hill. Aaron snorted and took another big swig. He still had Kathy's canteen, so he wasn't going to run out of water anytime soon.

And the Luger would take care of the Cryman.

They crested the ridge and took a moment to get their bearings. The land plunged down the other side into thicket, gorse, and whole curtains of Spanish moss. If they weren't careful, they'd get lost in that, even though they'd been here before. Every night the woods shifted into some other configuration, so experience was of no help.

There was sort-of-a-trail through the growth to the gullies, but it was hard to spot because it looked exactly like the millions of other game trails running all over the place. Mistaking one of those for the gully trail could lead them straight into knee-deep swamp water and quicksand. They spent a few moments thrashing around the edge of the growth until Stan grunted and said, "Here," and led the way into the brush. It looked like any of the other ways in, but Stan exuded confidence, so, fine.

Almost immediately it turned dark, but not cooler. If anything, the scraggy limbs and overhead vines had reached up and pulled as much hot air down to root level as possible. Not even a hint of a breeze anymore and the place became a shady steam room. Following the trail was harder, not only because of the dark, but the sweat pouring into Aaron's eyes. Even Stan-the-budding-Eagle-Scout had to call a halt several times to catch his breath and cast about for the right direction.

Odd. They'd been to the Gulches before and, sure, it was tough going, but it never seemed to be this hard. Maybe the Cryman was impeding them somehow. Aaron looked about nervously, expecting to see some monstrous shape lurking behind a curtain of moss waving its arms and gibbering some incantation, but nothing. That didn't mean it wasn't happening; maybe the Cryman was invisible during the day and stood right in front of them casting a slow-down hex. A pretty good one because, by the time they stopped for lunch, they hadn't gone very far.

"This is taking too long," Aaron complained as he propped against a less poisonous-looking tree and finished off the first canteen. He eyed the second one but decided he should wait.

"Here," Stan said, handing up an egg and bacon sandwich, to Aaron's delight and gratitude.

"Thanks!" Aaron grabbed it and wolfed it

down in seconds. Must have been hungrier than he thought.

"Idiot," Gary said to his brother, "Now you only got one." He leaned over and snatched Kathy's canteen away from Aaron. "Here's your payment for the sandwich." He guzzled, spilling more than he drank. Aaron glowered at him but couldn't say anything. Seemed fair.

"Take it easy on that." Stan yanked the canteen out of Gary's hand, spilling even more. Gary turned red, threatening to turn this into a brawl before the heat and steam discouraged him enough to sit back down, smoldering. "It's my water now," Gary said, pointing at the canteen.

"It's *all* of our water," Stan said, "and if we're not careful, we're gonna run out before we reach the place." With that, he shouldered the canteen strap and tucked it behind his back.

Despite losing possession of the canteen, the unexpected food, watching Gary get his comeuppance made Aaron content. He picked up a pine needle and twisted it like a helicopter, "How long before we get there?"

Stan was working on his egg sandwich. "An hour," he said.

"Huh," Gary snorted around a Ding Dong he was relishing. "Maybe we should run."

It was way too hot to take that suggestion seriously, so Aaron kept twirling the helicopter pine needle while eyeing the Ding Dong. He wished Gary had the same charitable impulses as Stan because he'd really like one right now. Or a Twinkie. Thanks, Kathy.

Gary read his hungry gaze, smiled around the Ding Dong, and gulped it all down in one motion, smacking his lips and licking his fingers with relish. "Um, um, um," he said. "Too bad we only brought two of those."

Half a Ding Dong plopped into Aaron's lap, startling and pleasing him at the same time. Stan was finishing his half and regarding Gary with a challenging look that Gary chose not to take up. "Let's go," Stan said and jumped to his feet. Aaron crammed his half-Ding Dong into his mouth and slid up the tree, ready to go.

Snap!

They all froze, eyes rounding as they, to a man, slowly turned in the direction of the twig break. The murk and undergrowth limited vision, but the sudden bird-and-locust silence proved they weren't hearing things: something was walking around out there. Aaron peered hard, trying to make out shapes, but it was all a heat blur.

A thud, followed by the swishing of branches, then another silence, and the three of them exchanged panicked looks, even Gary, who had gone pale. They took unconscious steps towards each other, an instinctive grouping of the herd. Of course, all that did was make it easier for the Cryman to catch and eat them. Frantically, Aaron looked behind, picking as clear a line through the woods as possible. If he had to run, he didn't want to trip over anything.

Smash!

Something big was crashing through the trees, right for them! "*AAAH!*" Aaron shrieked and the three of them convulsively spun on their heels and launched into the woods...

"Hey! There you are!" Darrell crowed as he pushed his way through the underbrush.

As fast as they were fleeing, the three of them stopped, as if a rope simultaneously yanked them to a halt. All three turned and stared at the grinning, little sweat-covered butterball. "You jerk!" Aaron shouted, "You scared me to death!"

"I'll say," Gary said, "You screamed like a little girl."

"Did not!" Aaron, flabbergasted, turned on him. Darrell was the issue here, dammit!

"Yeah, you did!" Stan burst out, "You scared me more than Darrell did." And all of them, including Darrell, pointed at Aaron and laughed, jeering, and calling him a scaredy cat.

This called for a change of subject. "What are you doing here, anyway?" Aaron, mortified, hissed at Darrell.

Darrell crossed his arms. "I'm going, too," he said, stubbornly.

"What?" Aaron couldn't believe it. "Yesterday, you said you weren't!"

"Well," Darrell's full-on-stubborn face set, "today I am."

"You weren't invited," Gary pointed out.

"I'm going."

Stan resorted to logic, "It's a long way, Darrell, and it's hot. You'll get too tired."

"Because you're too fat," Gary added.

Aaron whirled on him. That was true, but it wasn't Gary's privilege to say so. Only Aaron or another close family member, such as Kathy, had that right, and family dynamics required he close ranks with the fat little butterball who was ruining this expedition. "He is not!" Aaron shouted, hotly.

"What?" Gary goggled at him, "You say that all the time!"

Another truth, also immaterial, but it made Aaron's sudden defense of Darrell a bit problematic. Making it even more so was Darrell's throwing his arms straight down his sides, hands curling into fists while leaning forward, face blood-red in fury, and bellowing, "I am NOT FAT!" He gathered breath. "I'm HUSKY!!" he downright screamed Mom's favorite excuse for her chunky little baby.

And it was delivered with such conviction it suspended all argument. "Okay, okay," Gary said, "but the moment you fall behind, fatty, we're leaving you!"

Darrell, mad about the insult but pleased he'd won the argument, shut his wailing. Aaron inwardly groaned, knowing full well that Darrell would fall behind, cry each time he caught a finger on a nettle, fall over every single stump, and make so much noise the Cryman would know they were coming long before they reached the first turn. They'd all get eaten. Even worse, the little glutton would drink all the water and eat all the food before they even made the Gulches.

As if reading his mind, Darrell reached into his Batman knapsack and pulled out... a box of Twinkies. Aaron gaped at it. "Where'd you get that?" he asked.

"Mom gave it to me," Darrell said as he, with practiced motion, tore the box open and extracted two, managing to unwrap and swallow both of them in the process.

"Mom knows about this?"

"Yep!" said around a cream-cake mouth, "She said we gotta be back before dark." He looked around. "Where's Kathy?"

"With Cindy. Back at the farm," and he gave Gary and Stan a warning look.

Stan rolled his eyes but said nothing. "Yeah. With Cindy," Gary said in a tone that someone a little older than Darrell would have immediately picked up, but Darrell was too busy getting fatter. Gary threw an amused thumb at Darrell, "At least he brought food."

Aaron reddened but said nothing. Gary would soon find out how willing Darrell was to share.

"Let's go," Stan said, shouldered his knapsack, and pushed on. With Darrell licking Twinkie remains off his fingers, they all fell in behind.

Chapter 8

The gullies began as a red clay cliff looming above the swamp like a blood-coated castle. That was mostly illusion; the ridge fell so precipitously here that it made a notch in the swamp floor, giving the clay walls a height not really earned. But that didn't make them any less foreboding. A small, black, barely passable cut in the high wall allowed entrance to the gullies proper. When the four of them cleared the ridge, they came to a silent, nervous stop overlooking the notch.

They weren't confronted with the unknown; all of them had been here lots of times before. Despite the difficult route, it was a fun place — at least the first chamber just past the cut was — a big clay room with sheer walls reaching a good ten feet and crowned with teetering pines threatening to tumble down on them at any second. But the floor was smooth, interrupted by an occasional clay hummock, the whole arrangement making an excellent fort or battlefield.

And if they were here to play soldier, they'd have been through the cut and spread out over the floor in seconds, claiming territory. But they were monster hunting, a real monster that lived somewhere down a long, black, spider-and-snake infested tunnel that began around the corner from the first chamber. They'd been down it part way, of course, egging and daring each other on until they'd encountered the inevitable spiderweb clump or coiled snake – usually a king or garter, but terrifying nevertheless – and retreated, shrieking. None of them, even Gary, had ever gone its entire length. None of them knew what was at the end.

But that was due to terrors they knew, spiders and snakes and the danger of getting lost, not a monster so improbable that none of them had taken Gramma Eckhart's story seriously. That was before Aaron had seen it, meaning it was no longer improbable.

He shifted uncomfortably. Walking right into a bear's den and poking it was downright suicidal. "I don't know about this," he muttered.

"*Bock, bock, bock,*" Gary said, but

without enthusiasm, just reflexive Gary; even he was questioning the wisdom of going farther. Darrell, round-eyed, looked at Aaron, the words "Let's go home," already on his lips, when Stan said, "We've come this far," and stepped purposefully towards the cut. In seconds, he had disappeared through it. Gary, never to be outdone, gave Aaron a significant look and followed.

"Great," Aaron said and stepped up, but Darrell didn't budge.

"I'm not going in there!" he declared.

"Then stay out here," Aaron paused. "Alone." By the time Aaron made the cut entrance, Darrell was so close he might as well have been stapled to his back. Aaron smiled as he cleared the uncomfortably close entrance.

The chamber was damp but cool, the clay walls setting the mood for a monster hunt. Even the sun cooperated and fell behind a cloud, casting the chamber in shadow. Stan and Gary stood right dead in the middle, next to each other, arms folded across their chests and staring at the far turn. Aaron, with Darrell practically riding piggyback, walked up next to them.

"I don't know about this," Stan said.

Ordinarily, Aaron would have taken great satisfaction in that, but the air of menace emanating from the turn neutralized any sense of validation. Prudence replaces bravado at times like this. They all stood in line, brows furrowed, regarding the next step with some trepidation, except for Darrell, who had detached himself from Aaron and hovered back at the cut, shaking.

Stan broke the spell with a long sigh, "Let's at least take a look." Which was reasonable, and the three of them looked at each other and nodded, squared shoulders, and stepped off, in almost military precision.

"I'm not going in there!" Darrell announced from behind.

"Good!" Gary said, over his shoulder, "You'd just get stuck in the tunnel, anyway, fatty."

Guy never lost an opportunity, did he?

Aaron turned in time to see Darrell turn beet red and open his mouth to shout something along the lines of not being that fat, which, of course, would let the Cryman know they were here, in time for dinner. "Hush!" Aaron held up a warning hand, which Darrell acknowledged. "Stay here and stand guard."

"But—" Darrell spluttered.

"You can get away faster from here," Aaron pointed out.

Darrell pointed at the cut behind him. "What if it comes in?"

The three of them exchanged glances. That was a contingency they hadn't considered. "Then I guess we're all dead," Gary chortled, but no one else laughed.

"Yell for us and we'll come save you," Stan said, but Darrell wasn't convinced.

Gary looked at Aaron. "Give fatty the

Luger," he ordered.

"What?" Aaron was incredulous. "*We're* going to need it!"

Darrell, round-eyed, stared at him. "You've got Dad's Luger?" He blinked once, then reared back, "I'm TELLING!" he yelled.

Great. "Why don't you just send up a flare?" Aaron hissed at him, convinced an irritated Cryman would tumble out of the turn at any second, just to shut them up more than anything. Or through the cut, for the same reason.

Darrell, though, was more focused on the violation than any immediate danger of being eaten. "I'm telling Dad!" he crowed. "You're going to be in so much trouble!" And he turned, triumphant, righteous, and stomped towards the cut.

"No, you're not!" Aaron took three giant steps, reached out and yanked Darrell's knapsack, and the little twerp stumbled back into him, squalling. Any hope they had of sneaking up on the monster unawares was now long gone. "Shut up!" Aaron, almost frantic, clamped a hand over Darrell's mouth. Butterball struggled, trying to bite him, and Aaron considered punching him in the head.

Gary was on the ground, convulsed with laughter. "Get him, Darrell!" he egged, not even calling him "Fatty!" to make it look like he was now in support. Aaron raged, "Shut up!" and continued his struggle.

"Give him the gun," Stan said.

Aaron and Darrell's scrum ceased as though someone had thrown a bucket of ice water on them. Aaron blinked. "What?"

"Give it to him," Stan ordered and, without waiting, grabbed it out of Aaron's pack.

"Hey!" Aaron protested, but he was off balance and the pistol was in Darrell's hand before he could do anything.

Darrell hefted it, pleased, smile broad, eyes shining.

"You stand guard," Stan ordered, giving Aaron a tacit nod of acknowledgment. "Shoot the Cryman if it comes in," — he pointed at the cut — "or if it comes out." His finger flipped to the turn. "Just don't shoot us by mistake."

"He doesn't know how to use that," Gary snorted.

Darrell eyed him coolly, then expertly charged the pistol and depressed it, just like Dad had showed them. "Do, too," he said.

Gary's eyebrows rose, impressed. "Waddya know. Just don't shoot yourself," he chuckled.

Darrell frowned at him but maintained position, just like Dad had taught: "Boy, you don't point that thing unless you're going to shoot it. I ever catch you playing around..." and the implied death threat was ferocious enough they maintained Dad's protocols, even out of his sight. Besides, it was a grown-up thing to do.

Stan gave Darrell a look of approval and then turned, squared his shoulders and stepped around the corner. Gary and Aaron looked at each other and followed. Aaron glanced back at Darrell, still in gun-depressed mode, his face now a bit paler. Then they were inside.

Which was the right word, because the turn was a true tunnel, the opening shrouded by Spanish moss, its clay walls closing over the top of them. It was dank and smelly with a film of water on the floor; surprising, given the heat. It had the air of a tomb. No light here. Immediately, Aaron wished he had brought a flashlight, but who knew it would be this dark? Then a light snapped on ahead of them. Stan, of course. Always prepared.

Stan played the beam down the length of the tunnel. "Jeez," he said, because the end of it disappeared in blackness.

Sure seemed a lot longer and darker than the previous times they'd been here. "I thought this was a way into the other gullies," Aaron said, nervously.

"It is," Stan replied, uncertainty in his voice. "At least, Grampaw said it is. Maybe there's another turn up ahead."

"When you girls are done wetting your panties," Gary snorted, "we can go see." And he pushed Stan, who clucked in annoyance, but lurched forward.

Aaron frowned but followed, sticking close to Gary's back. He didn't want to hear further accusations of panty-wetting.

The floor was a bit sticky, and Aaron had

layers of clay on his Keds in seconds. It was annoying, and he scuffed on the occasional rock to clean it off.

"Would you stop making all that noise?" Stan whispered back and Aaron became more circumspect.

They came to the first spiderweb clump right away, and here was the point they should back out and go home, honor satisfied, but Stan brushed at it with the flashlight until the way was clear, except for tendrils of Spanish moss inexplicably hanging from the ceiling. Didn't that stuff need a tree limb to hang from? Nervously, Aaron peered upwards, but the top was a bare reddish glow and he couldn't see what anchored the moss. Must be a root poking through. After carefully examining the moss for any clinging black widows, he hastened after Gary.

After what felt like several hours, they had only managed about thirty yards down the tunnel, with no more spiderwebs or any snake encounters, when Stan froze. "What's that?" he said, the beam of his flashlight pointed ahead.

"What?" Aaron and Gary wheezed simultaneously as they crowded around him to look. Stan's beam focused on a lump on the floor ahead. They all stared, trying to identify it. It looked like a rock, but a furry one. "I think it's a squirrel," Gary said, and he pushed past Stan, seizing the flashlight and stomping forward. Stan tsked annoyance, but followed and Aaron was right behind him, heart in his throat. Had to stay with the light. The only safety was in the light.

Not a squirrel. "A weasel," Gary said, pushing at the dead lump of fur with his sneaker toe. It rolled on its back, now more recognizable, its face twisted in fury and pain, teeth showing. Broken open in the middle, its insides clean and empty, like a snapped candy straw with the sugar sucked out.

"What did that?" Stan asked, in some awe.

What, indeed? Because the kill looked fresh.

Almost in answer, a horrible smell crept from the tunnel's far distance. "*Erk*!" Stan said, putting a palm across his nose. "*Phew*!" Gary shook his head, as if that would dissipate the odor.

Instantly numb, Aaron knew that smell: old wet leather, mold and age, dried sweat and the sharp tang of manure.

The Cryman.

"Uh!" he tried to speak, but terror had overcome him. Stan and Gary stopped their odor evasion and stared at him. All Aaron could do was point a trembling hand back down the tunnel, as the odor wafted stronger from that direction. Stan shone the light down there.

It was still black, the light unable to reach the end. The blackness malevolent, pulsing, alive. The light shook as Stan's terror grew, and that made the darkness dance in the beam. The odor came in waves, flooding the chamber, and the black grew, regarding them, wanting them... "*aaAAAUH! aaAAAUH! aaAAAUH!*"

Those calls bowled them over with the force of a dynamite blast and they fell, legs tangled. The odor flowed over them like a tidal wave, and the black at the end of the tunnel suddenly loomed, rushing at them. "*aaAAAUH! aaAAAUH! aaAAAUH!*"

"Run!" Stan screamed, disentangling and leaping to his feet, the shared terror imbuing all three of them with instant agility as they jumped up and hurled back to the opening, terror-born track stars able to leap boulders and crevices and reach top speeds, even with clay sucking at their feet.

Gary was ahead of them, fear making him the fleetest, with Stan right behind. Aaron was in the rear, closest to the onrushing Cryman. The odor intensified and the ground trembled as the monster pounded closer. Any second, it would have Aaron. "Faster!" he screamed at Stan, pushing him, and all three accelerated.

They hit the turn and burst through the Spanish moss into the weak sunlight, limbs flying as they made for the cut. Aaron did not dare look back because the odor still engulfed him and the earthquake feet of the Cryman were still shaking the ground.

Darrell, the Luger in his hand, stood halfway to the entrance, goggle-eyed and stunned at the sight of the three bigger boys running for their lives. "What?" he yelled, as they raced past him.

"Run!" Aaron screamed as he zipped by.

Darrell needed no encouragement. Crying with terror, he flew after the boys. All of them reached the cut simultaneously, doing a Three (er, Four) Stooges imitation as they jammed it.

"*AaAAAUH! AaAAAUH!*"

Amazing how fear will make you slippery, and they all fell through and scrambled to their feet, all of them now crying like Darrell, who upped his game by shrieking at the top of his lungs as they all gained purchase and dug into the notch, seeking higher ground. They cleared the incline in seconds and pounded up the ridge, desperate to escape the woods and the Cryman's clutches.

"Aa-a-a-a-a-r-o-o-o-o-on!" Darrel wailed in a spine-breaking frequency laced with panic and horror.

Aaron whirled. Darrell was halfway down the ridge, sprawled on the ground, flopping his arms and legs in an effort to regain his feet after tripping over something. His eyes bulged, almost exploding out of his face, and tears blew out of them, clutching the Luger, trying to use it to lever himself up. "Aa-a-a-r-o-o-n! Don't leave meeee!"

Aaron gasped, his legs shaking towards the ridge, desperate to escape, but he couldn't leave Darrell, just couldn't. Darrell's free hand implored him and he was crying and Aaron dropped his heels and slid back...

Something black and shapeless loomed in the trees right behind Darrell, a shadow where one shouldn't be, moving against the light, huge, powerful, bending pines out of its way and leaning over the struggling Darrell. Aaron froze, unable to breathe, unable to move.

Darrell blinked at Aaron, then turned around to see what had blocked the light. He stared into the faceless black mass standing over him. Darrell's lips moved, but only wet sounds emerged, "*Uma, uhm!*" was all Aaron heard. The shadow massed larger, if that was possible, bending at what should have been a waist...

And smiled.

All Aaron saw were the shark teeth, perfectly outlined, floating in the massive black shadow that should have been a head. A blood-red tongue, huge and flat like a cow's, flicked against the smiling teeth. " *aaAAAUH! aaAAAUH!*" it called, triumphant.

"Mo-o-o-o-o-o-m-e-e-e-e!"   Darrell screamed into the shark teeth, then brought the Luger up. Three rapid shots, right into the maw. The teeth hovered, unfazed, then dropped on him. There was a flurry of movement, a blurring, then the black dissipated.

No Cryman.

And no Darrell.

Chapter 9

"Right about here?" the Sheriff, lean and wiry and pop-eyed, dressed in khaki, pointed a chaw-stained finger at the ground. Aaron nodded his head miserably. Yes, right there. That's where the Cryman ate Darrell.

"You sure?" Dad, raging, standing next to the Sheriff, clasping and unclasping fingers seeking a neck to break – guess whose? – glared murder and dismemberment at Aaron. Probably wishing the Cryman had grabbed him instead. Aaron nodded again. He still couldn't speak.

Dad and the Sheriff exchanged glances and the Sheriff turned towards the six or seven deputies behind him, and the two guys behind *them* holding the leashes of several dogs. Bloodhounds, mostly, with a beagle or two thrown in.

"Cody, Younger," the Sheriff gestured at the two plaid-shirt-red-suspenders-straw-hat dog handlers, "turn 'em loose. The rest of you," he pointed at the various-sized khaki deputies — fat, short, skinny, and combinations of all three — "get to it." All of them, Sheriff included, looked at Butch like he was crazy. Except Dad; he looked at Butch like he wanted to bite his head off. Just needed shark teeth.

Mom's hand on his shoulder tightened as the deputies spread out and the dogs, now excited and romping among themselves, headed down the hill towards the Gulches. Aaron looked up at her. Stricken, was the best one-word summary of her expression, a summary of the despair and horror over her missing baby. That was better than the wholesale complete and utter disbelief he got from Dad, Sheriff Oakley, and just about everyone else he had gibbered to about the Cryman eating Darrell.

Stan and Gary had been no help because they were already halfway to Gramma's house when Darrell got eaten. Gramma was already on the phone by the time Aaron collapsed, crying, in her kitchen, shooing the ladies off the party line so she could make the call, but not before telling them something had attacked the boys in the woods.

"Panther!" one of the old ladies had

exclaimed.

"Bear!" said another.

"Get off!" Gramma shouted and dialed.

Still shaking, Aaron was holding a cup of Gramma's herbal tea as the Sheriff roared up the driveway.

"What did you say?" The Sheriff, incredulous, head cocked, big Stetson pushed back on his head, beads of sweat perfectly marking the sunburn line on his forehead where hat met scalp. "Did you say the Cryman?"

"Yes," Aaron answered shakily, spilling tea. Big black shadow. Big shark teeth. Three shots. No Darrell. End of story.

Sheriff Oakley had blinked at him and blinked at Gramma and interrogated Gary and Stan and pushed his hat back even farther and stared at them and shook his head and then said, "Show me."

They led the Sheriff back to the slope before the Gulches, Aaron certain the Cryman waited for them, but there was nothing. No blood. No viscera. Just some scuff marks made by Keds. Sheriff Oakley pushed his hat forward and pulled out his gigantic walkie-talkie and, after fussing with it, got someone named Mabel to answer and made requests and deputies showed up, then the dogs, then Mom. Then Dad.

No Kathy.

No Gary and Stan. Gramma had marched them back to the house, followed by a short, fat deputy who was near to dyin' from the heat and whom the Sheriff thought was more useful taking statements. Cindy was here, standing behind Mom with a similar stricken look on her face. Somehow, that made it worse. If she had gone with them, maybe she could have saved Darrell.

The dogs started howling down the ridge and the Sheriff and Dad turned and headed that way, followed by the deputies, all of them sliding on the clay and pine needles in their haste. Mom gasped and her hand tightened; Cindy's face turned paler because all of them knew what that meant: the dogs had found something.

"No," Mom whispered, her hand seizing like a talon.

"*Ow!*" Aaron wrenched away from her, the first actual sound he'd made since the Sheriff marched them all back here.

She stared at him, face white, mouth working. "Why?" she asked.

"Huh?" Aaron blinked at her. Why what, Mom? Why did the Cryman eat Darrell? It was in the nature of Crymen to feed on little boys, he supposed. Or did you mean why did the Cryman come out of its hole in the first place? He didn't really know but, according to Gramma, it was drawn to the sweet perfume of trouble.

"Why didn't you save your brother?"

It was a psychic blow, so powerful, it could have been Professor X stopping

82

Juggernaut, and Aaron's legs weakened. She might as well have slapped him. Or, more accurately, stoved his forehead in with a sledgehammer. He slipped to one knee, his lips working, "I... I..."

I couldn't Mom. The beast was smoke, a shadow, predator teeth floating over Darrell, red-tongued and gleeful. So gleeful, so happy to see fat, screaming, terrified Darrell, the trouble in fatty's soul like a sizzling barbecue. Shot it, Darrell did, but it wasn't even fazed.

So what do you think *I* could have done, Mom?

Aaron would have summarized all that, but all he could muster was another, "I..." and then fell silent. He stared at the ground, at Mom's shoes. House slippers. She hadn't even put on a pair of sneakers when the Sheriff came calling. The slippers stood there a moment, then walked off in the direction of the baying dogs and the shouting men. Aaron looked up. Cindy was staring at him, Mom's question planted on her face, then followed.

"It's not my fault," he whispered to the pines and the sky and the Angry Face of the Lord, Who pointed an Angry Finger right at Aaron's heart. "Coward!" boomed the Lord.

Aaron fell to both knees at that, the shame driving him down. "What could I have done?" he whispered to God, but the Angry Face was turned from him, the Angry Finger still pointing. Aaron looked up at it, overwhelmed by a surge of his own anger. "Why didn't You?" he whispered to the turned Face, then stood and followed the sound of barking dogs.

Everyone gathered at the notch. The dogs howled and whined and shied from the entrance. Couldn't blame 'em. Cody and Younger were cursing the dogs and trying to push them forward, but they were having none of it. Dad and the Sheriff stood right in the entrance, and they conferred with a couple of the deputies.

"Shut them dogs up," Sheriff Oakley growled, and Cody yanked on chains until they did. "Billie," the Sheriff pointed at a particularly skinny deputy, "You and me," and the Sheriff ducked through the cut, Billie on his heels.

Aaron was on the upslope, tensed, ready to run when the Cryman burst out with half the Sheriff still in his mouth. It'd get the dogs and the handlers and the rest of 'em, including Dad vibrating there, his jaw working, and Mom and Cindy, clinging to each other a little farther back. That should keep it satisfied until Aaron stopped running, somewhere near Enterprise.

But nothing happened. The time stretched, silent except for the occasional whimper of a dog. Dad turned at one point and stared at Aaron, murder promised in his look, but Aaron didn't care. When the Cryman came out, they were all going to die.

"They's coming!" a fat deputy stationed near the entrance suddenly announced and there they were, Sheriff and Billie. Sheriff

Oakley was holding something wrapped in a towel and Aaron's heart leaped. Probably Darrell's head. But the towel wasn't bloody, indeed, was too flat to be a head, unless the Cryman had eaten most of it.

The Sheriff walked over to Dad. "Recognize this?" he asked, a question that caused Mom to gasp, probably thinking the same thing Aaron did, that it was a body part, but no. The Sheriff opened the towel revealing something metallic and gleaming in his hand, unrecognizable. Blinking, Aaron stepped down until he could see it clearer. What the heck was that? The Sheriff turned it in the light: the Luger, or part of it, the lower part only.

Bitten in half.

Chapter 10

Hobo, the Sheriff had concluded. "We git 'em out here on occasion," he told Dad and Mom and all of them, after further searches of the gullies and back woods, all the way out to Damascus, found nothing more.

No, Sheriff. Cryman.

Aaron sat on a stump behind the washhouse, watching the dark gather in the woods. It was safer out here, Cryman or no. Mom was not given to beatings, like Dad, but her words were just as cutting as she explained in excruciating detail why this was all Aaron's fault. When Aaron pointed out that it was she who had sent Darrell to join the expedition after Aaron had successfully left him behind, she had slapped him hard and ran, screaming, to the bedroom. Where she remained, barricaded. And inconsolable.

Thank God Dad wasn't here for that, or Aaron would have ended up impaled on a tree branch or something.

Dad was still out with the Sheriff. If there was any mercy in God and heaven, then Dad would stay out. Just stay out in the woods forever, searching for Darrell, having vowed to never come home until his boy was found. Which meant Dad would have to find and cut open the Cryman, which seemed a dim prospect. More likely, it would be the reverse.

Please.

Aaron sobbed, knowing it was a traitorous and evil thought, but he saw no other way to avoid the upcoming beating. Despite Mom's exquisite and quite detailed explanation, he still could not fathom how Darrell getting eaten was his fault.

His.

Let's disregard the fact that both of them had traversed the same pasture and ridges on thousands of prior occasions without mishap – save a bruise or two – that on this particular occasion, they had been accompanied by Stan and Gary, and that this was, on any other occasion, an innocuous summer day activity. Because something that shouldn't exist — the Cryman — had popped out of the cave and eaten his brother was not an indictment of the activity, or proof of Aaron's fault.

Yet, somehow, it was.

"Not fair," he whispered to the ground.

No, it wasn't, but Aaron was trying to remember when anything was. Even Oklahoma, encased in a golden glow whenever Aaron thought about the place, had been filled with vast unfairness. For example, Mom would, right out of the blue and for no reason he could see, banish him to a bedroom or refuse to let him go outside and play, even though Darrell was standing right out there in the yard enjoying the privilege, or would not let him have any of the stove-warm chocolate chips or lick the batter spoon until Darrell had at them first. And Dad would beat him for the smallest of sins, like clearing his throat at the dinner table, and tease and ridicule him for being a sissy because Aaron couldn't catch a fly ball.

But all that paled in comparison to this. This was a level of unfairness far above anything Aaron had experienced before, like an atom bomb to a firecracker. He did not want the Cryman to exist. He did not put the Cryman on Darrell. He did not call the Cryman.

Who did?

Aaron blinked at that. Who called the Cryman out of his hole? According to Gramma Eckhart, trouble called it. Trouble was its dinner, a rotten smell on the breeze that brought it out of its hidey-hole, grinning and slobbering and red-tongued, hulking through the woods to stand on the edge of the house and stare, hungrily, at him. And eat Darrell.

Why Darrell? What kind of trouble was in fatty's soul that the Cryman found so delicious? Aaron shook his head. Darrell was a spoiled little jerk, annoying, irritating, but he'd always been that. Why would that bring the Cryman to their doorstep?

What changed?

Aaron furrowed his brow. Nothing, as far as Darrell was concerned. Nothing at all that Aaron could see. They'd been here four years already, and there was the same level of anger and unfairness and fear now as the day they moved in. Dad beat them as often. Mom glowered at them and said they offended the Lord as much as always. Aaron was still a nerd. Kathy...

Kathy.

Aaron stared into the woods. Nothing moved there, but he kept a wary eye because maybe he had found the Cryman's lure. Kathy was the one with trouble in her soul, at least, a lot more than when they first arrived.

She had, over the last four years, become someone else. More distant. More alien. Her eyes traveled over the older boys and she ran into the night with Sawyer and she scorned Aaron's comics and telescopes and books with true malice, not jokingly as she did before. An air of sordidness wafted about her now, with her miniskirts and orange stockings and her eyes always on the boys, and boys' eyes on her. Even Dad looked at her like one of those centerfolds in Dad's Playboy magazines stacked up in a little corner of the garage, which Aaron had easily found, puzzled whether they had been purposely left out, and through which he leafed and stared as much as the boys did at Kathy...

"What happened?"

Aaron came off the stump and straight up into the air. "*Ack!*" he shrieked, stumbling over an ankle and landing, unceremoniously, on his rear.

Kathy stood over him. Ordinarily, such an excellent scare would have her doubled over, but her face was stricken, disturbed. "What happened?" she asked again, fierce.

"The Cryman got Darrell," Aaron said, staring up at her.

Her face turned crimson with rage, "That's so... stupid!" She stamped a foot. "There's no such thing!"

"How would you know?" Aaron couldn't believe how calmly he answered her. Maybe he was sick to death of being called a liar. "You weren't there."

He might as well have stood up and backhanded her. Her mouth gaped, and she stepped back, incredulity blanking her eyes. A surge of anger swept through him. "You weren't there. You left us." He pointed an accusing finger. "It's your fault."

"Ain't your sister's fault," a voice behind her, from the shadow of the washhouse corner, reedy and lilted with all the tones of open fields and autumn doves and stacked peanut vines.

Sawyer stepped out and looked straight at Butch with the same, honest, evaluating gaze he had for everyone. "Ain't no one's fault."

Aaron, still in the grips of the anger and fear that made him incautious, "Yes, it is. Darrell would still be alive if she hadn't gone with you!" And Aaron stood up, belligerent, chest thrown out.

Which was the posture and attitude that usually resulted in him getting pants'd or tripped, confirmation that bravery on his part was wasted energy. But Sawyer didn't hit him or noogie him or anything, just shook his head. "Would'na dun nothin'. The Cryman, he go and do what moves him."

Aaron stared. "What do you know about it?"

"Plenty," Sawyer stepped around Kathy, taking a wary glance around to make sure no one else was there. Not popular with the adults in this household. "And I'm tellin' ya, ain't your sister's fault. Ain't yours, neither."

It was like balm on the whipped back, a sense of momentary relief before the cat-o-nine descended again. Aaron swayed with it and blinked gratitude at this interloper, this troublemaker, the one stealing his sister away. "What do we do?" he whispered.

Sawyer hunched and looked as if he was about to provide an answer when headlights illuminated the garage behind them. Sawyer was gone so fast across the yard and into the woods that Aaron wasn't sure if the guy had actually been there. Kathy turned, facing the driveway as Dad's truck roared up, her face clearly pale in the false light.

Dad came stomping out of the cab at a full run, straight for Aaron and Kathy, murder and rage twisting his always angry features into a death mask. "Where the HELL is he?"

Answered almost immediately when Sawyer's truck peeled rubber somewhere over on the road – a surprise to Butch, considering the condition of those tires – and screamed away, towards Elba. Dad whirled to the sound, but the house and woods blocked his view. He whirled back, glaring at Kathy. "Get. In. The. House!" he hissed at her. Kathy dropped her eyes and, wordlessly, marched towards the back door. Not even a backward glance.

"And as for you..." Dad's look was venomous. He undid his belt.

Aaron braced.

Chapter 11

It was amazing how much pain a person could endure without dying. Aaron lay as still as possible, not wanting to activate any of the welts, bruises, and cuts that covered his legs, butt, and lower back. Dad had been more thorough than usual, taking Butch past the point where his screams and crying would, eventually, win him respite. Maybe the destroyed Luger was a crime too far, one no amount of pleading would ease. Especially if the base offense was killing your brother.

Killing your brother.

Aaron sobbed under his breath, fearful that would stir Dad out of his bedroom for Phase 2. Gingerly, he twitched fingers on the mattress next to him, confirming the absence of Butterball. How he had long dreamed of this day; what he would now do to take this day back. There had been plenty of opportunities to do so, like the moment when Gary had *bock*, *bock*-ed him and Stan asked if he was in. Should have said no, confirming for all time his cowardice, inducing a lifetime of chicken calls and contempt from those two. But, in retrospect, that was a small price to pay to ensure Butterball still lived, still sleeping next to him, raggedly breathing.

Wait...

What's that?

Some stirring, off towards Dad's bedroom, some rustling sound, and terror gripped Aaron, paralyzing him. So, Phase 2 commences. But it was just Mom or Dad turning fitfully in the bed, and Aaron let out a relieved breath. Mom's quiet sobbing had ended some hours before, mostly due to Dad's snapping at her to shut up. No noise, no movement, nothing from Kathy's room.

Probably snuck out of the window to be with Sawyer.

Sawyer.

Aaron frowned. Guy said he knew plenty about the Cryman. Well, if that was the case, why did he let Darrell go traipsing off into the Gulches to get eaten?

Because Darrell wasn't supposed to go.

That was true. Darrell had been successfully evaded. If it had not been for

Mom's intervention – so whose fault was it, Mom? – he wouldn't have been there, which raises some alternative outcomes. When the Cryman came pouring out of the hole, Aaron was the last one in line and would be the one caught.

And eaten.

Darrell saved my life.

Another wave of gut-shrinking guilt washed over him. The Cryman was coming for someone and Aaron wasn't as fast as Gary and Stan, so Darrell being there was a lucky event for him. Very lucky. Right now, Aaron would be the one digested in the fiery pit of the Cryman's stomach, his insides sucked out of the shell of his body left in the middle of the tunnel, a hollowed-out former boy with a rictus grin for the searchers to find.

But they hadn't found hollowed-out Butterball in the middle of the tunnel next to the hollowed-out weasel, had they? Only the sheered-off Luger. Aaron supposed the Cryman spat out animal carcasses and metal weapons but relished the whole boy.

Slowly, Aaron turned his head and stared at the empty mattress next to him. "I'm sorry," he whispered to it.

"Aa-a-a-a-ron, save me!"

Aaron gasped, a sudden spasm running up and down his body. Had he just imagined that?

"Aaron, why didn't you save me?"

Aaron's blood froze, as did his breath.

No, he had not imagined that! It was coming through the open window, from outside!

"Aaron, please! Please, help me!"

A scream formed deep in his stomach, building and battering against his lungs, and he fought it down to a sputter, struggling against it. If he let the very urgent scream out, then the torn, ravaged, half-eaten thing that used to be Darrell would know he was awake and come through the window at him, chewing and gulping until Aaron, too, was hollowed out, the shell of him left bloody on the bed and grinning sightless into the air where Mom would find him the next morning and say, "Serves him right!" and toss him out with the garbage and Dad goes whistling off to work while Kathy marries Sawyer and everyone's happy.

Except Aaron. He's dinner.

"Aaron, why don't you help me?"

Oh, God, it was getting closer! In a frenzy, Aaron yanked the sheets over his head, sobs escaping as he did. Sheets had the power to drive off monsters. But maybe not the ghosts of betrayed brothers.

"Aaron, pleeeease!"

"Go away!" Aaron sobbed to the sheets.

"Aaaaaaron!" the tone changed from the whiny, wheezy Darrell-voice to something deep and massive. Huh? Aaron pulled the sheets down and looked at the window. Something stirred beyond it, way back in the yard somewhere. Slowly, he crawled out of the sheets, leaving them in a position where he could easily re-bury himself should he need their protection. Like a soldier sneaking into an enemy camp, he crawled over to the window and, carefully, peeked out.

Pitch black out there, only the darker shadow of the washhouse discernible. Must be heavy cloud cover. Aaron squinted, trying to make out detail. It was silent, as if the darkness was a giant blanket muffling all sound.

Snap!

Aaron ducked down, trembling, and listened to the sounds of something enormous moving around somewhere past the washhouse. Aaron raised his head and took another peek.

His timing was perfect. Just as his eyes cleared the sill, the clouds parted and the moon shone down. In the yard between the washhouse and the back shed was the Cryman. It smiled, shark teeth gleaming in moonlight, its eyes opened wide and red as it stared, gleefully, at the paralyzed Aaron. Slowly, it brought up its massive, muscular right arm, hair hanging down it in folds, and turned its sharky gaze to it.

The Cryman held something, a whitish lump of some kind. As Aaron tried to make it out, a perfect beam of moonlight fell.

Darrell's head.

As Aaron, horror-struck, watched, the Cryman reached over with his other hand and moved Darrell's lips. "Aa-a-a-a-ron!" It mimicked Darrell's voice perfectly through its shark teeth. "Don't le-e-e-e-a-ve me!"

Aaron's knees turned to water and he collapsed into a ball below the window. He lay there for the rest of the night, listening to Darrell's puppet-head plead for help.

Chapter 12

Numb. That was Aaron's best one-word description of his condition over the following days, which weren't really 'days', just light and dark as the sun rose and set and Aaron went through motions of chores and eating, silent in the stiff disapproval of Mom and Dad as they went through their own motions — Mom cooking and housework and Dad to work and back and brooding. Aaron never saw Kathy. She might as well have been eaten, too.

People came by: the sheriff, with progress reports; neighbors with casseroles; even the preacher from the weird little church Mom loved on the other side of Damascus that advertised itself as Methodist, but whose hollerin' and fire-and-brimstone proved otherwise. All of them, individually and respectively, took time to gaze at Aaron in disapproval and incredulity, his story of the Cryman having made the rounds, spread by the party-line biddies. But Aaron was too numb to react.

He was not sleeping. At night, the Cryman came back, his Darrell-head-puppet crying and pleading for rescue and Aaron terrified, until he became numb. He didn't even bother to hide anymore, just stood in the window and watched the nightly performance.

Be nice if the Cryman got some better material.

He should just go outside and be done with it. The Cryman's mockery couldn't be any worse than being the Cryman's dinner. At least it'd have another head to use for the nightly shows. Perform for Kathy. Or Mom.

Aaron stirred from his breakfast, some toast or something, and stared at Mom. She leaned on the sink, looking out of the window. Aaron followed her gaze.

Nope, no Cryman out there in the yard doing Darrell-head puppetry.

"Mom," he said, "Can I go to the store?"

It was, pretty much, the first words he had spoken to her since Darrell became the Cryman's toy. She did not move, did not acknowledge his existence. Which, if he thought about it, was par for the course before Darrell got eaten.

Aaron waited a decent amount of time and then shrugged and pushed back and went into the den and got some change out of his piggy bank and out through the kitchen door. Didn't bother putting his plate away; give Mom something to do. He grabbed his five-speed and pedaled to the end of the driveway, paused and looked across the road at the pasture, but nothing stalked the ridge. He pushed off and rode to the store.

Ochs' Store, to be precise, at the top of the hill. It was the only place within biking distance where he could spend his allowance. Otherwise, he had to wait for Mom's once-a-week commissary trips or, when school was in session, the noon lunch break when he'd race across the street with Connor and buy Hershey bars at Melvis' Store in Damascus and then race back to the classroom before Gar and his hoodlum gang robbed him. Compared with the commissary treasure trove or even Melvis', Ochs' wasn't much of a place, but beggars could not be choosers.

He dropped his bike on the side away from the cement porch fronting the attached house where the Ochs lived and slipped around the corner. "Hello, Conrad," he said quietly to the black Chow, panting so hard in the porch's shade Aaron thought he might explode. It was certainly hot enough, and the feet-thick fur coat the dog had didn't help. He patted the dog and then let it lick his hand so he could see the black tongue. Gross, and he wiped his hands on his pants before entering the store, letting the screen slam *thwaaang*! behind.

Mr. Ochs, the world's oldest living human, sat behind the counter. Amenhotep or Methuselah, Aaron couldn't decide which, and he watched the mummy carefully to ensure he was still breathing. Yep. Aaron stepped to the candy rack in front of the counter and surveyed the offerings. Hershey Bar with Almonds, always a good choice, Fizzies, Bit o' Honey, Chick o' Stick...

...eh, not feeling it.

What he really wanted was something cold and wet. He went to the cooler, all decked out in a red Coke logo, opened it and fished around inside. Nehi Grape, Tab, RC Cola, nah, nah... bingo! With great satisfaction, he pulled out a Yoo Hoo, holding it out at arm's length. Cold and drippy and still lots of undissolved chocolate sediment on the bottom. He shook it hard and turned back to the counter. Mr. Ochs had barely moved, and Aaron examined him – yes, still breathing – and dropped fifteen cents — five of which was bottle deposit — on the counter. Mr. Ochs twitched an eye and flared a nostril and put out a tremulous, shaking, liver-spotted hand to sweep the coins into a box. "Thankee," he whispered.

"You're welcome," Aaron said and spun on his heel, snapping the cap off with the opener on the side of the cooler and took a giant swig of cold chocolate goodness, almost upending the bottle as he stepped through the screen, *thwaaang*! and down onto the drive...

"Well, lookee, lookee here."

Aaron, choking on the Yoo Hoo, stumbled back as Gar and his two henchmen, Cory and Steve, formed a grinning, malicious semi-circle around the door, trapping Aaron against it.

Aaron almost fell over the step and back through the screen. As he regained balance, Gar reached out and snatched the bottle from Aaron's hand. "Hey!" Aaron yelped, but Gar just smiled at him, tipped the bottle, and drained what was left in about three gulps.

"Aah!" he belched with great and — to the henchmen, at least — hilarious satisfaction, and then contemptuously pitched the bottle end over end across the road. He smirked at Aaron. "Thanks for buying that for me, Yankee."

Aaron got mad. "I didn't buy that for you! And I'm not a Yankee, I'm from Oklahoma. That's NOT in the North." Jeez, just how many times did he have to explain this, anyway?

"Well, it ain't around here, Yankee, and Cory and Steve saw you give me that Yoo Hoo." He turned. "Ain't that right?"

Cory, a head shorter but a stomach wider than Gar, his face so covered with freckles the skin in between was more like grout, laughed and said, "Sure d-yid!"

Steve, his one white eyebrow bobbing weirdly in his big-featured, dark-red face, simply nodded.

"That's a lie!" Aaron threw his chest out,

outrage making him reckless.

Gar stilled, stretching up to the full eight or nine inches taller than Aaron that he was, and thrust his face into Aaron's. "You calling us liars?" Gar's chew-imbued breath washed over Aaron, making him almost retch. He reeled back, Gar's red-stained teeth and mouth following him closely.

Gar gave a wink to his friends, "That's pretty funny, you callin' us liars." He paused. "Cryman boy."

Aaron blinked. Oh great. They knew.

Of course they did. By now, half the state of Alabama knew.

"So," Gar stepped back so he could get a full view of Aaron's tortured face. "Why doncha tell us what really happened to your fat ass brother, huh? Did you and those Dothan faggots cornhole him to death or somethin'?

Steve and Cory burst out laughing at that, Cory adding a chorus, "Cornholed him dead, ha!"

"What?" Stunned by that on a variety of levels, primarily because Aaron had no real idea what Gar was talking about. He knew it was something very dirty, but Aaron was woefully unschooled on the dirty side of life, and many of the lewd remarks and leers and snickerings that made up most of Gar and his friends' daily conversation went right over his head; something Gar and his friends knew and used to his detriment. This cornholing, for instance: Aaron had an excellent idea to what that referred, since Gar and his pals were obsessed with the term, but to use it in the context of Darrell's serving as a Cryman snack didn't make sense.

"What?" he asked, again.

Gar nodded sagely. "Yeah, that's it. After you and the other faggots got done with fat ass, fat ass said he was going to go tell mommy or something, so, what, didja knife him? Hit him with a club? C'mon." Gar moved in, putting a companionable hand on Aaron's shoulder. "C'mon, take us out there, show us where you buried him. We'll dig him up and then you can cornhole his fat dead ass again."

"Oh! Oh!" Cory was bent over with mirth. "That's gross!"

"Be softer," Steve's leering face hovered behind Gar, the white eyebrow twitching oddly, "Be easier for your little pencil dick," and Steve made the universal finger and enclosed thumb motion.

Aaron now knew to what they referred. Shock gave way to mindless, unthinking rage, which is the only way to explain what happened next.

Aaron punched Gar.

It was, in the history of punches, not much, just a glancing blow off the side of Gar's sloped head, poorly aimed and delivered, without any real force... but it was the shot heard around the world. Aaron did not know who was more flabbergasted, him or Gar. Gar, though, reacted faster.

"You sonofabitch!" Gar shrieked as he gathered Aaron's lapels in one meaty hand while drawing the other one back into a fist that promised to crash into Aaron's nose with far more significant effect than the little love-tap Aaron had executed. Steve and Cory were about a half-second behind Gar, but their faces darkened and they stepped forward to add punches as the opportunity presented. Aaron readied, sure he was going to lose the expensive braces Dad – after a lot of complaints – had paid for...

"Hyeah!"

The voice, shrill and saw-edged, knifed through all of them like a harpoon. Gar froze in punch-ready position, his eyes wide as he sought the source of that spine-breaking yell. Steve and Cory did, too, and Aaron turned his head.

Mrs. Ochs.

She was older than Mr. Ochs, if that was possible, but where he was inanimate clay, she was lightning in a bottle, a bustling big-hipped, flower-sack-dress-and-apron-wearing short ball of fury, infamous for slinging gum-stealing kids right out the door by their ears. She wore a sun hat about five times too big for her, the ends flopping down, but not enough to hide the ferocious glare blasting them from behind her pince-nez. She held a dirt-covered trowel in one hand. Conrad was at her other hand, making little *wuff* sounds deep in his throat.

She pointed the trowel at Gar and

shrieked, "What do you think you're doing, Gar Avis?"

"He hit me first!" Gar wailed. Like a little kid.

Aaron stared at him and considered those words.

He HAD hit Gar first, hadn't he?

Despite being on the edge of losing facial bones and paid-for teeth, a warm glow suffused him.

For the first time in his life, Aaron had defended himself.

"Well, iffen you said nasty things like that to me, I'da broke your head open, too!" She shook the trowel at him and Conrad's *wuff* became a full-blown growl. Gar let Aaron go and stepped back hastily, as did Cory and Steve.

Mrs. Ochs' evaluation of Aaron's punch was a bit overblown but, look at this! An adult was backing him up!

The day was just full of wonders, wasn't it?

"You just as white trash as you Daddy, Gar Avis. The whole buncha yew!" Her trowel swept across the trio. "I am ashamed to know ya."

Gar's face darkened and he took a threatening step. "I ain't trash!"

Conrad took an even more threatening step towards Gar, the growl continuous, and Mrs. Ochs glared. "You talk like you just did, you are! Now, git!" And she flicked the trowel at him.

Gar stepped back, but reluctantly, his face working. Aaron's jaw dropped. Was he crazy? Conrad would have his liver!

Mrs. Ochs' eyes narrowed and she reached down and gripped the black Chow by his lion scruff. "Boy, you better get outta here right now," she hissed.

Gar came to his senses and took giant steps out of Conrad's reach, Steve and Cory at his shoulders. "Get you later!" He pointed a threatening finger at Aaron and then stalked off around the side of the store, towards Damascus.

Aaron held his breath until the sounds of their retreat diminished and then he looked at the still-growling Conrad. "Thank you," he said.

Mrs. Ochs waved a dismissive trowel at him while soothing the Chow. "You stay away from them boys, you hyeah?" she said. "They ain't nothing but trouble."

Aaron nodded, "I know." He dropped his head and headed past her to get his bike, but her hand shot out and snagged him like a talon. Startled, Aaron turned to her, stunned by the sheer look of fright on her face. "And you stay 'way from that Cryman, too!"

"What?" Aaron was suddenly as frightened as her.

"It ain't done with you! It's been cryin' a spell and wants to keep walking. Don't listen to it. You don't, you hear?" and she shook him, the fear in her eyes almost manic.

Aaron broke away and stepped back, shaking from his own fear more than hers. She gave him one last terrified look and then whirled, disappearing like a wisp around the side of the house.

Aaron blinked. "What does that mean?" he called after her, but there was no answer. Conrad whined, licked him on the hand – gross! – and then followed Mrs. Ochs.

After a moment, Aaron did a Daffy Duck head clear and continued around the corner and reached down for his bike, pulling it up to mount, when he saw that the front spokes had been kicked out. "Great," he said. Must have been the Three Stooges' first action when they arrived. The bastards. Something else he now owed Gar. And Steven and Cory.

He walked the bike out to the road. Don't worry about the Cryman, Mrs. Ochs. Dad'll kill me when he sees the wheel.

Chapter 13

Aaron sprawled on the sawdust pile watching the hot white sky. It was late enough the sun had moved safely behind the pine tree screen, easing retina sear. Idly, he watched a jet's contrail penciling slowly across his view. Paris bound? South Pole bound? Didn't matter; he wished he was on it. Anywhere but here.

He'd hidden the bike in the garage behind some tarp, but it was only a matter of time before Dad found it and extracted, at the unfurling of his whip, a full explanation for the damage. It didn't matter that Gar and the other Two Stooges had kicked the spokes out while Aaron was cooler-diving. It didn't matter that Aaron had actually – actually! – smacked Gar.

According to Dad's logic, Aaron should have anticipated Gar's approach and taken appropriate precautions. Or shouldn't have left the house at all, putting the bike at risk.

Won't win this one.

Won't win anything.

It was a coin flip whether he was in more danger hanging around the house waiting for Dad to stumble across the bike or waiting out here for the Cryman to stumble across the creek. When he thought about it, the Cryman was actually the lesser evil: with the Cryman, at least he had the option of fighting back.

Fighting back.

Aaron played the Gar slap over and over in his mind. It was exhilarating. Outrageous. Thrilling. But, most of all, disturbing, because it was something he had never done before. Ever. Aaron had learned long ago that defending himself usually meant a far greater beating than originally initiated. Dad had taught him to keep his hands to his side, bucko, and, by God, don't cry, or you'll get whipped even harder and longer, for the simple temerity of disagreeing with the punishment. Raising his hands, even to ward off the blows, meant his death.

The same principle applied at large, so he'd never raised defensive hands against anyone who attacked him, even a fellow 8th grader like Gar – who should actually be a 10th grader – because he'd get an even harder beating. Yet, a mere hour or so ago, he'd not only raised defensive hands, he'd delivered a blow, albeit a weak one.

Apparently, he had a breaking point. Which was: an unfair accusation.

He had been unfairly accused of all kinds of crimes at many points in his life. There's no reason to think that will stop. To wit, his indictment, pending on Dad's discovery of the bike. But, on all of those occasions, there was some element of fault on his part. For example, he could agree with Dad that he should not have gone to the store, considering that he was still under condemnation for Darrell's disappearance.

Darrell's death, to be more accurate.

But, when the egregious accusation is, in every element, completely unfair, such as Gar's proclamation that Aaron had done something lewd and dirty to Darrell, then killed him and made up a story about the Cryman, he would, evidently, lash out.

Because the Cryman was real, Gar. And an ugly person like you, Gar, saying the ugly things you did, deserved to be a Cryman meal more than Darrell did.

Nervously, Aaron looked around the dimming trees, but no shark teeth grinned at him, no Darrell-head mouthed pleas, so he was safe.

For the moment.

But safety was relative and the borders were spinning rapidly away. Gar had promised retribution for the head slap, and it was just a matter of time before Gar and the Two Stooges caught up with him. Aaron doubted he would be able to lift a defensive hand then because he *had* slapped the cretin, hadn't he? So the retaliation was his fault and, therefore, he deserved the beating Gar was guaranteed to hand out, which meant he was back to nerd-coward positioning on the pecking order (just one slot above Connor), with a lot more beatings in store after that because he had the audacity to raise his hands in the first place. So he was now worse off.

And the Cryman was not done with him.

A chill ran up Aaron's spine. What, exactly, did Mrs. Ochs mean by that? Obviously, she believed in Aaron's Cryman, so it was some comfort that at least one adult did; but that was its only comfort because, clearly, she knew something about the Cryman that even Gramma Eckhart didn't, and that knowledge frightened her.

And if it frightened her, then it downright terrified Aaron.

Maybe the Cryman enjoyed head puppetry so much, it wanted a full set from which to choose, which meant it planned to add Kathy, Mom, and Dad – and Aaron – at some point. Include Sawyer and Gary and Stan, and the Cryman could put on a full-blown traveling puppet show, amusing the locals for decades to come.

Heck, maybe it could add Gar and the

Two Stooges.

Now, wouldn't that be great?

Yes, Aaron thought, yes, it would. If the Cryman went after Gar and Cory and Steve, and all the other bully jerks who lived here, life would vastly improve for Aaron and his brethren nerds. That made the Cryman a force for good, not evil, like that wrestler Don Carson who'd been a bad guy for years until he teamed up with Dick Dunn. Why, the Cryman could be a downright superhero, Nick Fury and his Howlin' Commandos, killing all the Nazis to make the world safe for democracy.

A twig snapped.

Gasping, Aaron sat straight up.

Oh no!

He'd daydreamed his way into the witching hour and the Cryman was on him! And it wouldn't be the superhero Cryman but the evil, shark-toothed creature living in the Gulches that played with Darrell's head and had now come for Aaron's. What had he been thinking, that something so evil could actually do good? Another twig snapped and Aaron whirled to the source, ready to bolt down the other side of the pile and flail blindly through the woods until the monster caught him. A shadow moved on the edge of the swamp, and Aaron gathered his legs to flee.

"Are you all right?" the shadow asked.

Cindy.

Aaron let out a long, relieved sigh and settled back down. "You scared me to death," he said.

She came up the pile. "Sorry. So, *are* you all right?"

Aaron looked at her. The concern on her face was genuine, her wide brown eyes lit with it. Something in Aaron stirred. "No," he said, and lay back on the pile.

She said nothing but sat next to him, her blouse lightly brushing his upper arm, Aaron was stirred again, but not in quite the same way. "Where's Stan and Gary?" he asked to distract himself.

"Back at Gramma's." She paused. "We're not supposed to play with you anymore."

Startled, Aaron sat up and looked at her. "Why not?"

She shrugged and looked off and Aaron didn't need an explanation, not really. Gramma — more likely, Grampaw — blamed him for Darrell's death, er, disappearance, too. Just like everyone else.

"So unfair," he whispered.

"It is," she said and then turned back to him. "Because it wasn't your fault."

Hello. Now this was a fresh breeze, and he gazed at her, unsure of the sincerity. "Everyone thinks it was."

"I don't. It was the Cryman."

He blinked at her. "You mean, you believe me?"

She nodded, her eyes still big and solemn. "Yes."

Relief washed over him, along with

gratitude, because there was no obligation on her part to accept his story. None whatsoever. She wasn't a relative or anything... just some girl.

Some girl.

He looked at her, those brown eyes, languid and soft and wide open, her lips compressed, a tilt to her head, inviting...

Aaron leaned forward. So did she.

Time stopped. Just stopped. All of nature did, too, as the trees and the bushes and the squirrels and Bambi all leaned forward in utter astonishment to witness this wonderful, life-changing moment: Aaron's first real kiss with a real girl. It was everything the movies and Disney and books and soap operas and Gene Kelly said it was — soaring, heart-pounding, breath-stopping, all glory and power. The world altered, the Universe opened: Galactus and Silver Surfer had barely scratched its surface. This warmth and softness and time-ending touch of lips, this was everything. Everything—

"Y'all about done?"

Aaron leaped like someone had shocked him with a cattle prod, toppling backwards and down the sawdust heap in an avalanche of shavings. He piled up at the bottom, did a very bad somersault to come out of the fall, and sat up, breathless, terrified and exhilarated, embarrassed and exultant. He looked back up the pile at Cindy, who sat, red-faced and cringing, but there, that light in her eyes, a light that met his. He smiled. So did she.

"'Cause if you are," Sawyer said, stepping into Aaron's view, "we got someplace to go."

Aaron blinked. Kathy stood next to Sawyer, grinning a bit, whether at the interrupted kiss or Aaron's clumsy dismount, he couldn't say, but there was also alarm and fear on her face. He looked at Sawyer, who was all grim, no amusement on his face at all. "Where?" he asked.

"Aunt Mary's," Sawyer said.

Aaron gasped. At an echoing one from the top of the pile, Aaron looked up. Cindy, no longer flushed, was ashen. And afraid. Aaron stared at Sawyer. "You mean, the witch?"

Sawyer nodded. "You asked what we do. We go see her."

Coldness ran through Aaron's limbs. Aunt Mary danced with devils, drank the blood of newborns, including her own children begot by the devil. She cast spells in the moonlight, shriveling men's eyes and turning their children into pigs, and she laughed at Jesus and spat at preachers. She lived off a grass trail, itself off a little dirt road way back on the other side of Damascus where the swamps converged and the snakes danced. Whenever anyone found themselves on that road, they said prayers as they hurried past. Even Gar was scared of her.

"She's evil," Aaron said.

"She ain't," Sawyer spat tobacco juice off to the side. "She's a white witch, not a black 'un."

Aaron furrowed his brow. "I thought she was Black."

"She a colored woman, but no black witch." Sawyer spat again. "You comin'?"

Aaron looked at Kathy. "Are you in this?"

She nodded, a hand on Sawyer's shoulder to steady herself, but she looked as scared as Aaron felt. A slide of sawdust and Cindy piled next to him, her hand on *his* shoulder. "I am, too," she said.

Aaron looked at her hand and then at her. She was still pale but determined, and she blinked that determination at him. Aaron's heart flopped between exhilaration and terror, but one more look in her eyes...

No contest.

Aaron set his jaw and turned to Sawyer. "Let's go," he said and stood.

Sawyer nodded and cut past the pile and into the woods, shadowed in the gathering dusk, leading the way to the creek trail. Kathy trailed behind him, still holding Sawyer's hand. Aaron stepped up, startled when Cindy slipped her hand into his as he pushed through the brush.

Wow.

He had a girlfriend.

Chapter 14

"We'll get in trouble," Aaron said.

The four of them crammed into Sawyer's cab, dangerous in itself because of the sharp edges everywhere, including the rusty springs protruding from the bench seat, avoided by only the most extreme of contortions. Kathy was jammed so tightly against Sawyer that she had to shift the column stick for him; a talent, Aaron suspected, developed over several previous runs jammed against Sawyer, whether anyone else was in the truck or not. Cindy was on Aaron's lap.

Cindy was on Aaron's lap.

Oh. My. God.

Her legs were folded over his, the top of

her head resting below his chin, one arm around his neck to steady herself while both of Aaron's circled her waist. Every bounce of the road initiated a responding bounce of Cindy's rear end and side and – ohmigod, was that a breast? – against Aaron's very willing legs and hips and... down there.

Oh. My. God!

Please let this go on forever. Please.

But, it wouldn't. Reality insisted on cutting into his pleasure: it was now past dark, and neither Aaron nor Kathy were home. Ergo...

"We'll get into *real* big trouble," Aaron escalated his earlier statement.

Kathy snorted, "You're such a girl."

Both Cindy and Sawyer laughed at that and Aaron's sudden mortification cut even more into the pleasure of his Cindy-wrapped body. "I am not!" he said.

"Yes, you are," Kathy asserted, "And stop worrying. Dad's not home."

"Huh? Is he working?"

"Who knows what he's doing," she muttered and Aaron left it alone because *whew*, good. Mom was easy; Dad wasn't. But if Dad was out, then there was a very good chance they'd get home before he did, depending on how long it took for Aunt Mary to steal their souls... best not think about that.

"Won't you get in trouble?" he whispered to Cindy.

"I'll handle it," she said with almost the

same level of scorn that Kathy had used and Aaron knew he'd just lost his first girlfriend. All the remaining pleasure of this ride, zip, out the window.

"Downshift," Sawyer ordered and Kathy did so and Aaron watched as the one functioning headlight — canted so far up it was almost useless — traced a path across the tops of the moss-shrouded pines looming from both sides of Aunt Mary's Dirt Road of Death. The trees looked like they were mad. He shivered.

They bounced hard all over the road, a combination of Sawyer's lack of shocks and excessive speed meeting the washboard contours and potholes. Cindy's presence on his lap changed from a breath-freezing source of joy to a teeth-gritting endurance of pain as her backbone slammed him down there over and over, like several well-placed dodge balls.

Better not let on, if he wanted her to be his girlfriend again.

So it was with a lot more relief than terror, that he greeted the truck's sudden lurch to a dust-shrouded stop and Sawyer's terse, "We're here."

"Finally," he said, trying to shift a leg to get circulation started.

"Am I hurting you?" Cindy asked, moving her legs in a way that, yes, hurt, but – Oh. My. God. – "No," Aaron almost sang it, "Not at all."

Kathy snickered. "All right, Romeo, how 'bout getting out, then?"

His face burning (fortunately, not visible

in the pitch blackness), Aaron reached through the open window and dropped the handle down, popping the door and almost spilling them like a Laurel and Hardy skit onto the ground, but he threw a numb leg out just in time and caught them.

And caught Cindy's rear perfectly in his crotch.

Wouldn't it be just great to sit like this for a while?

Cindy stepped down, though, ending that, and Aaron pitched after because Kathy was pushing him from behind and he almost stepped on Cindy's foot but stumbled out of the way, bouncing off the side of the truck and probably getting about seven (more) layers of rust and dust on him as Sawyer followed because, of course, the driver's door didn't work. Aaron irritably brushed off his pants and looked around. And gulped.

God, what a horrible place.

There was a half-moon — a devil moon — casting a half-glow of dead light around them. The pines were as thick as a hedge running right up to the poorly kept road, all of them linked and draped by the cancerous moss, their dead tendrils grasping at him in their eagerness to haul him up and hang him from the top branches. Peepers and frogs, probably carnivorous, chorused as they gathered their forces and edged closer to the road, to swarm out of the trees and crawl up their noses and eat them from the stomachs out. Lightning bugs everywhere, but they weren't really lightning bugs; they were the souls of Aunt Mary's victims, their flashing a frantic SOS: Get away! Get Away! Aaron was sure the Cryman waited for them in the shrouded trees, backed by an army of werewolves and vampires and zombies.

"C'mon," Sawyer said and stepped off the road and was gone. Just gone. Kathy didn't even hesitate but flowed right after and was also gone. No doubt, werewolves had them.

"I'm scared," Cindy whispered.

"Me, too," Aaron said and felt her start and put that warm, wonderful hand in his.

"We'll go together," she said and pushed the same way Kathy had, and Aaron had no choice but to follow. He wondered if God would give him special dispensation if he died defending his girlfriend from a werewolf. But, what if a vampire got them, instead? Aaron frowned. Then they were both damned.

Forever.

After scrambling through the moss and millions of poisonous spider webs that shielded the first line of trees, Aaron fell onto a rather clean dirt trail. How surprising. Someone had spent a lot of time cutting back the underbrush, no doubt to give Aunt Mary's zombie army a clear path for their unholy missions, but there were no zombies here now and Aaron was somewhat grateful for the effort. The half-moon lit the way well enough for Aaron to spot SawyerKathy — they were so close together, it was impossible to differentiate them into separate people — up at what looked like a bend.

The Sawyer part of the blob turned and waved them on impatiently, "C'mon!" he said and disappeared. Again.

Aaron hastened after, figuring numbers might stave off a werewolf attack, but, really, when was that ever true? Cindy must have been thinking the same thing because she was right there with him when he reached the point the blob had disappeared. It looked like a solid wall of spider-webbed pines and a chill ran through him because he was lost in the middle of the witch's circle, the ghosts gathering to snatch him away, when Cindy said, "Here," and tapped the ground between a little break in the trees with her toe. She then stepped through, dragging Aaron along.

The trees again reached for them, bony fingers clutching at Aaron's face and depositing worms to eat through his skin to his brains. Snakes wound through the overhead branches, seeking an opportunity to drop down his shirt and bite him until he swelled up, purple and fighting for breath. Aaron stumbled over roots, yanking Cindy off balance and threatening to upend them both and leaving them defenseless against the carnivorous frogs. Just at the point Aaron was convinced he was about to pitch forward into some kind of tar pit, the path cleared and they were standing at the side of a house.

Shack, more like it.

Mammy Yokum's shack, gangrenous in the half moonlight, clapboards peeling and moving somehow, although there was no breeze. The chimney was half-collapsed, bricks spilled down the roof, and plastic sheets flapped in the holes that substituted for windows. A red glow oozed through the plastic, probably the fires of a deeper Hell, as the demons inside giggled and grinned, anticipating the approaching meal. An old rocker sat on the porch, silhouetted by the swamp lights rising in the yard beyond it. Someone, or something, was in the rocker: a wraith dressed in black rags, skeleton bones giving it shape. The shape stirred and turned towards them. "Wacha'll want?" said a skull-voice.

It was a voice of ghosts and dead things, of fallen angels cast far from the eye of God, lost and bereft and damned, so damned. It grasped Aaron by the throat, choking off anything like a pure breath, a pure thought, and shook him. "*Urf* ..." was all he could manage.

"They're with us, Auntie," Sawyer's voice, coming from the front of the house, dispelled the corpse fingers. Aaron gasped for air and looked. Sawyer and Kathy stood on the bottom step of the front porch, watching them. Cindy tugged at his hand, further breaking the death spell, "C'mon," and pulled him alongside the other two.

The moon chose that moment to brighten and Aaron stared at the rocking chair wraith. The head shrouded in cerements, deep within its shadows two giant white eyes glowed. Simply glowed. A shock ran through him: there were no corneas, just two milk-white, luminescent orbs in Aunt Mary's head.

"I see you, boy," the skull-whisper floated across the porch and right at Aaron's ear, "I know you."

Panic flooded Aaron's heart because how could those sightless cue balls see anything?

"Yeah," Sawyer said, a bit irritably, "you know me, Auntie. I been here before."

"Weren't talkin' to you," Auntie responded just as irritably, the two sightless and all-seeing orbs twitching in the shroud and resting on Aaron. Impossible, but they did. "You, boy," she pointed a claw right at Aaron. "It on you."

The other three shrank back. Aaron, too paralyzed to move, stared at her, "What... what is?"

"You know," a contemptuous flicker of her bony fingers, then her claw was back on the armrest. "It found you. It always do. It on you now. Ain't gonna let go."

Aaron felt Sawyer and Cindy and Kathy exchange puzzled looks behind him, but they weren't really here. It was just Aunt Mary and Aaron now, and she was singing the bones and reading the black stars and seeing what stalked the woods and swamps with its shark teeth and puppet-heads.

Aaron had no idea how this witch knew what she knew, but she was right. "What can I do?" he gulped.

"You got two paths," the skull-voice caressed him, the orbs spun, and the red light flowing out of the shack danced. "One is thorny. One is black. The thorny one catch ya. The black one lose ya. You gonna walk one or the other."

Aaron blinked at her. "I don't understand. What paths? Where are they?"

The wraith leaned forward and a bony hand slipped out of the shroud and grasped Aaron's upper arm like a vise, drawing his terrified face into those ghastly orbs. "You standin' on 'em, boy!" she hissed. "You do what your heart want, you gonna get tangled all up! You do what your soul want, you gonna be in the dark. Forever!" and she flung him back, the breath of broken graves chasing him down the steps as something in the shack began laughing. He fell over the last step, only a last-minute grab by Sawyer keeping him from sprawling on the worm-covered ground.

"What?" Aaron shrieked, clutching at Sawyer's arresting fingers. "What does that mean? I don't know what it means!"

"Shut up, idjit!" Sawyer shook him and pushed him roughly over to Cindy, staring at Aaron round-eyed and frozen. Sawyer glared Aaron to silence, then quietly took Kathy's hand, cutting off what looked likely to be her own emerging scream. "Auntie," Sawyer whispered, "What we do?"

She had receded back into her tomb shadows, rocking a bit, the red glow inside pulsing in time with her motion. The orbs rested on Sawyer. "You gotta meet it head on," she toned, "You get the magic number 'fore you do."

Cindy, who was either too brave or too curious to be circumspect, spoke up. "What's the magic number?"

Auntie shrugged at Sawyer. "You know it. You meet that thing back where he live. You put it down."

"How, Auntie?" Sawyer took a step up the porch, but shadows swarmed the rocker and the shed and there was a swirling of some kind... and the rocker was empty.

Aaron gasped. The half-light flowed over the porch and cast along the path back through the trees, and the red light inside growled a warning. They didn't have to be told twice. Sawyer turned and followed the moonlight through the trees, Kathy clinging to him, Cindy and Aaron clinging to each other and on Sawyer's heels. Aaron glanced back. He swore a pair of milky orbs stared at him through the tattered plastic, until the red light flashed and took it away. Shaking with fear, he grasped Cindy's hand as they entered the tree line.

No one spoke all the way back to the truck, and they folded and pushed themselves into the cab in the same semblance of order as the trip here.

When they reached a real road, Aaron said, "That was stupid."

"T'weren't," Sawyer grunted, leaning into a turn.

"Yes, it was!" Aaron threw out a hand in exasperation as much as the crowded conditions allowed. "What's this path she was talking about? And what are we supposed to do?"

"That path yours," Sawyer said, dryly, "not ours. And, what we have to do, is get the Cryman." He paused, "At his home."

Aaron was aghast. "You mean, we gotta go back to the Gulches?"

Sawyer nodded grimly, the one-off headlight brightening him. Aaron shook his head. "No way I'm going back there!" Darrell's puppet-head danced in his mind.

"You're going," Kathy said, tight and controlled. "We're all going. With the magic number."

"What's that?" Cindy asked.

"Five," Sawyer replied.

Chapter 15

Five.

Five... what?

Aaron blinked at the dark ceiling, one hand self-consciously across the empty bed, seizing the place where Darrell used to be. Where his puppet-head would be, if the Cryman reached through the screen.

It was quiet. Even the crickets and peepers were subdued. Kathy and he had walked back into the house subdued; Mom served them a subdued, unquestioning late supper. Subdued Dad came in a couple of hours later and went to bed, subdued. Didn't even watch TV.

Like a spell had been cast on them.

One had. Aaron moved about restlessly. Aunt Mary had called it up like a fog, keeping Kathy and Aaron safe for the night. But fogs dissipate and, come morning, Mom and Dad would be back to their normal selves, two big distractions, making it very difficult for Aaron to figure out what the magic number five meant.

Five bullets?

Maybe that was the number of shots necessary to kill the Cryman: one in each knee, each elbow, and then the heart. Made sense. Cripple it, then finish it. But, man, that required steely resolve and incredibly good aim to place the bullets accurately while the Cryman roared out of the Gulches and up the hill and straight at Aaron, intent on removing his head and installing it alongside Darrell's. Sawyer should do it, then. He had to be a good shot, being a redneck and all, and was definitely filled with steely resolve. Visiting Aunt Mary was proof of that.

Five silver bullets?

Probably. Those worked on werewolves and the Cryman was sort of a werewolf, without the necessity of a full moon. That, of course, presented other issues, such as procuring said bullets. The Lone Ranger had no problem getting them, but that's because Tonto knew the location of a silver mine. Aaron didn't. He supposed he could grab some of Mom's silver necklaces and melt them into the bullet molds Dad kept in the shed, but what cartridge size? Where did he get the gunpowder? And the cartridges themselves?

Should probably leave that up to Sawyer, too.

Sawyer. Aaron frowned. Here, now, his life, tied up with Sawyer's. Dependent on Sawyer, in fact, because the Cryman was still out there and gunning for Aaron, and Sawyer's well-placed five silver bullets were the only things that would save Aaron from becoming a head-puppet. But he didn't like Sawyer. Sawyer was a rough boy, a redneck, only functionally literate, dirt poor, having more in common with Gar and his idiot friends than he would ever have with Aaron. Heck, the only reason Sawyer even knew Aaron's name was his attendance on Kathy, and, once Sawyer was done buzzing around her, he'd be off to another bloom. And then Sawyer and Aaron would be distant strangers, Sawyer's world of barely running trucks and 'possum hunts and tobacco chaw as far from Aaron's world of *Marvel* and Heinlein and telescopes as Mars was from Venus.

And Aaron gets eaten.

Nervously, he glanced at the window, but it was empty: all that filled it was moon-glowed night. What a situation; whether Aaron ended up as a Cryman snack or not depended on Sawyer's continued interest in this whole thing, which was in proportion to his interest in Kathy and in Dad remaining oblivious to the skulkings of those two about the house, something that would come to a quick and bloody end should Dad turn a corner at an inopportune moment and discover Sawyer and Kathy entwined about each other. Snap of a couple of necks and then there's Dad, digging unmarked graves somewhere past the creek, the Cryman at his shoulder, grinning and slobbering and gleeful at the chance presented to steal through the window and tie Aaron's head to its waist... another nervous glance at the window, but nothing.

Aaron had a sudden sense of time winding down, of time running out. Even worse, of events out of his control.

Perhaps it was best to get this thing done as soon as possible.

He considered the logistics. Seemed daunting. Silver, then bullets, then ambush: someone would have to go into the Gulches to lure the Cryman out and, since Aaron was the only one of the group with actual Gulch experience, it'd be his job. Great. He'd barely gotten away the first time; only the much slower Darrell saved him. And he'd been at top speed, even a terror-spurred percentage more, so how much faster could he actually run? Maybe if Cindy was at the ambush, urging him on...

Cindy.

A delicious chill ran up his legs and circled down there, a reminder of the delicious ride to Aunt Mary's. Aaron shivered with it, hugging himself and suppressing a giggle.

Didn't want Mom to come charging out and screaming that Aaron had no right to giggle, no right! You killed your brother, and there shall be no giggling! Ever! But, Mom, I've got a girlfriend. A real girlfriend. And the two of them are going to get the monster that ate Darrell, Mom, so it's okay. It's okay.

And it would take the two of them working together. If she stood on the ridge next to Sawyer as Aaron came pelting out of the Gulches, the Cryman hot on his heels, urging him on with screams of, "You're my boyfriend! I love you!', then he could outpace the monster and bring it within Sawyer's deadly range and, five shots of silver later, the Cryman dead and they're free, free, and then he kisses Cindy and they walk away, hand-in-hand, off through the woods and then they'd, they'd...

They'd what?

He frowned. Do sex, he guessed, that vague, frightening, thrilling act that everyone focused on, everyone wanted, everyone talked about, laughed about, sneering at Aaron's obvious ignorance of its mechanics. No longer. A walk in the woods after the heroic slaying of the Cryman and its mysteries revealed, its power harnessed. Cindy would be his sex slave, kneeling before him, afraid, helpless, eyes wide in terror as he slipped off his pants...

That didn't seem right. That seemed mean. Something Dad would do.

Aaron cast an eye down the hall. Dad had sex all the time, judging by the frequent rhythms and grunts from his and Mom's bedroom. Mom was always a little more transparent the morning after a night of grunts, as if this sex act, whatever it was, stole a bit of her soul. Perhaps that was the dark secret involved; the man grew stronger, bolder, more alive with each act of sex, while the woman disappeared. A slow-rolling Cryman. Maybe a man fed off the energies, giving him the strength to get up every morning and beat children and drive off in a cloud of dust and then spend the day insulting wimpy coworkers and playing vicious jokes on bosses and getting drunk at noon and running people off the roads on the way home then grab the woman and throw her on the bed for another round.

No wonder Mom didn't want Kathy to date Sawyer.

He regarded the dark at the end of hallway, straining to see if atoms of Mom floated there. Not that there'd been any grunt nights since Darrell got eaten, but maybe the process of sex was an ongoing destruction, like uranium dissolving in a reactor. Once the reaction started, it could not be stopped. The man fed off the power as the rod cooled to nothing. It was the way of the world.

Judging by his own strange urges down there and by most of the talk and actions on TV shows and movies, this sex thing was so hard-wired, so necessary, that it drove everything. Men must take the power, the women must disappear, like Dracula and Lucy Westenra, which is why the movie was so scary because it showed the results of sex. It was the modus of life, the heartbeat of humanity, a perverse, disgusting act, like Gar and his sick, stupid talk about Darrell...

Gar.

God, how he hated Gar.

Something rubbed against the window. Aaron looked.

The Cryman stood there.

Ice and terror ran through Aaron's soul, a glacier avalanche, and he was paralyzed, helpless. Nothing prevented the Cryman from tearing through the screen, grabbing Aaron's foot, and dragging him out and into his mouth, eating everything except Aaron's head, which would hang on the Cryman's waist, bound there by one of Aaron's intestines, for all eternity. Right next to Darrell. They would squall and snap at each other until the Cryman put its claws into their neck holes and put on shows outside Cindy's window, one night reaching in and grabbing her, too.

A small whimper escaped from Aaron's throat, best he could muster, as if screaming would do anything else but hasten his death. Dad won't respond, just yell at him to shut up. Mom won't even do that. Only Kathy will come out to see what was happening and she'd be gobbled up next. He stared at the Cryman, waiting.

It stared back, also waiting.

For what?

The ice that had frozen him began to thaw and Aaron recovered his limbs enough to draw his feet slowly away from the window, and then edge to the far side of the bed. He now had a fighting chance to get away as the Cryman came crashing through, but get away to where? Maybe the gun cabinet, in a hopeless effort to seize a shotgun and put five rounds into the thing before it reached him, or maybe out of the kitchen door in an equally hopeless effort to outrun it, because Cindy is not standing on the road at this time of night urging him on. But what other options did he have? Aaron braced and turned full on the monster, getting ready.

It hadn't moved. Wasn't even grinning its sharky grin. Just stood there, swaying a bit, shrouded by hair and dark, it's breath rumbling, watching Aaron.

Expectant.

Hungry.

And Aaron, suddenly, knew what it wanted.

To be fed. From the trouble in his soul.

Aaron took the Cryman in, felt its need, its expectation, which only he could fill. "Gar," he whispered.

The Cryman started, leaned forward a bit, and smiled, its shark teeth tomb-gray in the moonlight. "And Cory. And Steve."

The Cryman's smile widened with each word and its breath came faster and louder, almost resembling a locomotive gathering steam. It lurched and Aaron quailed, sure this was it. But, seconds later, it was gone, only the deathlight filling the window.

Gasping at a sharp pain in his calf, Aaron reached down, his fingers brushing against something jammed into his pajama leg. He pulled, tearing flesh, warm blood flowing. He held the object up to the deathlight.

A thorn.

Chapter 16

The fog continued, testament to Aunt Mary's power. Mom didn't see Aaron, even when she served him a breakfast of toast and eggs. Dad didn't either, thank God, as he lurched out of the door and to the truck, backed out, and gone to work. Kathy didn't come out of her room, and neither Dad nor Mom made any comments about that.

No comments were made about the blood on his leg, either, but not because of Aunt Mary's power; he'd lain in bed, covered up with sheets, until Mom was engaged in the kitchen. When Dad had cleared the bathroom, leaving a cloud of Aqua Velva in his wake, Aaron slipped in and cleaned up, examining the deep wound in his calf. It had scabbed over already, ugly and red, and Aaron held the thorn up to the light for inspection. It was smooth and hard, like a piece of wood carved into the shape of a talon. Aaron had never seen one like it and wondered where he had picked it up.

On the Thorny Path, of course.

He shook that thought away and flushed the thorn down the toilet and scrubbed the blood out of his PJs as much as he could, stuffing them into the bottom of the hamper where Mom may, or may not, notice them and then may, or may not, screech at him about messing up his clothes. The fog might hold her long enough to spare Aaron. Or might not.

Mom retreated to her bedroom after clearing up the breakfast plates and Aaron quietly knocked on Kathy's door, but all he heard was a muffled, "Go away," so he did, drifting into the living room and watching TV. Just news shows on, the same stuff happening now as it did the last couple of weeks, couple of months, years: Vietnam, of course, with President Nixon making some visit there, and a Kennedy in trouble because a girl drowned in his car.

Darrell getting eaten, and Aaron's subsequent daily beatings, meant he'd missed Apollo 11's return to Earth and the crew getting locked up in a cylinder in case they'd brought back moon flu. But Mariner 6 had flown past Mars and taken some pictures, better than the ones Mariner 4 took, and Aaron scrutinized them as they flashed past: no cities and no John Carter, just craters and plains. Disappointing. Maybe when Mariner 7 sent back *its* pictures, there'd be something more to see, like Thark or Helium.

Aaron gazed out of the picture window at the ridge. The lower pasture was empty; couldn't blame the cows and the bull because it looked murderously hot out there. Heat waves already rising, run-over kids obscuring the distance, Aaron wondered if they were playing with the Cryman in the woods. That would be a bigger incentive for the cows to stay hidden.

A bike appeared on the road from the Opp side, the kid pedaling it bent over the handlebars and obviously struggling to make it up the hill. Aaron blinked. He knew that bike, and its rider.

Connor.

Surprised, Aaron went out of the front door and stood on the covered porch as Connor sliced the bike across the road, almost creamed by an 18-wheeler coming down the hill, blowing its air horn in anger, as the bike hit the bottom of the driveway. By the time Aaron cleared the juniper screen lining the drive and stepped onto the gravel, Connor was halfway up, puffing and wheezing as he pushed the bike along.

"Hello!" Connor screamed and waved maniacally. "Man, it's hot out here!"

"Yeah," Aaron agreed, as if the sudden drenching of his armpits wasn't proof enough.

D. KRAUSS

"What are you doing here?"

"Came to see you!" Connor yelled. Top volume was Connor's normal speaking voice.

Aaron was incredulous. "You rode all the way here in this heat?"

"Yeah!" Connor wiped inexpertly at his brow. "How else was I going to get here?"

"Your Mom could have dropped you."

"*Pffht*," Aaron waved a dismissive hand. "She's too busy praying for the gift of tongues or something."

"What?" Aaron laughed that into two syllables.

"Nothin'," another dismissive wave. "Got anything to drink?"

Aaron got two glasses of sugar tea and brought them out and the two of them sat in the screened-in porch attached to the side of the house, the ceiling fan on, enjoying some slight relief from the heat. Connor gulped his straight down and then screamed about his freeze head and Aaron, of course, had to outdo that and then both of them had to repeat the process with two more glasses. By that time, they were somewhat cooler and filled with tea and well-being.

"So, why'd you come?" Aaron asked.

Connor shrugged. "Seemed like a good idea."

"'Cause, you know, you've never come over before."

Connor cast a wry eye at Aaron. "Was never invited."

True. It was bad enough Aaron had to endure association with Connor at school, so he felt no need to solidify the relationship with mutual home visits. Connor lived five or six miles away, which was the best excuse Aaron had for ignoring Connor's constant pleas to come over. His appearance today, then, was all that more extraordinary. "So, why'd you come now?"

"Because of everything that happened. You know..." and Connor made a 'you know' gesture and, yes, Aaron did know.

"So." Aaron blew out a breath in exasperation. "You wanna hear about the Cryman. How it ate my brother. Then you can laugh at me, too. Right?" Aaron finger-slapped his glass and it sailed across the patio table, bounced off the screen and clattered to the floor.

Wow. Didn't mean to do that. Thank God it was plastic or he'd be in trouble.

"Nooo," Connor's rising tone gave his eagerness away, but he was wise enough not to show it. "I heard all of that already. I just came to, you know..." and Connor paused.

Aaron threw out his hands. "No, I don't know! What?"

"To help you kill it!" Connor yelled.

Speechless, Aaron stared, round-mouthed, at the little dweeb. Connor was short and encased in a terminal sunburn that turned his skin, his eyes, heck, even his hair, rust red. His arms and legs were mismatched, longer than his short body should allow, and they fired in different sequences whenever he moved so that Connor ran and walked and played basketball as though having a series of epileptic fits. It was embarrassing to be around him, especially since his full-volume snorts and laughs and talk drew constant attention, something the little spastic guy could really do without.

And the idea that this... this... dweeb could kill the Cryman was just too astonishing.

Aaron laughed. A genuine, humorous laugh, not the one of desperation and frustration and fear he'd been making since Darrell was eaten, but a real belly laugh. He pointed a mirthful finger at Connor. "You?" he chortled, "You're going to kill the Cryman?"

Connor had gone even redder and he glared at Aaron. "Yes, I can help kill it!"

"How?" Aaron full-on laughing now. "What are you going to do? Nerd it to death?"

"No!"

"You got silver bullets? Five of 'em?" Aaron slapped the side of his own face in hysterics.

"What?" Connor looked at him, baffled. "The Cryman's not a werewolf!"

Aaron dropped his hands and tilted his head into the confrontation angle. "How do you know?"

"It's Bigfoot!"

"Bigfoot?" Aaron sat back. Bigfoot, the mysterious apelike creature some guys had filmed walking away from them into the woods. "That's out in California." Aaron was dismissive.

"Uh, uuuh!" Connor's tone was triumphant. "Bigfoots are everywhere! They live in the woods and swamps. They eat meat!" He looked at Aaron sideways. "They eat people."

A vision of Darrell's puppet-head grinning at him made Aaron shudder. "It's not a Bigfoot. It's... a devil," and his eyes went off and dark as he saw things Connor could not even guess about.

Connor sobered, his eyes wide, but then set his lips. "All the more reason to kill it."

Aaron shook his head in disgust. This kid. "And just how are you going to do that?"

"Blow it up," Connor said, his arms crossed in satisfaction.

Aaron blinked. "Blow it up." He paused. "Are you crazy?"

"No." And Connor kept that satisfied look.

"Blow up a devil," Aaron rolled his eyes. "You can't blow up a devil. They're magical. This thing is... magic." Visions of a dark shack and white orb-eyes flashed across his mind, and he felt a stab in his calf again, the thorn wound. He shifted.

Connor shrugged. "Maybe. But you can trap it in its lair."

Aaron considered. If they could collapse the Gulches around the Cryman, then maybe it wouldn't be able to dig out for a while. Enough time for them to get away. Or collect silver bullets. "How?" he asked. "With a grenade? Dynamite? I don't have anything like that."

"Neither do I."

Aaron threw his hands out. "Well, then, this is stupid!"

Connor's face twisted up in delight. "We make a bomb."

Aaron stared at him. "Out of what? Black Cats? We'd need like a million of them!"

"No, dummy," Connor snorted, "Out of mercury and nitric acid and ethanol, and ammonium nitrate."

"What!?"

Connor sighed. "You mean, you've never used your chemistry set to make bombs?"

Well, no. He'd done the volcano and made crystals, but chemistry was boring. He'd rather be outside with his telescope looking for Neil Armstrong's footsteps. That is, until the Cryman showed up. "Have you?"

Connor's eyes shone. "Yeah! Big ones!" and he made a *pekhwww*! sound as he moved his hands in imitation of a nuclear explosion.

"And you didn't get into trouble?"

Connor shrugged. "No one heard me. I was way out in the woods."

"Your parents didn't get mad at you?"

"Ha! Them?" His laugh was derisive. "All they care about is saving souls. They have no idea what I'm doing." He paused. "No idea." That last he whispered.

A bit disturbing, but if Connor could

make a bomb that would kill the Cryman... "It's going to have to be a real big bomb."

"No problem. We can make it as big as you want! Where's this thing live?"

Aaron described the Gulches. "Hmm," Connor scratched his chin. "Probably fifty pounds will do it. We'll put it in the tunnel entrance, bring the top down. It'll take it years to dig out!" Connor crowed.

Years. Time enough to grow up and reach eighteen and get out of here, just get out of here, leave the Cryman and Dad and his beatings and everyone's accusing eyes and Darrell's puppet-head far behind, Cindy by his side, driving off into the sunset...

"Fifty pounds, huh?" Aaron considered. "Kinda heavy, doncha think?"

"Anything less wouldn't work. We'll also need fulminate and a fuse. Fulminate's not a problem." He paused. "Didn't you tell me once that your Dad has some kind of field telephone?"

He'd described to Connor, one day at recess, one of Dad's favorite games: he'd make him and Darrell hold hands while Aaron held on to one end of the telephone wire, both of them crying, "No, Dad, no!" as he yelled at them to shut up and stop being crybabies and he spun the crank and the shock ran through Aaron and Darrell and they both screamed and dropped the wire and ran inside, Dad laughing at them, "That didn't hurt!"

One advantage of being a head-puppet

now, Darrell, you don't have to put up with that crap anymore. "Yes."

"Know where it is?"

Yes.

Moments later, the two of them were in the shed, squatting over a canvas bag that Aaron had pulled from one of Dad's Army trunks. "An EE-8!" Connor yelped as he, almost lovingly, pulled the handset out and admired it. "You don't see these babies much anymore."

"Huh?" Aaron stared at him. "How do you even know what this is?"

Another shrug. "I just know." Connor pulled out the wire coiled around the set. "At least a hundred feet," he nodded in approval, then narrowed his eyes at Aaron, "You sure this works?"

"Trust me." Aaron ruefully rubbed his hands.

"All right!" Connor put it all back and helped Aaron repack it in the trunk. "We're in business!"

There was such enthusiasm in his voice that Aaron felt his hopes soar. To be rid of the Cryman! Just have to plant the bomb...

His hopes crashed back to earth. "In business?" Aaron threw exasperated hands upwards. "How are we in business? Have you even been to the Gulches?"

"Well... no."

"Then how are we going to get fifty pounds of explosives all the way from your house and across the pasture, where, let me tell you, a real bad-tempered bull lives, then up the ridge and down the hill and squeeze through the opening and set it all up without the Cryman eating us, or blowing ourselves up?"

"Don't forget the field telephone and the fulminate detonator."

"Okay, I won't forget those, either!" Aaron's volume now matched Connor's and they were in danger of being discovered, mid-plan, but, who cares? It was a stupid plan. They couldn't pull it off, not by themselves...

Not by themselves.

But with Sawyer and his truck to haul the stuff up and distributing the rest of it between Aaron and Cindy and Kathy, they could do it. The five of them working together...

Five.

A wave of certainty, of realization, almost made him lose his balance, and he stumbled back. "Not silver bullets," he breathed.

Connor cocked his head. "Huh?"

The five of them. The magic number five. He looked at Connor. "It's going to work."

"Of course it is."

A joy seized him as he grabbed Connor's shoulders, the first sense of joy and hope he'd felt since the Cryman had borne Darrell away. "It's going to work!" And he was almost dancing Connor around the shed.

"Okay! Okay!" Connor pulled away and straightened his shirt, obviously pleased at Aaron's new enthusiasm. He watched as Aaron kept up the victory dance until heat drove him back inside the shed.

"When?" Connor asked.

Aaron thought. As soon as possible, obviously. But have to take into consideration the time necessary to gather the materials and manufacture the bomb, and then the earliest time possible after that when the five of them could safely come together to execute this plan...

Monday.

They would do it on Monday. Dad would be at work; Mom would be in the state of exhaustion brought on by attending Dad over the weekend; Connor's parents would be doing whatever Monday thing they did; Aaron would have time to brief everyone and assign roles to the five of them. The Magic Five.

"Monday," he said.

Connor grinned. "Perfect! Mom and Dad are usually deep in the throes of some evangelical ecstasy by noon or so, so I'm free." He looked about with satisfaction. "Okay. I'll go get started. You do the same." And he tornadoed out of the shed, onto his bike and gone, a 2000-decibel, "See ya!" trailing after him.

Aaron simply waved him out of sight, his joy soaring. This was going to work. If he could convince the others, that is.

Chapter 17

"That's the stupidest thing I ever heard!" was Kathy's first, and derisive, take on it. An hour or so of pleading hadn't changed her mind one bit, but at least she agreed to tell Sawyer. He was the key, anyway. If he thought it was the stupidest thing he ever heard, then they were sunk; they all might as well head straight over to the Gulches and become Cryman puppets.

Surprisingly, Cindy had been easier to convince. He'd called her on the phone, ready to hang up if anyone else answered, but she did and, after ensuring the party line was clear of nosy old ladies, he gave her the highlights. She was doubtful until he pointed out there were now five of them. "Oh," she said, quickly followed by an even brighter "Oh!" as the implication became clearer. "It's gonna work!" she said with the same level of enthusiasm that Aaron felt and, after they hung up, he walked out on the porch and surveyed the distant ridge with some satisfaction.

It will work. The Magic Five will bury the Cryman under tons of Alabama clay. Forever.

A vehicle pulled up the driveway. Dad's truck. Uh oh. Home a little early, and, if Aaron wanted to avoid being assigned to an insane task like cleaning all the rocks in the garden with a toothbrush, he'd best look busy. Stepping hastily off the porch, Aaron looked about for some kind of pleasant time-consuming task that would mollify the beast and his eyes fell on the front of the riding lawn mower sticking out from under the garage overhang. Perfect. Dad finds him astride the tractor, looking earnest and concentrating on the controls as if about to start it and mow the acres. Without being told. What a good boy am I. Besides, mowing was an infinitely better task than cleaning rocks with a toothbrush, so he took a somewhat graceful leap off the porch and had already turned towards the overhang when another vehicle pulled up behind Dad's.

A sheriff's car.

Dad, stepping out of the truck, spotted Aaron and froze him with a yell of, "Boy!" As if the sheriff's car hadn't done that already. "Get your ass over here!"

A wave of terror slammed into Aaron. Oh

no! They'd found Darrell's body, and the Cryman had arranged it to look like Aaron had done all the terrible things Gar had said he did and they were here to arrest him and throw him in front of a big, mean, wigged judge who would scream at him as everyone in Cofield County thronged the room jeering and pointing and calling him evil and dirty and the judge sentenced him to a life of breaking rocks, the Cryman standing in the back, giggling. Oh no!

Aaron's legs turned to Jello and he stumbled over the lawn through a thin spot in the junipers, putting him between Dad's truck and the Sheriff's car. "Ye... yes, sir?" he quavered.

Dad was on him, grabbing Aaron's T-shirt in a frenzied and powerful fist of iron, almost jerking him off the ground. "You better tell me where you were yesterday!" Dad roared.

"Wh... what?" was all Aaron could muster because he'd been here all day yesterday.

You know that, Dad.

"Take it easy." Sheriff Oakley stood in front of his car, staring at Dad like he was crazy. Dad glared at the Sheriff, then shoved Aaron at him, taking a step back but still full of power and rage.

"You better answer everything the Sheriff asks you. Everything!" Dad's chest heaved.

Aaron, terrified, looked at the Sheriff, who gave Dad a cool glance and then looked at Aaron. Oh no, here it comes: did you do unspeakable things to your brother and then kill him to cover it up, boy?

A shriek of "No! Don't send me to the salt mines!" was already on his lips when the Sheriff pushed back his hat and asked, "Son, do you know someone named Gar Avis?"

The shriek died but remained ready for launch. Gar. Who he had named to the Cryman last night. What's this? A dread formed in his stomach but no, no way, it was too fast. More likely, Gar had told Sheriff Oakley his personal theory regarding Darrell's disappearance. "Yes. Yes, sir."

"How 'bout Cory Dyess and Steve Semple?"

The Three Stooges. What's this? "Yes," he answered, the dread climbing to his throat but, wait, c'mon. Be smart here. Be scientific. It's just too fast, too soon. The Cryman had no time to do anything yet. So, obviously, Cory and Steve had backed up Gar's story. Three witnesses were enough to convict anyone, right? He could almost picture the wigged judge and those three idiots standing in the back of the courtroom laughing at him after lying on the stand.

The Cryman had set him up. To feed off the trouble in his soul.

Great.

"When's the last time you saw them?"

"Last day of school," rose to his lips, but what if the Sheriff had already spoken to Mrs. Ochs? Then he would be caught out, a liar, all the proof necessary to show he was the exactly the picture of perverse murderer that the Three Stooges had painted. "Yesterday," he said, reluctantly.

"Where was that?"

Aaron pointed up the road. "Ochs' Store."

"Who said you could go to the store?" Dad bellowed and took a threatening step towards Aaron, who shrank against a juniper, one of its branches jabbing him in the same spot the thorn had. He resisted an urge to rub it.

"I said to take it easy." The Sheriff, irritated, glared Dad off and Aaron was, momentarily, safe. Perhaps he should leave with the Sheriff when this was over. Perhaps he was going to leave with the Sheriff anyway, whether he wanted to or not.

"What'd y'all talk about?"

"Talk?" Aaron blinked. "About nothing. They're not really friends of mine." So far, very true statements.

"Nothing?" the Sheriff pushed his hat back again. "You sure? Mrs. Ochs said you had some kind of fight with them."

Good thing he didn't lie earlier. And there was no point in lying now. "They were mean to me. They broke my bike."

"What?" Dad, eyes popping out of his skull. "You let them?"

"You want to do me a favor and walk away?" the Sheriff said it easy, but there was an iron in his voice that promised some kind of unfortunate action if Dad did not comply. Dad, his face a mottled, furious red, looked at the Sheriff as if he was actually considering defiance. But then he whirled and walked around to the front of his truck. Out of earshot. But not out of glare range.

The Sheriff eased his hat back to the point of impossibility, then squatted down to Aaron's level. "You ain't in trouble, son," Sheriff Oakley said with a gentleness in contrast to the previous iron, "I just need to know if them boys said anything about going somewhere. Running away, maybe."

Aaron was now thoroughly confused. "No, Sheriff. They didn't say anything like that." Au contraire, they had strongly indicated a desire to stick around and get him later. "Why, Sheriff?"

"Well, them boys up and gone, son. Just up and gone. Weren't in their rooms this morning. We been looking all day. So, if you remember something... boy," the Sheriff's voice was now all concern, "You all right?"

That concern was justified, because Aaron's face had drained of all color, the world had swayed, and his breath was just a wheeze – Sheriff, I can save you a lot of trouble – because Aaron knew exactly where the Three Stooges were right now, or, at least, their heads. The thorn gash throbbed and ached.

"Son?" the Sheriff had grasped Aaron's shoulder, alarmed.

"I..."

Get control, you idiot! Or you're off to jail!

Aaron shook his head. "I'm all right. It's just... what with Darrell and everything..."

The Sheriff nodded, full sympathy on his face. He looked over where Dad was fuming in front of the truck. "Son," the Sheriff said, softly, "Do you need some help?"

Aaron regarded him. Yes, Sheriff, yes, I need help with that Cryman you didn't believe me about. It's real and it does my bidding. Submitted for your consideration, the Three Stooges are missing. After I named them. We need to stop the Cryman, Sheriff, before it does more of my bidding. So what do you know of explosions and setting them in a way that the Cryman, with its growing collection of head-puppets, is trapped forever in its lair, crying and screaming to be let out, let me out! And have at Aaron and Kathy and Sawyer, and his Cindy. "No," he said.

"Well," the soft voice continued, "if you do, you call me at the office. Just go through the operator." He patted Aaron gently on the shoulder, stood, frowned at Dad one more time, then got in his car and drove away.

Dad was on Aaron before the Sheriff had cleared the driveway. "Show me your bike. Now!" he yelled, the promise of retribution clear and firm in his voice.

Aaron did.

Promise kept.

Chapter 18

"A-a-a-ron!"

As expected, Gar Avis. Aaron stared at the midnight ceiling. He had not slept. The beating and the throwing of his perfectly good bike – it just needs a new wheel, Dad, that's all! – into the woods and his banishment from supper, with Mom's approval, and Kathy screaming at Dad to leave Aaron alone, earning her a head slap, several of them, actually, followed by banishment to her room — and now, the puppet show he'd been dreading all day — had made sleep ridiculous.

"Go away," he whispered.

"Ah, c'mon, Aaron, come on out and play with us. We got your brother right here! You know what we're making him do?" and then Gar and Cory and Steve all laughed nastily.

Wow, the Cryman's an excellent ventriloquist, able to make three voices at once.

Four.

"Aaron!" Darrell shrieked, "Help me! They're doing bad things to me. Real bad!" and his voice choked off.

"Go away," Aaron whispered again.

The thorn wound throbbed and pulsed, as if it had broken open, and Aaron carefully felt down there. Yep, blood.

"C'mon, Aaron!" Gar, again. "You'll like this. Come look. We'll show you what to do with that Cindy girl."

What? As much as he had steeled himself to remain fixed on the ceiling for the duration of the show, her name coming up surprised him, and his head snapped over to the window.

Shark teeth. The Cryman filled the frame, holding Gar's head and Darrell's, pushing their faces together like they were kissing. It then slid Darrell's head down lower and lower, below Gar's head, right about the middle of where Gar's body would be if he had one. The Cryman then motioned Darrell's head back and forth...

"Augh!" Aaron yelped, as he realized what Darrell's head was kissing. A strange feeling of both revulsion and excitement flooded through him, as the thorn burned and burned.

"That feels so ni-i-i-ce!" Gar chortled,

joined by Cory and Steve, who were looking on from their positions strapped to the Cryman's waist. "When's it my turn?" the Two Stooges individually wailed.

"Help me, Aaron!" Darrell cried, or something like that. It was hard to understand him because it sounded as if he was choking on something.

"Go away!" Aaron said.

"Hey, Aaron!" Gar turned an evil eye at the window. "I think Cindy could do this better, don't you? Think we'll go pay her a visit after we're done here." And the Gar head smiled so broadly one of his cheekbones popped through.

"Leave her ALONE!" Aaron shrieked and lunged at the window, but trapped by sheets that pulled and pulled at his leg, the thorn searing and on fire, Aaron scrambled and tussled, further entrapped, and could not reach the window nor the wound...

Crack! A blow to the side of the head. *Crack*! *Crack*! Two more in quick succession and Aaron reeled as blows kept raining down, but not from paws and talons or gigantic hair-covered monsters...

A different monster. Dad.

"Boy!" Dad yelled as he unwound another series of slaps at Aaron's head and shoulders and whatever else was exposed, "What the HELL is all this noise?"

Well, Dad, Aaron felt like saying, that would be you beating me to death, but Dad was obviously referring to the earlier screams elicited by the puppet-head show, so it might be a bit imprudent to give voice to that thought. Aaron took a moment while ducking Dad's hands to check the window but, of course, it was clear. "A nightmare!" Aaron shouted between Dad's slaps, "I was having a nightmare!" Because Dad sure wasn't going to buy Puppet-Head Theater.

"Nightmare?" Dad sneered, "I'll nightmare you!" and the slaps continued as Aaron puzzled over the logic behind that... concluding that a beating for his reaction to a monster outside his window doing lewd things with the heads of its victims was, indeed, another kind of nightmare, one of those helpless ones, like falling. So he braced, taking two or three more rounds before Dad, at last, tired of it. By then, Aaron was sobbing the contrite I-was-wrong tears that Dad required before he was satisfied a proper lesson had been conveyed.

"Go to sleep!" Dad said as he stalked away, muttering "Nightmare!" disdainfully under his breath.

Sleep? Aaron huddled under sheets, trying to gain solace. Gonna have to knock me out for that, Dad, but he didn't express that thought, either, because he didn't really want to get knocked out, so, idiot, suppress all urges for smart-assery, be quiet, listen, wait for Dad to go back into the bedroom...

There. Door closing.

But... that was Kathy's room.

Puzzled, Aaron cautiously lowered the

sheets and stared down the hall. Too dark to see anything. Maybe he should get up and pretend to use the toilet.

Are you nuts? Dad will flush you down the toilet in pieces!

And, besides, he might have only heard Kathy getting up for a bathroom visit. But Dad would have yelled at her and she would have made some snarky remark about being unable to sleep with all this shouting and hitting going on and *whack*! her own head slap. Nothing like that happened.

Just her door closing.

Aaron took a breath and held it, straining to hear. Silent, so maybe he'd misheard. Sound can play tricks at night, especially when there's a Cryman outside the window providing entertainment. He glanced fearfully at the window, resigned to seeing shark teeth, but no, and Aaron figured the show was over. For this night. Tomorrow, though, was already scheduled, with a guest star: Cindy.

And that was a problem, because, not only would he lose his very first – and, no doubt, very last – girlfriend, he'd lose the Magic Five. No Magic Five: no stopping the Cryman.

Maybe he should run across the road and pound on Grampaw's door screaming for Cindy to run and hide because the Cryman was coming.

Uh uh.

Dad would cut him apart with a machete

before he even cleared the front yard. If, by some miracle, he actually made it, Grampaw would shoot him through the door. And all for naught, because the Cryman can go wherever he wants with impunity and may have already acquired a Cindy puppet-head. It had no problem acquiring the Three Stooges, did it?

He craned his neck to look at the kitchen divider and the phone sitting there. Call. At least a ringing phone would alert Grampaw, driving the Cryman away. Or... maybe get them all out of bed and in a position where the Cryman would have an easier time adding all the Eckharts to his troupe.

What other option do you have?

Slowly, Aaron shuffled across the fold-out, trying not to squeak springs or make any other noise that would bring Dad back on him. His calf hurt every time he shifted, and he was probably getting blood all over the place. Great, another set of PJs to hide. Gingerly, he reached a hand to the phone, mentally reciting the Eckharts' phone number so he wouldn't mess it up—

Someone spoke.

Aaron cast an eye fearfully at the window, but it remained empty, so it's coming from somewhere else. He listened. A muttering, somebody trying to keep their voice down. Cautiously, Aaron withdrew his hand, making sure he didn't knock anything over, and then sat up.

The muttering went on then rose in

volume, sharp, "Shut up!"

Dad.

And then quiet again, but Aaron had triangulated and was no longer in doubt; Dad was in Kathy's room. Another sound, undertoned, furtive, and it took Aaron a few moments to catch its rhythm — Kathy sobbing, while trying not to. Along with another sound, one that he had just heard...

Darrell's puppet-head as it kissed Gar.

Chapter 19

"What was going on last night?" Aaron hissed at Kathy over their toast as Mom, still in Aunt Mary's fog, went off to the washhouse. Dad was long gone, ignoring Aaron when he strode through the den and out of the door with a funny look on his face, like a murderer savoring a victim.

Kathy gave him a cloudy glance and shrugged. "I could ask you the same question."

"The Cryman," was all Aaron said.

Kathy came somewhat back to life as she threw him a scornful look. "Yeah, right."

"It was here!" Aaron insisted. "It had..." – four puppet-heads, one of them our brother. That may be a bit hard for her to take. – "...big shark teeth," he finished weakly.

"Uh huh," the clouds returned.

"You don't believe me?" Aaron was incredulous. "I'm telling you, it was out there!"

"You just dreamed it."

"I didn't dream it! It. Was. Out. There!" Aaron emphasized every word with a stab of his finger on the table.

"Uh huh."

Aaron sat back, bewildered. "Well, if you don't believe me, then why in the world did you go to Aunt Mary's?"

Another shrug. "'Cause Sawyer was going."

"But!" Aaron spluttered, "you heard what Aunt Mary said! Even Sawyer believes it!"

"Doesn't mean I do," and she was done with the subject and back on her toast.

Aaron was baffled. All this time, he thought he had his sister's support but, apparently, he'd been wrong. "So, then, you think Sawyer's an idiot?" He paused. "Too?" Aaron left all the implications of that intact.

"Of course he's an idiot," another scornful tone. "And, yes, so are you." And then, more softly, "So am I."

Aaron sat for a moment gaping at her, then pushed away and stomped out of the house and down the driveway, so mad he could just spit, which was a phrase he had never truly appreciated until now. He flopped down hard on the edge of the drainage ditch that ran underneath the front part of the driveway and actually spat, right into the dirt. An unfortunate wind showed up at that exact moment and flipped most of it back in his face. He wiped at it angrily.

Perfect.

Just one more in a series of crappy things he'd endured over the past twelve hours or so.

Head in hands, elbows anchored to knees, Aaron viciously kicked his heels into the ditch wall. He didn't look up when the occasional car went by. If he did, he would just scream. Scream! Gawd! Kathy had been lying to him all this time! Lying! And to Sawyer, too! Acting like she was part of all this, but she was just laughing at them! Laughing!

He gazed at the red dirt below him as another implication slowly sank in... he was in this alone. Completely alone. Kathy was just playing along, all a big joke to her, and she would tire of it and tell Sawyer he was an idiot for believing in boogeymen and Sawyer would blush and say, "Yere ri-ight!" or some other yokel thing and go off with Kathy and there would be no more contact with Aunt Mary and there's Aaron, facing the Cryman with only Connor and Cindy for support.

We're gonna get eaten.

Was three a magic number? Aaron supposed it was, but Sawyer had said five, and he'd gotten that direct from Aunt Mary, a real witch, so it did not matter if three was magical or not. This situation required five. Three wasn't going to cut it, especially *this* three. Connor? Oh, don't make me laugh; that kid was far more cowardly than Aaron, despite his love of blowing things up. Connor was far more of a weakling, too, which was saying much. There was no way Connor could lug fifty pounds of nitroglycerin, or whatever he was making, all the way over here without dropping dead of a heart attack or breaking his arms off or something. And when the Cryman came roaring out of its den, Connor would just cry and pee his pants. As for Cindy, she might already be a head-puppet after last night.

Aaron peered through his fingers at the Eckharts' house. The rusted metal roof shimmered in the heat glare, but, otherwise, everything was still. No sheriffs, search dogs, ambulances, no Grammaw running around the yard screaming about her missing granddaughter. Maybe they haven't found Cindy's empty bed yet. Or maybe they had and didn't think anything of it. Cindy might have gone out to milk the chickens or something at dawn like always, and they wouldn't worry until maybe dinner time, when Grammaw would frown and check the bedroom and then ask Gary and Stan where their sister had gotten off to, and they'd shrug and look blank and then the sheriffs, search dogs, and ambulances would descend on the Gulches, led by a hysterical Grammaw.

Aaron levered to his feet and balanced his way down the ditch's edge, clear across the front of the yard, until he stood at the end of it. He should go over there and see. But Grampaw would seize him by the back of the neck and strip his skin off his bones, and then Gary, always looking for a chance to torment, would rub salt all over him. Stan would try to wash it off but then suggest Aaron go home and never bother them again, because you killed your brother and everything.

Just as Aaron was working up the courage to go and get his bones stripped, Cindy stepped around the side of the distant house. Relief flooded through Aaron and he yelled, "Hey!" and waved his arms frantically.

She stopped, head swinging about until she located him, and waved back just as frantically, a sign she was glad to see him. A warm glow, not associated with the sun's brutality, cascaded up and down his stomach and he made an exaggerated point into the woods. She gave him a thumbs-up, and Aaron took off through the sideyard, hitting the trail and reaching the sawdust pile in record time.

Seconds later, Cindy burst through the creek screen, also in record time. "Hey!" she called, flushed, looking pleased, and stepped towards him.

So, what do you do when your girlfriend shows up? Aaron felt awkward, unsure, and took a hesitant step. Cindy must have felt the same awkwardness because her hands flapped about and she looked off, and then solved the problem by stepping forward and giving him a kiss on the cheek. She beamed at him, took his hand, and led him up the pile. His heart soaring, Aaron allowed himself to be led. They settled at the top, facing each other.

"I'm glad you're all right," Aaron said. "I thought the Cryman might have got you."

"You did?" Her eyebrows rose. "Why would you think that?"

"Because—" Aaron was all prepared to explain the disturbing puppet theater last night when something occurred to him. He narrowed at her. "You believe me about the Cryman, right?"

She looked as if he had just slapped her. "You know I do!" Her mouth open, the wound obvious.

Yeah, he did. "I know! I'm... sorry! Sorry!"

The damage, though, had been done. "How could you say that? I went with you to Aunt Mary's!"

Aaron stared hard at her hurt, beaten expression, then collapsed, shaking his head miserably. "I'm sorry. It's just that Kathy told me she didn't believe it and, well." A helpless flop of the hands.

"Oh." Cindy nodded. "I knew that."

Aaron started. "Knew what? That Kathy thought I was crazy?"

"Um-hmh." Cindy was now all better and turned to survey the woods. "She's just following Sawyer."

Huh? How is it that Cindy, a relative stranger, was more attuned to his sister than he was? Must be girl ESP. "So, does that mean we no longer have the magic number?"

She turned back to him, brow furrowed. "What do you mean?"

"I mean, if Kathy doesn't believe it, we're only four. And if Sawyer goes off with her, then it's only three. And then it won't work. And then we'll all be puppet-heads."

She was startled. "What?"

So he explained.

By the time he wrapped up last night's puppet show, she was completely white, her eyes almost out of the sockets. "Oh my God!" she breathed. "Has that been happening every night?"

"Well..." and he thought about telling her of thorns and their bleeding wounds but decided that might be a bit too much. "No. Not every night."

"So it knows about me," she said to herself and panic seized him.

"I didn't tell it!"

"I know," she said, absently, "It's a monster, it knows everything."

Whew. He wasn't going to get blamed for this. One crisis resolved, now onto the main question: "So?"

"Hmh?" Puzzled at first, then she nodded. "Oh. The Magic Number." She cocked her head and chewed on her inner lips, a rather endearing set of traits that delighted Aaron as she thought it through. "No," she said, after a moment, "It'll be okay. It doesn't matter if Kathy doesn't believe it. Or if anyone else doesn't. As long as you do."

His turn to be puzzled. "Why?"

"Because it came to you first."

That, somehow, made sense. "But, if Kathy won't show up and Sawyer doesn't either, then we won't have five."

She smiled. "Oh, she'll show up. Because Sawyer will."

"What if she tells him not to?"

She tsked. "She won't. Besides, even if she did, he'll come, and she'll follow." She paused and frowned a bit. "She's not ready to dump him yet."

"Huh?" Aaron's eyebrows rose. "She's going to dump him?"

Cindy smiled, which set a delicious dimple in her chin, "You're so cute." And she affectionately pinched his cheek.

Aaron's heart soared, and he knew, just knew, he was blushing so hard his face was the color of sunset. Cindy laughed and leaned forward and so did he—

"What the HELL!" roared a voice and Aaron leaped backward, right off the top, somersaulting down the side of the pile at about sixty miles per hour until he hit the bottom, landing on his neck and wondering why it didn't break. He rolled and sat up and rubbed his head. Maybe he really, really, shouldn't try to kiss a girl while sitting on top of a sawdust pile anymore.

Especially with Grampaw bearing down

on him like a T-Rex cornering its prey.

"I TOLD YEW! TOLD YEW! Stay away from this boy!" Grampaw roared with some incongruity because he was fully focused on Aaron while, obviously, yelling at Cindy. Her whimpers from the top of the pile confirmed where Grampaw's wrath was truly directed, although he still bore down on Aaron with what could only be murderous intent.

Aaron merely watched as the giant thumped towards him. He was too disoriented to get up and run and besides, die here, now, at Grampaw's merciful hands, or later, at Dad's merciless ones? Aaron prepared himself, giving a quick prayer to God, asking that He stop the Cryman on Monday, even though Aaron's impending death meant the Magic Five was effectively dissolved.

But Grampaw stopped short right in front of Aaron, breathing fire but making no move to stomp him into hamburger. He glared at Aaron, then swirled his fiery eyes up the pile. Aaron followed the gaze, seeing Cindy up there trying to make herself small. "Git!" Grampaw barked and threw a talon back towards the creek trail. "You git to the house right now!"

The pile shook and an avalanche of sawdust cascaded over Aaron's head, making him splutter, and he slapped at his eyes to clear them. Cindy moved hastily out of Grampaw's reach and towards the trees.

Grampaw spun to watch her progress.

"Don't you ever see this boy again!" A jab of the talon at Aaron, now shaking Cindy's sawdust shower out of his hair. "He'll get you killed just like he killed his brother!"

Whoosh! All the air in his stomach, gone. Grampaw might as well have punched him in the stomach. Aaron stared open-mouthed at the raging old farmer, who was still glaring Cindy out of the area. "I didn't—" he uttered in sawdust-tinged protest.

"SHUT UP!" Grampaw whirled on Aaron, his voice as powerful as the X-Men's Banshee, driving him at least three inches deeper into the pile. Astonished, Aaron lay there, chained by voice and outrage and injustice.

"And you two!" Grampaw roared again, turning back towards the woods. This puzzled Aaron until he looked around the insane farmer monster and saw Stan and Gary on the edge of the clearing, stupefied, as Cindy slipped behind them, a frightened rabbit seeking refuge. "You keep your eyes on your sister! You don't let her see this one" — another talon stab — "ever again! You hear me?" And without waiting for acknowledgment, his glare of judgment, of hate enveloped Aaron. "Murderer!" he spat, spun, and stalked off.

Stan fled before Grampaw, his face a mix of terror and helplessness as he quick-glanced Aaron before running after Cindy, no doubt to share her refuge. Not Gary. He stood a moment, looking straight at Aaron, a slight smile on his face, scorn and exultation in his eyes. He turned slowly, triumphantly, and followed the mad parade down the trail.

Aaron didn't have limbs or breath or speech for at least a minute. As he recovered, the woods quieted and got hotter, if that were possible. He finally regained control of his body and wiped the last of the sawdust from his lips. "I am not a murderer," he said, then rolled to his feet and went home.

Chapter 20

Night.

Finally.

For the first time in weeks, Aaron welcomed it. Now, Grampaw, I'll show you who the real murderer is.

After stumbling back to the house from the sawdust pile, Aaron had stood quietly by the washhouse for a moment, then mowed the lawn and trimmed the nice bushes near the side porch and raked up, and was waiting at the top of the driveway when Dad came home from work. "Is there anything I can do?"

Dad, in a good mood, blinked and chuckled. "Sure. Paint the shed." Meant as a joke, but Aaron had almost fallen over himself collecting paintbrushes and old half-empty cans of white paint and went at it. Dad, surprised, watched for a moment, then jumped right in, taking great pleasure in correcting Aaron's every move, while letting Aaron know just how much of a doofus he truly was; why, without Dad's help, Aaron wouldn't know which end of the paintbrush to hold, idjit.

So, the day passed rather quickly, if not dangerously.

At dinner, Aaron was bright and deferential and complimentary and Dad was amused and Mom suspicious and Kathy... not sure. She remained fog-bound (Aunt Mary apparently still had her) and everything bounced right off, including a couple of snide remarks Dad sent her way. Aaron washed the dishes under Mom's stony supervision and then stayed quiet and invisible in the back of the living room as Dad watched his Westerns and comedies, periodically stretching out an empty hand so Aaron could fill it with a fetched beer. In this way, the evening waned and the dark descended until Dad called out, "Bedtime!" and made some other snide remark that bounced right off Kathy as she and Aaron headed to their respective beds.

Finally.

"I am not a murderer," he whispered to the dark.

He breathed deeply, calm, centering himself, like Kato taught the Green Hornet to do, and slowly, he looked at the open window.

The shadows were deeper because the moon was lesser. The dark, humid and heavy, tried to convert into a fog different from Aunt Mary's but wasn't quite there. Aaron probed the night with ears and eyes and other senses he shouldn't have and then scrunched down as a coldness he shouldn't feel crept up his spine. He knew what it meant, that he was about to invoke forces and powers well beyond his ken, as if he'd stumbled across the Eye of Agamotto and fooled with it, unintentionally throwing the Earth into another dimension. With great power goes great screw-ups.

Well. Fine. So be it. He didn't start this fight. Whatever he used to end it was fair.

"Come to me," he whispered.

Aaron felt those words pass through the screen and waft through the dark, quieting the errant peepers, turning off the fireflies, gently moving the wildcats and skunks and foxes aside, questing. Until...

...the Cryman heard.

A ripple in the thick air, a displacement, as something huge and terrible moved through the night. Everything else fled: animals, bugs, decency. God.

Aaron waited. He felt it track its progress across the yard as it approached the window and stopped just outside his view. Aaron smiled. The Cryman did not need to make a confirming appearance; Aaron knew it was here, and it knew he was there. The two of them in accord, in perfect synch, the heartbeat of the dark.

Aaron sensed the Cryman's growing anticipation. The breaking point almost reached, Aaron whispered:

"Grampaw."

Hesitation, and then a grin he could not see but didn't need to. The air thickened, a brief salutation, and then the mass drifted off, heading towards the woods and the trail and the road.

Now you'll see the real murderer, Grampaw.

A searing pain ripped Aaron's shoulder blade, and he bit down hard, almost breaking a tooth, to keep from crying out. Slowly, he reached back, probing until he found the protrusion and, biting down even harder, pulled it out, ripping more skin than was necessary. He slipped the bloody, wet thing into the dim light.

Another thorn.

Contemptuously, he tossed it in a corner, rolled over, and slept better than he had in weeks.

Chapter 21

Apparently the fog had formed in Aaron's room sometime after he fell asleep. It hid him when Dad left for work and covered him when Mom got up to resume her go-through-the-motions chores. Covered his chores, too. He didn't see a single chicken that he fed, a single weed he pulled. As for the shed painting – eh, no longer necessary.

He was in control of greater powers and didn't need to pretend. The fog did that for him. He went inside and watched fog-bound TV until the phone rang, a tinny, distant wet sound you hear across a bog.

"It's for you." Kathy held the phone out, her smirk too insinuating for Aaron's taste and he frowned as he took it. She was being a much bigger smartass than usual, wasn't she?

"Hello?" he said, warning Kathy off but all she did was step one or two feet away and stare at him, the smirk permanent.

"Hello."

Cindy.

He warmed and couldn't help it, smiled. Kathy grinned evilly and made kissy faces at him. Aaron frowned at her while saying, "How are you?" He hoped the frown didn't convey.

"I'm... okay." There was a definite frown in her voice and Aaron's brow furrowed, Kathy's transition to monkey motions no longer distracting him.

"What's wrong?"

"It's Grampaw."

Aaron's heart leaped and now it was his turn to smile evilly, and he didn't care if that conveyed or not. Kathy stopped her scratching of monkey armpits and stared at him, wary.

You best be.

"What about him?" And before she could answer, he added. "Is he right there, telling you to get off the phone and not talk to the murderer?"

"What?" Cindy was confused by that. Kathy was downright astonished, her eyes wide and uncomprehending. Aaron thoroughly enjoyed this because he already knew the answer to the question and sneered at Kathy, who took a step back, alarmed.

"No," Cindy gave the already known

answer. "He's—

"—'cause that's what he called me," Aaron drove right into her sentence again. "Out there by the pile. Did you know he said that?"

"No." Subdued.

"Well, he did." Aaron paused. "He shouldn't say things like that."

"Aaron," she said.

"What? Going to make an excuse for him?" and he felt a rage, an odd, strange, vicious thing creep through his stomach. He looked at Kathy. She took another step back. He grinned.

"Grampaw's missing."

A couple of heartbeats went by... Aaron knew this was coming, but still, the proof of it silenced him.

"Did you hear me?"

"Yes," Aaron finally responded and the rage retreated, cooled... no, settled, as if the viciousness he'd felt earlier, that flipflop in his stomach, was now hiding behind something else.

Guilt.

"Missing?" he breathed.

"He... he was out early this morning, didn't even have breakfast with us but he's done that before and he always comes back a little before noon to eat when that happens, but he didn't come back at dinner and Gramma got worried and told Gary and Stan to go look for him and they did and came back and said they couldn't find him and now... it's late and he's still not back."

Aaron waited, his breath shorter, Kathy looking at him strangely, head cocked, worry plain on her face.

"Did you... did you call the sheriff?" he asked. An eyebrow raise from Kathy.

"No," Cindy was miserable. "I wanted to, but Gramma said no, everyone would get all upset for nothing, he was just being an old fool and would come back soon enough..." her voice trailed. "Aaron," she whispered, "do you think it was the Cryman?"

Something obscene and filthy crowed deep within Aaron's stomach, slapping the guilt aside, and burbled up his throat to give voice: "Well, of COURSE it was!" so that she and everyone else who offended him, who crossed Aaron, the Walker of the Thorny Path, would know what fate awaited. But he swallowed hard against it, the counterwash of panic and fear becoming a plug in his throat. Kathy took a step towards him, her mouth parted in concern.

There was a sudden drop of line tone, an obvious change in the background hum, a scattering of white noise and then snatches of words and laughter dopplering from a distance and suddenly filling the earpiece, "Hello? Hello?" A screechy, chaw-infused voice burst over the line. "Who's this? Get off the line, I gotta makes a call!"

"What?" Aaron, startled, pulled the phone back and stared at it.

The voice screeched through the earpiece, "I said you kids get off this line! I gotta make a call and you kids are just tying it up. The nerve of you! We grownups gotta talk, so you git!"

"Maybe we should," Cindy said, bowing before the power, the authority of an adult, some bonnet-wrapped, wrinkle-faced, old biddy who wanted to call her other bonnet-biddy friends and laugh and gossip about canning and beans and old Hiram and his favorite pet cow.

The rage. The cold of it. The sheer... POWER of it.

"No," Aaron hissed into the phone. "We were here first. You wait until we're done."

Cindy gasped. The biddy did, too, but only for a half-second. "Why!" she screeched. "You little brat! You don't be tying up this line when adults gotta talk business!" said with such self-righteous surety.

"What business?" Aaron snarled. "How many jars of jam you're gonna put up this hyeah year, how your lumbago is doing the fandango on your head-o, what kind of cows you're gonna ride on the way to the market where you're gonna sell your *bayeans* and co-O-O-rn and chow cho-o-o-o-ows?" Aaron exaggerated the Alabama accent well past the point of mockery.

"Well! I never!" Biddy was certainly perturbed now. "You are just the rudest boy! You tell me your name right now!"

186

"You first, granny," Aaron even made an exaggerated bow at the telephone.

"Granny! Why... you! You!" The old lady was so flustered she couldn't even get a good retort out! Ha! "This is Miss Dumphy over hyeah at Paysonville! Now you tell me who—"

"Thanks, Miss Dumphy!" Aaron shouted her down, the shocked silence now greeting him so sweet, so wonderful. "Be seeing ya!" And he hung up. He smiled at Kathy, goggling at him.

Yeah. Be seeing ya. Real soon.

Chapter 22

"Get up!" Mom, an insistence in her voice so fierce that Aaron thought the house was on fire. "What? What?" he yelped as he kicked his way out of the sheets. Oh no, the Cryman was in the house, had sniffed out the impending attack on his lair, and was now dispatching the main participants! Mom was trying to save them. But she couldn't.

"We're going to church," Mom announced as she grabbed the sheets he'd reflexively pulled tight against his chin, as if that offered any protection.

Huh? Aaron stared at her uncomprehendingly. Church? What? With everything that's happened you want to go see a bunch of church biddies who will dip their heads together and make whispered judgments, right at the perception level, of Mom's competence as a mother and Aaron's role as a murderer?

Yeah, church biddies? Want to meet the real murderer? Like Grampaw did?

Grampaw was part of the puppet show theater last night, quite a convivial addition as far as Aaron was concerned because Grampaw spent the time giving Gar and Steve and Corey what-fer as Darrell, hanging from the Cryman's waist, cheered him on. Aaron actually giggled at a point or two, the horror receding to the background as the show reached crescendo. When it was over, Aaron whispered, "Miss Dunphy of Paysonville," and suggested, for the next show, that Grampaw and Miss Dunphy engage in the same behavior that Gar had forced Darrell into, something the Grampaw head readily agreed to undertake. So, things were set.

And if the church biddies wanted to join the group, then Aaron was happy to recruit them.

"I said, "Get up!" Mom screeched that and Aaron goggled at her because this was a deeper intensity than Mom usually expressed for church. Sure, she was a stickler for attendance and observing the hundred thousand rules of church decorum that applied to every single aspect of human existence and respected (downright loved) the handsome young Pastor Conroy, who smiled a dazzling set of perfect teeth from his Rock Hudson face as all the ladies swooned, and all the men muttered but what could they do? Church was a lady thing and the men were helpless before it.

"Alright! Alright!" Aaron acknowledged, more to ameliorate her attempts to grab the sheets off him because he had something to hide...

Another thorn.

Right after last night's naming, a longer and more painful one scoured a line from the top of his right hip all the way to the top of his knee, quite deep, quite bloody. He cried out as the thorn made its way, keeping a fearful eye on the back bedrooms, sure that Dad would come roaring out, but nothing. There was a lot of blood and the wound was so deep Aaron was convinced he'd have to get stitches but, after a while, it stopped hurting and bleeding so much. Another set of bloody things Aaron would have to surreptitiously change, sheets as well as PJs, and he was running out of both. And luck. There was no way he could keep Mom from seeing the blood if she got the sheets away from him. There she'd be, shaking the evidence in his face, "What's this? What's this?"

She best not do that, or she might get her name mentioned one night.

A bolt of horror ran through Aaron, making him jerk upright and earning him a startled glance from his still-agitated Mom. He regained immediate control and ensured the sheets stayed well above any blood evidence. She frowned, said, "Hurry up!" and bustled off.

Whew.

You can't give Mom to the Cryman, Aaron.

It's bad enough the thing got Darrell. But, send up Mom? He'd get a thousand thorns for that, shredding him down to bone, and he would walk around the rest of his life with skin hanging from his face in streamers: the Mark of Cain, the mark of one who put the Cryman on his own mom. People would run away from him, screaming. The Sheriff would clap him in irons and throw him in the deepest dungeon available, where he'd rot and bleed and try to put his skin back together. And God turns His back.

Hadn't He already?

That was another shocking thought, but Aaron didn't jerk upright at that one because he saw it as inevitable. Aaron had chosen the Thorny Path, and God will not walk it with him, His Strong and Protective Hands reaching through the brambles and plucking him out of its midst. When you cast your lot with the devil, there is no hope. Instead of an eternity with Jesus, he'd follow the Thorny Path straight to Hell's Gate, where laughing demons would stick red-hot pitchforks into him, right into the same wounds the thorns left. He'd scream and scream for a thousand years and then become the next Cryman, stalking the

Gulches and finding boys with trouble in their souls and tearing off the heads of the boys' enemies. Until some other path-walker replaced him.

He had to get out of this.

Get off the Thorny Path, anyway. That meant moving to the dark path, which couldn't be much worse. Could it? Wander around blind and helpless, groping his way and crying because he was so alone and so lost. But, at least, no more thorns. And no more Cryman.

And no God. So what was the point of going to church?

He almost voiced that, but Mom was in the kitchen and that would bring her screeching back – and no, don't do that — take advantage of the opportunity. Springing up, he made a low-profile dash all the way to the bathroom like a guerrilla moving into cover, sheets bunched in his hand, and had the door shut before Mom could look up and ask about the mess.

Whew.

The sheets were pretty bad, as were his PJs; he washed them out as best he could and stuffed them below the other bloody clothes filling the hamper and knew it was just a matter of washday Monday until discovery.

Monday. Tomorrow. When everything will be set aright.

He dashed out, modesty towel wrapped around his important parts, and snatched clothes out of the utility closet that served as both the hot water heater's space and his storage and back into the bathroom and there, corduroy pants and a pocket shirt, church-approved young man's wear. Quick brush at his brush cut, frowning examination of the three or four pimples erupting across his cheek – forget them, not poppable – okay. Wary glance at the hamper to ensure no blatant evidence and then he stepped out.

Mom was standing there. "Let's go."

Taken aback, Aaron shifted into a defensive stance. "But, I haven't had breakfast yet."

"Then you should have gotten up earlier. Let's go!" and she made a somewhat threatening shoulder move at him that made Aaron raise hands.

What is this?

A thousand protests rose to his lips but he was real close to Dad and Mom's bedroom, and if he gave her a hard time, there was a good chance the door would burst open and a slavering Dad rush out, ready to dismember. Aaron had enough problems with a ready-to-dismember monster, thank you very much, so he went, "Man!" and stomped to where his loafers were and put them on and was out of the door, Mom pushing him in front of her.

"What about Kathy?" he groused. If he had to suffer, it was only fair a sibling suffer, too.

"She's not coming." She pushed him off the porch and towards the garage.

"What? Why not?"

"This is for you and me." She paused. "Only."

Which meant no Dad, either. He looked back at the house. That will make this a real fun morning for Kathy. Mom looked back, too, but there was an odd expression on her face, like she knew this was a mistake. Dad should go with them.

"Why just us?" Opening gambit.

She whirled on him. "Because you need to find God!" a finger raised heavenward, dramatic expression of sincerity. She held that posture for a moment, then it collapsed on her. "And because I lost Him."

Him? Which him? God, or Darrell?

Aaron didn't dare ask for clarification or provide one of a million responses to why he shouldn't go, all of them along the lines of 'I am on the Thorny Path, Mom, and will never find God again, He will never seek me' but the look on her face, so stricken, so broken... Aaron didn't say another word but slipped around the back of the Skylark and got in the passenger side.

He stared straight ahead, not trusting his reaction should he see Mom's grieved face because he would burst out in confession and explanation: Mom, I am on the Thorny Path, and that's why you lost Darrell. And God. Mom would sever his throat because he had called the monster that ate her baby and drove God out of the house. Not that he minded an execution; it was deserved, but it would be the end of her. So he watched the driveway recede as Mom, wordless, backed down it and swung the car around on the road and punched it. It took him a moment to realize they were going the wrong way.

"Mom," he chided, "First Methodist is that way," and he thumbed back at the rear windshield.

"We're not going there," she said, somewhat grimly.

"Then where?"

"The Evangelical Church."

"What?" Aaron stared at her, dumbfounded. The Evangelical Church? "But... that's Connor's church!"

She nodded, "I saw him here the other day. That's where I got the idea."

"But... Connor!"

"Isn't he a friend of yours?"

No, Mom, he is not. He is an embarrassment, an albatross hanging from Aaron's neck. But tomorrow, Mom, he and I and the other criminals will rid this world of the monster who ate your baby.

He looked out the window. "I suppose," he said, quietly.

Chapter 23

How Mom found the church was a mystery because she switched and turned and cut through some of the most bewildering series of back roads, both gravel and dirt, before emerging through a hedge break into the grass field that served as the church's parking lot. It was actually a nice-looking building, traditional white wooden square raised somewhat on pilings so Aaron could see underneath it, with a steeple in the front overlording the iron-railed steps leading from an expanded gravel patio up concrete steps. Which was packed with people making their way from the field to the inside, all of whom turned as if on signal and stared at the Skylark as soon as Mom broke through.

THE CRYMAN

They didn't look friendly. Not at all.

As Mom maneuvered her way through the haphazardly parked cars, Aaron studied the congregation, paused on the steps. To a man, woman, and child, they frowned at him, as though he had just walked into their living room and farted. Ordinarily such a thought would make him giggle, but there was a sense of danger here, as if these people were annoyed at his presence. Scanning the faces quickly, he did not see anyone he recognized, which was a bit of a surprise. This was a Holy Roller church, and if there was something the peanut farmers around here thoroughly enjoyed, it was Holy Rollers.

One summer night, Aaron had found himself perched on a hill with about six or seven peanut farmers watching the goings-on inside a Holy Roller tent pitched below them in the middle of a field near Enterprise. How Butch got there, much less with a gaggle of Damascus peanut farmers, had something to do with a football game playing in the nearby Enterprise High School stadium and some girls he didn't know, who got bored with the game dragging the peanut farmers along with them, with Butch somehow attached. Guess because he knew one or two of the farmers. Didn't matter; one of the girls, a brunette with a medium-sized hump on her back but otherwise quite cute, was leaning against his knees watching the show below. And it was quite the show.

"Lookatdat!" Bingo Watts, one of the more jovial farmers who had some blonde girl without a hump wrapped around his neck, hollered, and yes, lookatdat: a very large woman wearing what looked like a white muumuu was in the middle of the fold-down chairs swinging her enormous arms and stomach in a sequence quite reminiscent of a tornado's spin, her head thrown back as far as her gigantic neck would allow, mouth wide open and screaming, "Ektel! Ektel! Ektel!" or something like that. Two very tall black women, dressed like models on some fashion runway with their hair done up in beehives, stood on either side of her, grabbing at the tornado arms and screeching, "Sister Rose! Sister Rose!" or something like that.

"What in God's name?" Aaron said.

Which elicited peals of laughter from Hump and Bingo and just about everyone else. "Boy, you ain't never seen this afore?" Yad Semple, another member of the peanut-farmer Hall of Fame, queried.

"No," Aaron said, growing ever more amazed, "I don't think anyone on this planet has."

Which elicited more peals of laughter, all appreciative, and got him a peck on the cheek and a "You're funny!" from Hump and Aaron figured he was in high cotton, especially when, at some cue only visible from inside the church, the entire congregation rose and threw arms up and shouted "Hallelujah!" and then back down and then up "Hallelujah!" over and over, and a choir somewhere out of view belted out Black gospel that got all of the peanut farmers clogging and dancing and laughing.

Overall, it was pretty entertaining.

But then it all dissipated — congregation and Sister Rose, her attendants, preacher and choir and tent and peanut farmers and Hump, whose name and phone number he forgot to obtain — and Aaron was alone on a moonlit hill, a bit stunned by how quickly things move, as Dad, in a rage because he had to look for Aaron, descended on him.

He wondered if this would be like that.

"Let's go," Mom, impatient, and Aaron stepped out of the car with much trepidation, leaned on the open door, and regarded the congregation regarding him. It didn't exactly go silent, but the conversations hushed to give the line a chance to pass judgment before resuming whatever they were discussing before the Skylark so rudely interrupted. Probably whose infant they were going to sacrifice at service today.

You know, with the Cryman and everything, that's just not funny.

Mom launched from her side of the car and made a beeline for the steps, not even bothering to check if Aaron followed. Hastily, he stepped around the car and was at her shoulder, figuring it'd be harder for the Witch Hunters to get them both. As they approached, the congregational scrutiny intensified and

Aaron suppressed an urge to check his zipper because these people were sure staring at something. A tall woman with brown hair, and the biggest white sunhat ever, made broke from the line, and intercepted them with the biggest fake smile Aaron had ever seen outside of a used-car commercial.

"Haagh! Ayund weal-come!" She held out a white-gloved hand and tipped her fake smile and arched eyebrows at them. "Is thyis y'all's first time hyeah?"

Oh my God, Aaron felt like he'd get diabetes from all the sweetness. And lose IQ points from the absurdly over-the-top Southern accent.

Mom must have felt the same on both points because she stopped and coolly regarded Miss USA. "Yes," brusque answer and Mom moved at the line, forcing entry into the Queue of Judgment, Aaron at her heels.

Miss USA, unperturbed by the brush-off, followed them with, "Wa-yal, y'all are just most welcome. Thyis is Gawd's house," — expressed with a hushed tone of reverence and a palm raised skyward — "and all Hyis childrens can enter." And she took her diabetes smile and slim Metracal figure off to a taller man in a suit bearing the most beatific smile and expression of sincerity possible to form on a masculine face in the line behind where Mom had penetrated. They beamed at each other in the holy light of God's Love and Aaron stared. Was that the pastor and his wife?

They're Connor's parents? Well, that certainly explained a lot.

As if by some unacknowledged signal, the queue flowed forward up the steps and through the open doors, the tide carrying Aaron along irresistibly. Somehow, the currents and countercurrents deposited Mom and him in some middle aisle, flanked on either side by very sincere-faced and beatific-expressioned families who turned their otherworldly love on them in greeting and welcome, ensuring there was absolutely no way Aaron could escape. Nervously, he glanced at Mom, but she was intent on the front, where Mr. and Mrs. USA had, by virtue of the tide, been deposited on either side of a pulpit on which draped one of the most enormous Bibles Aaron had ever seen. So, pastor and wife, indeed. And Connor's parents, evidenced by Connor himself standing to the side of the dais, his eyes locked on Aaron, jaw dropped in pure astonishment.

That makes two of us.

Connor's gaze swept back to his parents and he made a little cut motion across his throat, which Aaron interpreted to mean, "Cool it, " not "I'll kill you." Cool what, Aaron had no idea, but he acknowledged it with a cut motion of his own, puzzled by Connor's expression of evident relief. What's going on?

No time or opportunity to answer that because Mrs. Connor's Mom suddenly produced a tambourine, which was quite a good trick, and began shaking it like the opening to *Green Tambourine* and Aaron wondered if this would turn into a rock concert when the congregation to a man, woman, and child all stood and clapped hands in rhythm. Confused, Aaron stared at this display until Mom's four-foot-long fingernail jabbed him in the ribs and he jerked to his feet and, after a few off-rhythm attempts, matched the handclaps, looking at Mom in bewilderment.

Mom, this isn't how the Methodists do it.

Seeking clues, Aaron scrutinized as much of the clapping congregation as he could. Okay, typical southern Alabama good-ole-boy redneck cast to most of them. Sunburnt and wrinkle-eyed and the years of soil and toil evident in strong backs and the little red patches of veins on faces, men and women alike, but there was an animation as the clapping kept pace with Mrs. Connor's Mom. White people, but there were some black people scattered here and there, some with entire families, very surprising because you simply didn't see that in the Methodist church. Black people had their own churches with which Aaron was slightly familiar, Dad having driven by one or two of them on some Sunday morning and the door opening and a line of well-dressed Black people coming out clapping their hands and singing as they passed, Dad sneering, Mom ignoring, Aaron intrigued. Clapping like this congregation was doing right now. There was even an entire Asian family on the other side of the aisle, brown-skinned like

Polynesians and Aaron wondered if they were Viet Cong. How the devil did Viet Cong end up in Alabama? And clapping in rhythm with White and Black people, at that?

Mrs. Connor's Mom sang, low at first, the jangles of the tambourine covering it and Aaron strained to hear. "This is the day the Lord has made, this is the day the Lord has made," softly, growing in strength with each iteration, the emphasis on every fourth syllable, like a stab. Like a chant.

The congregation picked it up at the same softness, growing in volume as the clapping increased in volume and speed and then foot stomps, not so hard at first, and Aaron looked around, concerned. Where they all going to rush the pulpit or something? It got louder with every third iteration, the stomps turned downright stampede-like, a frenzy building throughout the entire congregation.

Including Mom.

Aaron gaped at her. Mom, all inside herself and subdued and invisible in the same room as Dad, was clapping and downright shrieking the chant, downright dancing the stomp. Her eyes cast heavenward, her face straining against itself as if her very soul wanted to break free and soar the seven Heavens and escape this world, this pain and sorrows.

His mom, whose only animation was in cooking and admonishing Aaron's violations of the millions of rules the Lord had made, was rapturous over the day He had made. She was in the grip of something Aaron had never suspected, powers and forces that ought to be relegated to scary books and fairy tales and Biblical times, but he'd seen it, hadn't he? Was in the grip of it himself, wasn't he? But not the Lord's power, oh no.

The devil's.

He gasped as Mom's frenzy matched the congregation's and he almost saw the pure, holy light beaming down from the rafters and enveloping the dancing, singing, praising people who sought the power of good and love, a light that passed over and around him, leaving him in darkness. A black curtain in the middle of bright columns, the part of the church left out of holy blessing.

Where the devil's boy walked the Thorny Path, no light could penetrate.

Already suspicious glances came his way: a redneck breaking the frenzy to stare at him, a slattern pausing mid-dance to eye him suspiciously. Even Mom. "Clap with me!" she insisted, bringing her beating hands in front of his face, "Sing with me!" and now her enraptured face in front of his, "For Darrell! For Darrell!"

Repelled, Aaron shifted out of range, but the pew arrested his retreat. For Darrell, Mom? Darrell is a bauble on the Cryman's belt. He entertains nightly and is far beyond God's reach. Your screeching means nothing.

"Brothers and sisters!" a booming but

reedy voice cut through the shouting and hoopla, an arresting voice and Aaron moved around Mom's insistent face to see. Mr. Connor's Dad, standing tall and central behind the pulpit, one palm to the heavens, the other drifting over the giant Bible as if invoking powers, his eyes bright and otherworldly, transformed into something alien, the very fire of God blasting from his face, transporting the congregation from this world of sin and sorrow into the Throne Room Itself. Except for the boy in the back, shrouded in black horror.

"Brothers and sisters!" Downright shouting now, the tambourine beating so hard it was losing all sense of rhythm, Mrs. Connor Mom leaning into her husband, her face working in ecstasy. "We are the Lord's and He is Ours!"

"We are the Lord's and He is Ours!" shouted back from the congregation, even Mom, who had turned fully back to the front.

"Open your hearts to His Power!"

"Open your hearts to His Power!"

"Open your souls to the Spirit, and OPEN YOUR THROATS!"

That last was bellowed with enough force that Aaron wondered if Mr. Connor's Dad was a mutant. Not Banshee but Professor X, because everyone did as he commanded. "*AAAAAAAHHHHH!*" a continuous nonsensical note thrown from every open mouth towards the heavens, not musical but a raw shouting of nothing but emotion; which emotion Aaron couldn't say, but Mom was in it, Mom called to heaven, too.

The note rose and fell and renewed with more power, if that were possible, and now there were other notes, or words, or something like them, accenting the one note, words that sounded ancient and Biblical but which made no sense to Aaron. That "Ektel Ektel" he'd heard on the hill outside the tent.

What is this language? And why can't he understand it?

Simple. You walk the Thorny Path. And the language of the Lord is forbidden you.

Repulsed, Aaron leaned right then left, hemmed by the Lord's anointed, and knew his very touch would burn them, and they him. Thorns will score him from head to toe and the congregation, Mom included, will spin and fingers point and scream the holy language he did not understand, but he can guess what it means: "Devil child!" "Devil!"

"Devil," he whispered, but it was lost in the roar, and a hand fell on his shoulder and he shrieked, also lost in the uproar, and this was it, the Lord's rendering, and he will be torn limb from limb and the parts mailed across the four corners of the country so all can see what he had done.

"C'mon!" Connor, shouting in his ear.

Aaron blinked at him, uncomprehending, because this should be his judgment, his death, not rescue, but Connor pulled on his sleeve and pushed through to the end of the aisle and Aaron followed, wondering how the shouting, now frothing, now singing people, did not see him. Mom did not see him.

Of course. They can't see him on the Thorny Path.

The invisible monster boy slipped past the frenzied, holy people and out through a side door, following Connor onto the lawn.

Chapter 24

"Whew," Connor grinned, "They're all pretty worked up already."

Aaron blinked at him. "What?"

Connor made an impatient gesture at the door they'd just exited. "Them. The lemmings. It usually takes a bit longer to get them up and hooting. Dad usually has to do a magic trick or two, but, today, man." And he shook his head.

"You call them lemmings?"

Connor gave him an owlish look. "What would you call them?"

"Uh," Aaron was at a loss. "I guess I'd call them the congregation. Aren't they your congregation?"

"Not mine." Connor wiped his glasses on

his shirt. "The parents. And not yours, either." He put his glasses on and stared at Aaron. "Just what are you doing here, anyway?"

Aaron made a helpless gesture. "Mom made me come."

"Why?"

More helpless gestures. "I guess... she... Darrell." That was all he could say.

Connor regarded him a moment, shrugged, then stepped towards the back of the church. "Well, since you're here, let's go see what I've got."

"What you've got?" Oh no, some spazzy bottlecap collection or something equally nerdy.

Connor raised an eyebrow at him over his shoulder. "For tomorrow."

Oh. Yeah. Tomorrow.

Monday. When they will put all this to rest.

Somewhat eagerly, Aaron fell in behind as Connor led the way over a grassy trail that topped the rise behind the church and fell towards a ramshackle ranch set in a clearing at the edge of some woods and a pond. A couple of goats perched on the pond's banks bleated at them and an old yellow dog wobbled off the house porch and headed towards them, big smile on its face and an oversized tail wagging in time with its walk. "That's Simon," Aaron introduced. "He's good, he won't bite you or anything."

Aaron doubted the old dog had enough ill will or even the energy to do anything violent as it wobbled up and *woofed* at them happily. He patted it on the head and it wriggled happily and fell in with them, as Connor skirted the house and headed towards a shed set on the other side of the pond. The goats bleated at them as they walked. "Are those yours?" Aaron asked.

"I guess." Connor waved a hand dismissively at the expectant goats. "Mom wanted them to do some cheese and stuff but she's never done anything with them. I think we should eat them."

"What?"

"They're annoying. Only want to be fed all the time. Besides, goat meat is pretty good."

"You've eaten goat?"

Connor gave him a mischievous smile but said nothing and shooed the goats off as they came closer, Simon adding a bark or two in emphasis. "Won't you get in trouble?" Aaron asked as Connor pulled the shed door open.

"For what?"

"Being away from the church."

"*Pfhht.*" Connor gave his opinion. "They won't even know I'm gone until sometime tomorrow." And he stepped onto the raised floor and gestured Aaron inside. Hmm. That may also explain why Connor was so... Connor.

It was surprisingly larger inside than the shed dimensions indicated, and Aaron took a moment to take it all in. Old, like one of those falling-down barns that dotted the Alabama countryside, but this one remained upright, probably more by prayer than maintenance because the walls were gapped boards allowing streams of dust-filtered sunlight to zebra-stripe the place. Lots of building materials leaned against various walls or were stacked in corners, awaiting projects that, judging by the layers of dust on them, would never be started. The roof was rusty tin and, amazingly, still intact with hundreds of thousands of wasps and other mad bees conducting dogfights up there, a few of them dropping down to see about Aaron and Connor. Connor swatted at them absently as Aaron dodged kamikazes.

Connor flipped a switch: thick yellow wires stapled above it, ran up an exposed stud and across a beam to a gigantic fluorescent light suspended above a mad scientist's table; that was the best description of it as the bulbs blinkered on and exposed the tubes and Bunsen burners and flasks filled with oddly colored liquids, with various electronic devices scattered across its length, and a stool pulled up the center. Lots of other mad scientist paraphernalia was stacked underneath the table, which was really nothing more than a homemade bench, five or six two-by-fours laid across stacked concrete blocks.

"Welcome to my laboratory," Connor chuckled in his best Vincent Price. Which wasn't that good an impression but Aaron giggled as he swept a hand across the scene, "What *is* all this?"

Connor looked at him like he was stupid

or something. "Where I do my experiments. Don't you have something like this?"

Well, no, Aaron didn't mess much with chemistry sets, which even he thought childish now, but this setup was light years beyond those kid toys. This was a serious lab.

Connor snapped his fingers. "Oh, that's right, you're a space guy," and he waggled a hand dismissively and Aaron supposed he was right. He scrutinized the flasks. "So what are you doing?"

"Making the bombs, of course." Connor reached under the bench and hauled up a tin bucket and dropped it on top, causing an alarmed Aaron to step back. Connor laughed, "Relax, they're not ready yet."

"Oh." Aaron felt simultaneous relief and embarrassment. Tricked by the little dweeb. "What do you mean, 'they'?"

Connor reached below again and hauled up two more buckets, setting them all in a line and stepping back with satisfaction. Aaron peered at them skeptically. "Bucket bombs?"

Connor grinned so wide, Aaron thought his face would split and nodded vigorously. "You betcha!"

"How?"

Connor shrugged. "Nitrate. Under compression." He patted a nondescript sack leaning against a bench leg. "The tricky part is the fuses." And he flipped a hand over some Bic pens and tubes scattered behind the buckets. Aaron had no idea what he was looking at, his suspicion heightened. "So they'll be ready?"

"Oh yeah."

"And your parents won't give you a hard time?"

"*Pfhht,*" again with the razz, "they don't know what I'm doing in here." A pause. "They don't know what I'm doing most of the time." A look of sorrow flashed across his face.

Aaron didn't understand that. Connor's hands-off parents were a blessing. One of Aaron's fondest wishes was a world without parental interference. It would make things so much safer, no more belts off and flaying at the flimsiest provocation. It would make things easier.

Like killing the Cryman.

"So what time are you guys picking me up?" Connor asked as he fooled with some particularly dangerous-looking flasks.

"Uh..." Aaron didn't really know. "In the morning I guess."

"You guess?" Connor cocked a puppy head. "Haven't you guys planned this out yet?"

"Well, no. I mean, I don't know if Kathy's even talked to Sawyer yet or not."

Connor gaped at him. "Geez, Louise! We doing this, or what?" At his normal 2000 decibel level.

"Keep it down!" Aaron cast a worried glance at the door.

"Don't worry about them." Connor flicked a dismissive finger towards the yard. "They're all frothing at the mouth and rolling on the floor by now." Gimlet eye at Aaron. "Including your mom."

"No, she's not!" said hotly.

"Yes, she is." Said confidently.

This was one of those increasingly frequent moments when Aaron was on the verge of hitting someone. Unlike Gar, Aaron didn't expect a devastating retaliation from Connor, other than him falling down and screaming bloody murder. Like Darrell used to whenever Aaron smacked him. Before he was actually murdered. So he stepped forward, fist raised to his chin level, preparatory to striking. "You take that back!"

Connor didn't back up, simply looked at Aaron mildly, which was rather unexpected and made Aaron hesitate. Connor might know kung fu or something. "Trust me," he toned, "she is. I know the look."

Which Aaron had to admit was quite likely. Connor had a lot more experience with the type than anyone else. He dropped the fist, feeling helpless. "I don't know what's going on." And he felt a sob rising in his chest and no, oh no, don't do this, not in front of this spaz, this dweeb, this embarrassment, this... only friend Aaron had.

Sympathetic hand on the shoulder. "It's okay. She's dealing with it her way. We're gonna deal with it our way." Dramatic gesture at the buckets. "By blowing up the Cryman." Raised eyebrows. "Tomorrow?"

The surety of it steeled Aaron. Yes, Mom,

you pray and sing and seek the solace of the Lord, even if it's through spouting nonsense into the air, and tomorrow I will seek vengeance on your behalf, with the help of your Lord.

Who has turned His back on me. But not on you.

"Tomorrow," Aaron assured. And seized Connor's hand, pact, accord. With his only friend.

Chapter 25

Mom hummed that annoying "This is the day" ditty all the way home and as they went into the house and while she threw together the breakfast she had earlier denied him. She maintained a half-beatific smile the whole time and was otherworldly, not here, and Aaron wondered if Aunt Mary's fog still held. Or maybe another fog.

And, wow, French toast, a special treat and Aaron did not know who to thank, Aunt Mary or Connor's parents. So he decided for the go-between, "These are great, Mom!"

She turned from the sink, her face unreadable, studying him and Aaron felt an uneasy flipflop in his French-toast-filled stomach. "They're Darrell's favorite," she toned and turned back to the never-ending wash of dishes. Aaron didn't feel like breakfast anymore and, after appropriate moments, pushed back and walked away. Mom didn't turn.

Not Aunt Mary's fog, the Cryman's.

Because his bedroom/den was right next to the kitchen, Aaron thought it better to put some distance between him and Mom, so he headed through the dining room door and glanced to his left and froze. Dad was in his chair, his dark curls popped over the back of it and his beefy arms splayed on either upholstered side, one hand grasping a drink that looked suspiciously like RC Cola, probably with the requisite splash of whiskey. Aaron logged his forearm Tank Destroyer tattoo, the snarling black panther resting against a tank silhouette because Dad had driven one in the Big One, and it was appropriate that he emblazon that on his arm. Everyone who gets shot at and shoots back ought to emblazon that event on them somewhere.

Aaron wondered if he should get a Cryman tattoo.

"Where you been?" growled from the other side of the chair, which was a bit startling. How did Dad know he was there? Because he had eyes in the back of his head and saw everything. Well, most everything. Right, Cryman?

Aaron almost giggled when he replied, "Church."

"Uhm," Dad grunted, which might be approval, Aaron couldn't tell. The television was showing *The 20th Century* and Walter Cronkite was going on about the Suez Canal or something and it looked interesting, but if Aaron moved to the couch, he put himself in Dad's range, and there was something in Dad's posture, as little of it as Aaron could see, that warned he's in a weird mood, like an old Western gambler who had successfully played an ace from his sleeve. Probably best not to poke the bear; Aaron quietly slipped back out of the door and down the hall.

At the living room door, which actually led directly to the television side of the living room/dining room combination, Aaron held his breath and zipped past it, confident that the angle between doorway and Dad's chair was steep enough to block Dad's view of him, but not his shadow, and when there was no "Hey, boy, bring me a beer!" or "Go outside and mow the lawn!" sighed in relief and, surreptitiously, tapped on Kathy's door. "Hey, it's me!" he whispered. No answer, even after a few more attempts he feared were dangerously loud enough to catch Dad's attention. He opened the door and pivoted inside.

Hmm. Dark and empty. No Kathy wrapped deep in the sheets and duvet, which were thrown back almost violently. Aaron put the shade up to give him more light because she was probably going to jump out, "*Boo!*" scaring him to death, but no such attempt and no evidence she was here, so she must be outside somewhere. Quick survey out of the window but not in sight. A little odd. He figured she'd wait for him.

He opened the closet door, the only true closet in the whole house save for the one in Mom and Dad's room. This one served as combination Aaron/Kathy and, until recently, Darrell's main storage, with the water heater closet serving as Aaron's satellite storage that he'd begun using as Kathy had become quite circumspect about him and Darrell, and just about everybody, bursting into her bedroom unannounced and without her permission. A rule that did not apply to Dad or Mom, of course. Kathy owned the majority of the big closet mostly because of clothes and shoes, the volume of which mystified him because all she ever wore were tops and jeans and Keds. Aaron's portion was a fraction of hers but sufficient for his needs, containing his clothes and, more importantly, the giant stack of precious comic books and *Creepy* and *Famous Monsters* magazines holding down one corner. There was even enough room for a small bookshelf next to the stack, and Aaron patted it affectionately. It held his favorite books: *The Golden Impala*, *Knee Deep in Thunder*, some favorite Hardy and Power Boys, and that extraordinary *The Forgotten Door* with its other dimension of peace and happiness where Aaron so wanted to go. So badly.

"Take me now," he whispered to the cover

and steeled himself for a miracle that did not happen.

He looked down at the comic stack, a *Famous Monsters* on top, the one with Barnabas Collins on the cover, and wondered if there was a Cryman issue. If not, maybe he should write something and send it to them. Hmm. That would make him rich and famous, and Aaron had a sudden vision of himself tooling along a beach road in a red sports car convertible, wearing a pair of sunglasses and a long white scarf trailing behind. Nice. But he'd need photos of the Cryman. Maybe he could snap a few with Kathy's Polaroid Swinger before they blew up the monster tomorrow.

Speaking of Kathy, where is she?

Frowning, Aaron stepped out of the closet and made another recon out the window — no Kathy — and then out of the bedroom and past the living room with no interception by Dad, and past Mom still at the kitchen sink forever and ever dishes without end amen, and out into the backyard. Hot. Too hot, and she wasn't in the shade of the washhouse or the shed and there was no way she would be in the chicken coop, so that left one place...

Yep. Sitting on top of the Magic Sawdust Pile.

Aaron ascended, intending a "Hey, how long you been here?" but saw the stone of her face and far distance in her eyes. He choked the words and settled next to her. The top of the pile was large enough to afford distance and, thank God, because she obviously didn't want to be bothered. But there were many things to discuss, and Aaron didn't know what an appropriate period of silence was in this situation so, after what was probably not an appropriate period, asked, "What are you doing?"

"Nothing," toned flat and disinterested.

"So how long you been here?"

She shrugged noncommitally, and Aaron found himself right back where he started. He shifted restlessly, dangerous up here, and a small sawdust avalanche started, but must get things going. "Do you know where Mom and I went?"

Another shrug. Aaron was getting irritated. C'mon, this is important! "Connor's church."

No reaction, not a show of interest. So let's stir things up. "Don't you think that's weird?"

"No, because you're weird."

Well, okay, slapped him back, but at least she's responding now. "I didn't pick it," he said in defense, "Mom did. That's what's weird."

"Not so weird." She stretched and a bit of relief ran through Aaron because she was coming to life. "She doesn't want to see those old prune-faces at our church."

That made sense. "But, Connor's church?"

"She doesn't know anyone there."

That made sense, too. Still. "It was

weird."

She grinned at him. "Then you fit right in."

Despite the insult, he warmed because she was back. Or pretty close to it. "Do not," more defense, "but you should have seen it. Lots of hootin' and hollerin'."

"Yeah?" She picked idly at some loose sawdust. "Sounds like fun."

"Nooo," he heartily disagreed. "It was more scary than fun."

She stilled, a hooded look in her eyes. "You have no idea what scary is," and turned away from him.

Hello? Cryman, remember? Aaron was incredulous but, to give her benefit, he had never told her about puppet-head theater, so her only measure of whatever he thought scary was based on oblique events, at least oblique to her. She hadn't actually seen anything, had she? And she didn't believe him in the first place. Maybe best not to try and convince her that he was, indeed, quite familiar with scary, thank you very much.

"Fine." He let his irritation show in compensation. "Connor showed me the bombs."

"Hmh?" Kathy came back from her full distraction and looked at him, confused.

"To blow up the Cryman? Tomorrow?" Stay with me here, will ya?"

"Oh." She shook her head in exasperation. "He's actually made them?"

"Well..." Technically no. "He's assembling

them today."

She laughed. "He's going to blow himself up."

Aaron couldn't disagree with that and expected, any moment, a mushroom cloud to rise in the air, marking where Connor's house used to be, but in the event he didn't evaporate himself and five square miles around the church, then the plan goes forward. "So Sawyer's ready?"

"Ready for what?"

Huh? He gaped at her and wondered if he should do a Three Stooges head knuckle to wake her up. "Tomorrow. The Gulches. Blow it up. Ya know?"

"*Pfhht*," she gave her opinion about that, "I haven't even told him about it."

"Told me about what?" This from Sawyer, who made the best-timed appearance possible, stepping into the clearing from the roadside at just the moment Aaron was about to explode all over Kathy, like a badly made Connor bomb. For a rare instant in his life, Aaron was glad to see him. Kathy wasn't, seemed more bored than anything and was also unsurprised, so Aaron figured she'd called him earlier. Odd, her disinterest, considering the felonies they planned for tomorrow.

"About blowing up the Cryman," Aaron summed after giving Kathy a few moments to take the lead, which she didn't.

Sawyer stepped to the base of the pile and furrowed his brow. "What?"

Aaron gave him the Cliff Notes' version, culminating in his survey of Connor's bombmaking factory this morning, the whole time Sawyer's brow furrowing even deeper, if that was possible. "Lordy," was all he said.

Aaron glanced at Kathy to see if she intended to join this conversation, but she looked even more disinterested. What the devil? "So," Aaron said as he kept an eye on her, "are you with this?"

Sawyer raised shoulders. "I guess," he said, "it'll be fun."

Fun? Aaron stared at him. Maybe in a redneck peanut-farmer way, but blowing up a significant geological formation to entrap a monster was hardly a day picnic. Maybe Sawyer was having doubts, too. "You do still believe all this, right?"

Sawyer started a bit. "What? The Cryman? You know I do." And he looked downright insulted.

Relieved, Aaron threw a superior glance at his apostate sister, which Sawyer caught. Waving a hand in dismissal, he said, "She don't, I know that, but it's still fun."

Now it was Aaron's turn to be startled because what was this dynamic? Sawyer knows his girlfriend thinks he's a hick for believing in the Cryman, but he's here all the same? And she hasn't broken up with him?

Maybe boyfriends/girlfriends could stay boyfriends/girlfriends even when they think the other is stupid.

To underscore this, Kathy rolled her eyes and said, "You're both idiots," and slid down the pile to stand next to Sawyer, who laughed and they hugged and Aaron was learning lessons. "And weird, don't forget that," he added.

Kathy actually laughed at that and gave him an appreciative look and Aaron grinned. All was not lost. "So tomorrow?"

"Yeah, yeah," Sawyer waved him off because he had something much more interesting to attend to now, specifically, Kathy.

"After Dad's gone to work," Aaron briefed.

"Yeah, yeah," another wave off and hand-in-hand, he and Kathy headed towards the road trail. Aaron guessed this was the last time he'd see either of them until late this evening. "Is it still the Magic Number?" he called.

"Huh?" Sawyer turned to him, puzzled.

"I mean, with Connor."

Sawyer frowned, telling Aaron there was no magic in the number four, so he added hastily, "Cindy's coming with us."

Sawyer smirked in some derision and Aaron felt himself grow red, but the hick gave him a thumbs-up. "That's five. That'll do." And he and Kathy disappeared, leaving both their smirks behind.

Aaron took in a deep breath. Okay. Okay. Everything will be okay.

Chapter 26

Aaron was on the couch. The news was on, and Dad was sitting in his reclining chair opposite, beer in hand, completely absorbed by Roger Mudd. Mom was doing something in the kitchen and Kathy was... elsewhere. Still. With Sawyer, still. Who cares?

Because Monday was coming.

Monday was coming.

The arrangements were already made. In the morning, they'd go to Connor's and collect everything and then the Gulches, lay Connor's bombs, and ignite them with the field telephone wire.

The cave collapses, killing or trapping the Cryman, and Aaron is released from the Thorny

Path...

...and becomes a dweeb again, at the mercy of the Three Stooges.

Well, not *that* group of Stooges, who will remain forever under tons of clay alongside the Cryman, forever grousing and snapping at each other while making Darrell do unspeakable things to them. Another group of Stooges. There's always a group of Stooges ready and willing to take over the time-honored mission of dweeb torment.

Who would it be? Probably Carlton, the fury-eyed skinny peanut-farmer kid, who had an unnatural hatred of Aaron based on no reason he could surmise other than Aaron got straight As. Peanut-farmer kids didn't like the idea of anyone doing well in school, thereby having more options than being a peanut farmer. A peanut farmer you are born, a peanut farmer ye shall be.

But Aaron wasn't born a peanut farmer, so why was his choice of something other than peanut farming enough to raise the ire of Carlton and *his* Two Stooges, Cray and Joseph? Aaron wanted to be an astronomer, even had the requisite telescope, although he was having a tough time with math (which, he suspected, meant he wouldn't do very well as an astronomer). But even a bad astronomer was better than a great peanut farmer.

So, there he'd be. Defenseless. Again. Putting up with the daily insults and sneers, books knocked out of his hand every time he turned around, laughed off the baseball field, tripped, punched, pushed... the usual, all starting up in about two weeks. And the new Stooges would have the advantage of Darrell's disappearance (his death, you mean, but no one knows that. Yet.) and Aaron's Cryman story as torment points. Aaron would have to put up with it because he'd no longer have recourse to simply whispering a name. No shared joy of watching the Cryman's menagerie grow and grow until the Cryman could put on puppet-head *Ben Hur* if he wanted, Aaron laughing at the antics.

The power will be gone.

That raging, sweet, lustful sense of power that came with each naming, with each scouring of thorns, *pfhht*. Gone. Today, he was the Walker of the Thorny Path, the Cryman's master, and could make it do his bidding. Just had to put up with having his flesh torn. And bad puppet-head theater.

After Monday, though...

Do you really want to give that up?

Aaron squirmed, a dangerous move, but Dad didn't even glance over, riveted by something Roger was grimly talking about. "Holy God," Dad muttered.

Aaron looked at the screen. There were shots of some mansion with cops and ambulances running all around it, some bodies covered with tarp, and the word "Pig" scrawled across the front door in what looked like blood. Aaron chilled. "What's that?"

"Shut up!" Dad snarled, "I'm trying to listen!"

Aaron shut up. And watched. Some guy who looked like a police detective was saying they had a "weird murder" on their hands. Five people butchered, one of them an actress named Sharon Tate, who'd been in *The Valley of the Dolls,* a movie which Mom and every other girl in America liked, but Aaron didn't. *The Wild Bunch* was much better. Sharon Tate was pretty; at least, her star photo showed she was. What she looked like now, Aaron could not guess.

"Damn druggies!" Dad snapped as the "Pig" door was shown again, the blood suddenly brightening and wriggling and dripping and calling out to Aaron. His chill went glacier because he knew, right then, it wasn't some drug user who'd killed those four people.

It was a Walker of the Thorny Path.

The shark-tooth grin superimposed over the "Pig" door and Aaron's breath stopped. Whether the Cryman had done it, ripping the four people and beautiful Sharon Tate into head-puppets, or another kind of monster, invoked by a Walker like Aaron; someone who soared with the same raging, sweet, lustful sense of power that came with each naming, whispering "Sharon Tate," and releasing the dragon. A brother. A blood brother. He gasped.

"Terrible! Just terrible!" Dad fumed, his face turned down with righteous anger. "All them damn hippies and all them drugs, them damn Hollywood people getting all in it? What do you expect?"

Yes, Dad, what do you expect when we taste the power of the Thorny Path? Someone is named and the named are eaten, their heads part of puppet theater, forever. There is no end to the Path. It careened across the earth, to and fro and up and down, its victims enriching its soil, its future victims quaking and helpless and waiting for the Path to cross them, for Aaron and his blood brothers to cast their hateful, murderous eyes on them for any offense, any reason, and point their bloody fingers and send the Cryman to its duties.

"No," Aaron whispered.

"Yes!" Dad was in full righteous joy, hands folded, a gleam in his eye at the pretty Sharon Tate, now stretched across the Thorny Path. "Serves them right!" he crowed. Satisfied. So satisfied.

Aaron stared at Dad. Was he on the Path, too? Was Aaron merely following along, a chip off the old block? Did that mean, decades from now, he'd be a raging, lustful creature who beat his sons and screamed at his daughters and cowed his wife and took great pleasure in the tearing of the thorns and the tearing of pretty young actresses?

"Yes," Aunt Mary whispered in his ear.

No. No, I will not become him. I will leave the Path.

On Monday.

Chapter 27

"What's with you?" Kathy, giving Aaron a suspicious glance as they bounced along in Sawyer's truck.

What's with me? What a stupid question, Aaron thought. Grampaw's head, along with old Miss Dunphy's dried-up one, had last night put on the command performance Aaron had asked for earlier, to the howls of the watching Stooges and Darrell — and to the faked howls of Aaron, who couldn't let on that he was revolted and terrified and wanted off the Path lest the Cryman got suspicious, ate Aaron, and made his head tell the truth and uncover the plot, and the rest of the Five, including you, Kathy, became head-puppets instead of, right now, heading over to collect Connor and his bombs, meet up with Cindy and wire up the Gulches – where the rest of Grampaw probably resided – to kill the damned thing.

"Nothing's with me. Nothing at all." He leveled his gaze out of the windshield.

Kathy frowned and attended the road, not required to shift because there was room for the three of them. Where Connor would sit was a mystery; Sawyer and Kathy hated the kid, thought him an uber-dweeb unworthy of even looking at Sawyer's truck, much less ride in it. That Connor could make explosives was the only reason Sawyer agreed to this, but such a skill did not mean Connor got a break. He'll probably have to ride on top of the cab or in the bed of the truck, a very dangerous proposition, the giant rusty holes making the bed more sieve than transport. And if the bombs didn't work, well, then Connor gets to walk home. With an angry Cryman on his trail.

On all their trails.

The more Aaron thought about this plan, the more unworkable it seemed. First of all, bombs? Powerful enough to collapse a tunnel? Made by a kid? More likely Connor's "bombs" were a super firecracker, like those Aaron made by tearing open about 100 Black Cats, wrapping the gunpowder tight in newspaper, and then lighting it. Satisfying bang — more accurately, fizzle — but hardly the kind to bring down a cavern. The only thing they'll actually bring down is the wrath of the

Cryman.

Because the Cryman was magical, supernatural, a force of evil, and things like that weren't killed by conventional means. Try shooting a vampire and see what happens. So what could a bomb do to a demon? Bury it, okay, strong possibility, but it's a demon. They love caves and dark places and tunneling through them. Aaron pictured it now: the Cryman glances up at the explosion, basks in the avalanche, then laughs and makes his puppet-head slaves eat a way out. Then it goes looking for the bombers.

Maybe we should call this off...

"We're here," Sawyer announced as the truck precariously rounded a curve and went up a driveway past the Church of Crazy People, following it around to the ramshackle ranch house and onto a gravel pad between the house and Connor's lab. Aaron blinked at the dust, expecting Connor's Bible-thumper parents to come tearing out of the back door dressed in sackcloth and throwing ashes at Sawyer and his Sin Truck.

Sawyer must have thought the same thing because he looked around suspiciously, dwelling on the Oldsmobile sitting in an open garage past the house. Looked like the parents were home, so this thing gets cancelled before it even gets started.

What a relief.

Aaron was gathering breath to advise Sawyer that it probably was in their best interests to skedaddle, when the back door flew open and Connor flew down the steps. "Hey!" he screamed, "You ready?" The kid passed in front of the truck at full tilt and headed towards the lab, disappearing inside. Sawyer and Kathy looked at each other and burst into scornful laughter, giving Aaron scornful looks. So, this is your best friend, huh, Aaron?

No, he's not. Despite appearances.

Aaron set his lips in a grim line and endured the laughter, watching the back door for the expected, and wanted, appearance of the plan-killing parents, but nothing. A moment later, Connor appeared at the back of the pickup, struggling with a giant pail. "Help me with these," he wailed at top volume.

Sawyer turned about to look at the pail because, no rearview mirror, then shrugged at Kathy, and Aaron got out at Kathy's sharp elbow in his ribs and they all queued out of the passenger door, Aaron and Sawyer reaching Connor at the same time and both making a grab at the bucket handle because Connor was stumbling and in danger of dropping it and Lord knows what happens when someone drops a bomb.

"Take it easy, kid!" Sawyer said.

Connor rose straight up, avoiding Sawyer's hands, hefted the bucket up to his chin level, and then let go.

"Ack!" Aaron yelped and dove for the ground, sure he was about to be atomized. Sawyer stood there, jaw dropped. It was too late for him.

The bucket hit hard, testament to its weight, bounced a couple of times as Aaron went fetal, braced for the blast wave and heat and dismemberment. The only explosion, though, was Connor bursting into gales of laughter as he collapsed to his knees, pointing at Aaron. "Oh, man! Look at you!' he crowed.

Aaron scrambled to his feet, terror now giving way to rage and he pushed Connor away. "You idiot!" he screamed, "Are you trying to kill us?"

Connor, still laughing, shook his head. "You're the idiot. It's ammonium nitrate. It won't go off if you drop it."

Sawyer stuck a toe uneasily at the canted bucket. "It won't?"

"No," Connor chortled.

Sawyer looked at him and grinned. "Good one," he said. There was a gleam of respect in his eyes.

Connor glowed under it, his dweebness shed. For the moment.

"Now these," Connor, still in Sawyer flush, whipped a plastic bag out of his pocket, "are a different story." Gingerly, he handed the bag to Sawyer who, taking the cue, gingerly examined it. Inside were five or six tubes made out of the Bic pens Aaron had seen on the lab table, the ends sealed and wires running out of them. "Look like blasting caps," Sawyer said.

Connor nodded in approval. "Pretty much. It's fulminate. We stick a couple inside the buckets, wire 'em up to the field phone, spin the crank and, boom!" He made a gleeful atom bomb movement with his hands. "You did bring the field phone, right?" Raise of eyebrows at Aaron.

Aaron snorted and threw a thumb at the truck. "Of course I did." His contribution to this fiasco fulfilled. Made it easier for the Cryman to surmise his involvement, when it digs its way out and finds what's left of the phone.

Sawyer tilted a head at Connor. "Did you say 'buckets?'"

Three of them, Sawyer, all sealed with wax, all at least fifty pounds apiece, maybe more. Even Sawyer puffed a bit when they got the third one into the bed, precariously tied down between the rusty holes. Maybe they wouldn't explode if they rolled about, but Sawyer wasn't taking any chances. Connor kept the fulminate close, a handy way (Aaron suspected) to avoid hauling the other buckets so that Sawyer and Aaron ended up doing most of the work.

During all of this, Aaron expected Connor's parents to leap out and put a stop to such nonsense, but the door remained closed. "What about your mom and dad?" Aaron, finally, asked.

Connor waved a hand in dismissal. "Don't worry about them. They're in their closets. Will be all day," and he grinned and helped Sawyer latch the barely hanging tailgate, rust coming off in waves as they did so.

Sawyer cocked his head at the three buckets. "So those'll really work?"

"Yep!" Connor at full enthusiasm.

Sawyer shook his head in admiration and then looked at Aaron. "How come you don't know how to make those?"

Connor made another dismissive wave. "He's an astronomer, not a chemist," and, merrily, strolled around to the cab and queued next to Kathy, who looked at him like he had leprosy. Sawyer smirked, confirming Aaron as the new uber-dweeb, and headed to the passenger door and led the queue back inside.

Aaron, his face burning, squeezed in next to Connor. Kathy stared at the little jerk as though he had passed gas, trying to put as much space between her and Connor as the confines of the cab allowed. She was mostly unsuccessful, and Connor had a dreamy look — pressed against a girl and riding in the truck of the coolest guy in south Alabama, with three giant bombs in the back. He must have died and gone to dweeb heaven.

Nervously, Aaron glanced behind at the bed and then longingly at the back door, but no parents emerged. Dang.

Good thing nitrate did not explode on impact because the ride out to the Gulches was just one long jolt as Sawyer careened across back roads along the south side of Damascus. Aaron expected any moment for Connor to be proved wrong about the buckets and all of them blown to pieces and out through the cracked windshield, but that's a satisfaction Aaron didn't really want to experience.

Connor, though, was more concerned about the fulminate, because he kept a hand clasped tight against his shirt pocket, trying to ease the bumps and sways, his flush of victory slowly turning into the paleness of concern.

But, nothing exploded as the truck slapped to a halt in a cloud of dust against a dirt trail between a set of pines. "Gotta walk from here," Sawyer said as he tumbled out, a half-revolted Kathy preceding him and stepping as far from Connor as the embankment allowed, grateful to be no longer in physical contact with him.

Connor, a silly grin on his face, pushed impatiently at Aaron, and the two of them walked around to where Sawyer manfully tried to unlatch the tailgate without busting its one intact hinge. "How far is it?" Aaron asked.

"'bout a mile, mile and a half," Sawyer said as the gate, miraculously, opened without falling off, and he jumped up to untie the buckets.

Aaron and Connor exchanged looks. Mile and a half? With fifty-pound buckets?

Great.

Chapter 28

"Grueling" was the best one-word description of the hike, for Aaron and Connor, that is. Sawyer carried his bucket along the crappy trail that ran across the peanut fields and through the swamps, swinging it back and forth like a cotton boll or something, while talking and laughing with Kathy, who carried the field phone and the canteens. Apparently, Sawyer could carry an anvil without breaking a sweat.

But Aaron was definitely breaking a sweat, his shirt soaked through within the first ten feet of travel. What did you expect, hauling a ton of bucket bomb in 100-degree heat? Connor was worse off, even more sweat soaked and struggling harder than Aaron, which provided a small amount of satisfaction. Aaron's dweeb status was now slightly elevated above chemistry boy over there. Slightly.

They stopped frequently, Aaron and Connor having to catch their breath and regain their strength every five minutes or so. Sawyer said nothing, beelined for whatever shade was available while Kathy flopped next to him, giving the two dweebs murderous looks of contempt. If Connor harbored any fantasies about Kathy's succumbing to his chemistry boy charms, they were dashed by Connor's draining of the canteens before they had gone a half mile. "You don't get this one!" she snapped as she grabbed the last full canteen out of Connor's reach, daring him to protest. As if Connor, or Aaron, had the energy.

Sure, they would die of thirst and heat prostration long before they reached the Gulches. Aaron wondered if dying in a heroic, albeit incomplete, effort against evil would give him a better chance of entering heaven. Probably have to do some fast talking at the Pearly Gates, but this should give him some amount of offset against that whole Thorny Path thing.

Finally, after what felt like seven or eight arm-numbed, sweat-drenched hours, they burst through a thick hedge and stumbled into the small clearing at the base of the Gulches. Aaron collapsed on the ground, not caring as his bucket rolled away. Let the dang thing blow up; it would be a mercy. He looked back at the trailhead they had just dismounted. "I didn't know that was there."

Sawyer, wiped his brow with a big red bandanna, the only sign he might have been affected by the hike, shrugged, and said, "Ain't no reason you should. You usually come from that way," and he pointed up the slope back towards where presumably the pasture and house lay.

"Yeah, but I live here." Indeed, he did. He knew the Magic Sawdust Pile and the creek trail and even the hidden peanut field a mile or so behind the house where, in the autumn, great piles of peanut stalks rose, providing a place to hide while waiting for doves to fly in during the season while snacking on the raw peanuts missed by the combines. These were his woods, his Gulches, and nothing should be a surprise.

Like the Cryman? Aaron pressed his lips together.

"Don't mean you'd know about it," Sawyer squeezed out his bandanna and wiped again.

"How do you, then?"

Sawyer smiled a bit. "I was a kid once, too."

And there it was, the put-down. Subtle, and probably not even intended as such, but one, just the same. Aaron, despite being almost fourteen, was merely a kid, a baby, still in short pants and getting his butt wiped by

Mommy, and because he liked comics and telescopes and schoolwork and cartoons, this kid-ness earned him the sneers and insults from those oh-so mature peanut farmers masquerading as Damascus School students. While Aaron spent Saturday mornings watching *Mr. Peabody and Sherman*, they were out plowing fields and breaking horses and marrying and having kids and simply didn't have time for stupid kid stuff, playing Army or reading *Spiderman* or looking through telescopes at moon landings. They were far too grown-up for that.

Aaron frowned darkly at Sawyer. Yeah? I'm just a stupid kid?

Who controls the Cryman, then?

A cloud enveloped the sun and a chill breeze slipped through the clearing, a touch of warning to it, and Aaron looked up guiltily. Sorry, God.

"Man!" Connor wheezed noisily around his designated canteen, sucking down the last few drops, "Is it hot!"

"I'll say," Kathy said dryly, taking an obvious survey of Connor's sweat stains while rolling her eyes at Sawyer, who chuckled and squeezed more out of the bandanna.

Connor, missing it, eyed the last canteen. "Can I have that, anyway?" he wheedled, courting danger because what had Kathy already said?

She studied him the way she regarded a cockroach, turned and gave the canteen to

Sawyer. He took a big drink, probably emptying the thing, and then poured what was left over his bandanna, taking a face-and-neck bath with it. Grinning, he draped the bandanna around the back of Kathy's neck and pulled her, squealing, into him for a kiss.

Aaron watched. So did Connor.

Aaron wasn't sure what Connor was feeling, although the wonderment and rapture on the dweeb's face provided a fairly decent clue, but Aaron was bouncing between disgust and thrill. Disgust because this redneck ignoramus was slobbering all over his sister; thrill because it relived his own moment with Cindy, although that wasn't half as enthusiastic and slobbery as the performance in front of him. This was intense. Well-practiced, even, and Aaron wondered how many Sawyer-lessons Kathy had been taking. And what else they'd been practicing.

Now thoroughly disgusted, Aaron kicked at his bucket. Connor immediately broke his kiss trance and looked at Aaron with alarm. "What?" Aaron said. "I thought it wouldn't blow up if you hit it."

"Shouldn't," Connor said, "but, in this heat, you never know."

Aaron examined him for guile, but Connor looked sincere so, discretion being the better part, stopped his next bucket kick. That Connor did not grin in response put some weight to the warning.

Sawyer was done lip wrestling with Kathy

and pushed her back, both blushing, she more than he. He craned his neck, examining the sun's angle. "Near noon," he announced, "Maybe we should get this show on the road."

Connor jumped to his feet with an enthusiastic, "Yeah!" and fussed with his bucket.

Aaron peered up the ridge. "We can't yet," he said.

"Why not?" Connor, puzzled, stared at him.

"Cindy's not here," Aaron pointed out.

Connor threw out "who cares?" hands. "So?"

"Need five," Sawyer said, examining the notch at the bottom of the cliff. There was an uneasy expression on his face. Aaron understood that.

"Five what?" Connor was now even more puzzled.

"Five silver bullets," Aaron felt like saying, but that would just further confuse the issue and only serve as a private joke with himself.

But Sawyer, still examining the notch, said absently, "Magic Five."

Aaron almost applauded. Sawyer got it.

That, of course, did not clarify things for Connor, who remained confused, but shrugged it away and went back to fooling with the buckets. Aaron noted the wax seal on his was looking mushy, probably from the heat. He frowned. Would that affect it?

"So, where is she?" Kathy asked Aaron while searching around in her pocket and pulling out... a cigarette pack.

Aaron's eyes bugged. Cigarettes! He watched in amazement as Sawyer produced a lighter and Kathy dipped the end of the cigarette into the flame, suddenly wreathed in smoke. Sawyer took the pack, tapped out a cigarette expertly, and flipped it into his mouth after rolling it across the back of his hand. Winking at Aaron, he lit his off Kathy's.

When did this start?

"That's not a very good idea," Connor toned, staring fixedly at Kathy's cigarette as he rested one foot on the bucket. He obviously didn't mean the Surgeon General's warning, and Kathy and Sawyer exchanged alarmed looks then, hastily, took giant steps up the hill, putting as much distance between them and the buckets as the slope allowed. Again, Connor looked serious, and Aaron wondered if errant cigarette ash could find its way through the softened wax and blow the buckets, eviscerating all of them right here. He took his own hasty step away.

Kathy resumed puffs and looked at Aaron. "So?"

"She'll be here," Aaron replied, then stared at her cigarette. "Since when do you smoke?"

"Since whenever," Kathy dismissed that. "When will she be here?"

Good question, and far more important

than the date and time Kathy took up smoking, but cigarettes, Kathy? Cigarettes? Like Mom and Dad, smoking a carton or five a day? Really? He felt the distance between him and Kathy increasing.

"Well?" Kathy was more irritated, the cigarette held before her like a dagger, and Aaron figured he'd better say something, but what? Cindy should have been here already. At least, that was the plan before Grampaw got turned into a head-puppet: she was to arrive at the looming ridge and wait until Aaron and the others showed up. But they were supposed to get here a couple of hours ago, and maybe she got tired of waiting. Or maybe Gramma was extra vigilant, what with the gone Grampaw, and wouldn't let Cindy out of her sight.

Or maybe the Cryman paid her a visit after last night's puppet show.

"I..." Aaron said, more to make noise than anything because he really didn't have an answer. Desperation formed in his stomach like hot ash and he needed to stall because Lord knows what Kathy would do in the next few minutes, stomp off or make kissy noises at him or break out a cigar, when there was a severe rustling in the trees and bushes above them. Aaron paled. Oh no! The Cryman had smelled out the plan – or the cigarettes – and descended on them in full shark-toothed fury!

Sawyer and Kathy whirled to meet the noise, the expressions on their faces signaling they thought the same thing, and Aaron readied to flee past the bewildered Connor — using him the same way he'd used Darrell to escape — when Cindy appeared at the edge of the berm, smiled, waved cheerily and said, "Hey!"...

...followed closely by Stan and Gary.

"No," Aaron whispered.

"Sorry I'm late," Cindy said, stumbling down the angle and pulling up next to Sawyer and Kathy, her brow furrowing at the smoke.

"Yeah," Gary snorted, "Sorry we're late." He eyed Kathy's cigarette with amusement, while Stan eyed Sawyer without amusement.

"You two can't be here!" Aaron said.

"Who sez?" Gary challenged, looking down at him from the height. "This is our woods."

While technically true because Grampaw did, indeed, own the property, Gary was an infrequent visitor to the farm, so had less claim than Aaron did, but that was an argument for another time because there was a different, more urgent and possibly fatal reason.

Five. Just five.

He made a helpless gesture at Cindy.

"Gramma wouldn't let me leave without them," she explained.

Well, just dandy. "Because of Grampaw?" he asked, unable to keep the bitterness out of his voice.

"No," she frowned, looking off, "Grampaw's just out on a drunk. He's done it before," and looked at her brothers for confirmation.

Wanna bet? Aaron thought, but kept that to himself.

Gary's sneer widened as he pointed straight at Aaron. "It's because of you, Romeo."

Cindy flushed a deep red as Aaron felt he'd been slapped. Both Sawyer and Kathy burst out laughing. Even Stan looked amused.

"Romeo?" Connor exclaimed behind him, "What's THAT about?"

Aaron spun on him and then spun back to the laughing jackasses, then stared at the still-flushing Cindy. He had a sudden realization that she was far too embarrassed to let on that she was, indeed, his Juliet.

And that was a camel straw too much.

"Great!" He threw hands upward in defeat. "Just great. We might as well all just go home," and he dropped his hands and headed for the lower trailhead, kicking the bucket out of his way and earning a gasp from Connor.

"Where you going?" a surprised Sawyer called.

Aaron turned, taking in the jeers and scorn of Gary and Stan and Kathy, and the averted eyes of Cindy. "I'm going home," he announced. "Home. Because it's not going to work now."

"Huh? What?" Connor was staring at him. "Of course it will!"

"No, it won't!" Aaron leaned into that, driving a startled Connor back. "It won't! Five's the magic number! Not seven!" and he stomped an irritated foot.

"Seven's better," Sawyer said in the astonished silence following.

Aaron blinked at him. "You said it was five."

Sawyer dropped the cigarette and crushed it under his boot. "Five's a good number. It's Jesus' wounds. But seven, that's the perfect number." He paused. "The number that makes you safe."

Safe.

Aaron studied Sawyer, who nodded assurance. Then he turned to Cindy, no longer flushed with embarrassment, but excitement.

"Well, what are we waiting for?" Gary crowed. "Let's blow something up!"

Chapter 29

Easier said than done.

First, the logistics. The buckets had to explode in a location guaranteed to bring down the Cryman's Hole. The most likely place was right about where they'd found the weasel carcass, which meant those placing the buckets had to do so in uncomfortable proximity to the shark-toothed Cryman lurking somewhere in the back. The Cryman had reacted rather strongly to mere trespassing before, how much more to a direct attack?

"I'm not going in there," Aaron announced.

"Me, neither," Stan seconded. Smart decisions, given their previous experience.

"Chickens!" Gary laughed. Obviously, not one to learn lessons from experience.

"Well, if you're not going," Connor pointed at Aaron, "then I'm not either." Which was either Connor deferring to Aaron's experience, or refusing to go anywhere without a fellow dweeb.

Which was a problem, because, of all of them, Connor *had* to go because he was the only one who knew how the bombs worked. Indeed, he was the only one who could prepare them. So, naturally, an argument broke out.

It went on for five minutes or so, Stan and Aaron holding forth on the fairness of it because, after all, they had already been exposed to the danger, which Gary countered by declaring he was going in despite also having been previously exposed, which proved he was braver, which led to a secondary argument about the difference between bravery and foolishness.

Both Cindy and Kathy suffered this for about thirty seconds, then both declared *they* would go in and place the bombs if Aaron and Stan were...

"Too scared!" Kathy sneered, making two syllables out of that last word. Which shut both Aaron and Stan's objections right down because there was no way two girls were going into the cave; first, girls simply didn't do things like that and, second, boys were never, ever more scared than girls. The quickest way for Aaron to lose any possibility of Cindy as a girlfriend would be pointing out girls' limitations and boys' superior courage. Apparently, Stan realized the futility of making the same points to Kathy, so the argument then veered to the girl's inability to wrestle fifty-pound buckets down the tunnel or defend themselves should the Cryman put in an appearance...

"Shut! The! Hay-el! UP!" Sawyer's voice bulled through all of them, silencing the magpie screeches that the several cross-cutting arguments had become. They all did, turning angry and frustrated faces to him as one.

"*I'm* going in," Sawyer pointed at himself. "So are you!" Subsequent finger points at Aaron and Connor.

Aaron paled and protests rose to his lips but those were cut off by Gary snapping, "Well, I'm going, too."

"Fine." Sawyer made that decision, too. "You can help haul buckets. You," a couple of fingers at the girls, "will run the field phone" — the two exchanged satisfied glances — "while you," a point at Stan, "will keep them safe." A pause as Sawyer let the assignments settle in. "Got it?" He glared at each of them in turn.

Got it.

"All right," Sawyer said and grabbed a bucket. Gary grabbed another one, acting like it wasn't heavy, but Aaron saw, with great satisfaction, the strain on his face. Connor and he took the last one and, with much bumping and stumbling, the whole parade made its way through the notch and onto the first chamber floor.

Where they all stopped and made a collective gulp.

The chamber was as damp and cool as always, but it had an evil feel to it now, the trees lining the top seeming to lean and gibber at them: lunatics shaking their witch's hair. It was only the breeze, but a breeze only present here, stirred by the restless spirits of Cryman victims, Aaron supposed. He watched the moss shiver, expecting any moment for the tendrils to merge into Darrell's screaming face, or Grampaw's.

"This is a scary place," Connor whispered.

Aaron looked at him. Connor was round-eyed and defensive. So was everyone else. In a way, Aaron was relieved. He wasn't the only one spooked.

Sawyer, grim in the face of his new leadership role, pulled the now-cold cigarette out of his mouth and flicked it away while eying the moss doing its odd dance. "Faster we do this, faster we're gone," he said. Sawyer turned to Connor. "What do we do?"

Connor shook himself out of the spell and reached for the field phone, which Kathy mutely gave up. They all gathered to watch as Connor pulled the spool out of it and attached the copper wires to the terminals of the case. He then yanked enough wire out of the spool to give them a lead. "We'll have to spin this out," he said as he gestured with the spool, "as we're walking down the tunnel until we get to the end of it. The wire, I mean. Then, I'll attach it to a fuse in each bucket" — he carefully patted the plastic bag in his pocket — "and we all come out here, turn the crank and, boom!" Atom bomb gesture again, but no smile. This was now serious business.

"How big a boom?" Stan asked.

"Big," was all Connor said.

Stan frowned, straightening and looking towards the turn. "Where will you set the phone?"

"Right at the entrance to the tunnel," Connor said.

"Isn't that too close?"

Connor shrugged. "It's a hundred feet of wire. We have to make sure we put the buckets deep enough to collapse the tunnel."

"But," Stan persisted, "won't that mean we'll get blasted, too?"

"No." Connor waved that away. "We're not going to set it off from there. We'll have slack when we come back out and can move the phone farther away." Connor stood and peered at the turn. "In fact, we can pull it around the corner of that wall before setting it off. That should be far enough away."

"Far enough away?" Gary sniffed, "We're already far enough at the entrance. The buckets will be way down the tunnel," and he looked at Connor as though he was stupid or something.

A look Connor returned. "The tunnel will throw the explosion right back at us. That's why miners never stand at the entrance when they're using dynamite, no matter how deep. Don't you know that?" and the look turned derisive.

Gary reddened and took a threatening step forward, a pound-the-dweeb expression wrinkling his face.

Stan stepped between them. "He's right," Stan said, putting a palm in Gary's chest, "We gotta be clear of the tunnel AND the turn before the bomb goes off. So, once it's set, we gotta get out of there. Fast," he emphasized.

"Fine," Gary smacked the hand away, "We'll get out fast." His eyes bored into Connor. "Most of us will, anyway."

Connor's jaw dropped in surprise, and then concern, at the implied threat.

"Knock that talk off," Sawyer cut the tension. "We're all gonna get out before the bomb goes off. All," he repeated and looked hard at Gary, who dropped his eyes but not before giving Connor another look.

Sawyer pointed at Connor's pocket. "You said a fuse in each bucket, but you've got more than three."

"Yep!" Connor said, brightly. "That's in case they don't ignite." Another gingerly pat of the pocket.

Sawyer blinked. "What are you talkin' about?"

"We only need one of the three to blow

'cause it'll chain react the other two. But, sometimes, fulminate doesn't react."

"Wait." Kathy regarded him like he was crazy. "You mean, if it doesn't go off, we'll have to go back in and replace the fuses?"

"Yep!" Connor said it brightly, again. "But, shouldn't have to. Should work."

They all exchanged glances as Sawyer shook his head ruefully and snorted, "Well, here's prayin' to God it blows the first time, then."

"Well, we ain't gonna blow up nothing unless you guys get moving!" Kathy snarled and that was the impetus they needed. Aaron and Sawyer and Gary each grabbed a bucket as Connor led the platoon to the turn. They all hesitated there, and Stan cautiously peered around the corner, staring for a few moments before saying, "Looks clear."

All of them peered to verify, looking like an Our Gang totem pole of kid faces checking around a doorway, which would be funny under other circumstances, but not when staring down the tunnel to Hell.

"Okay," Sawyer said and they stepped around, all so tight against each other they might as well be one fat kid. Connor placed the phone on the ground just under the tunnel entrance and pointed at the crank on the side. "Whatever you do," he said to Kathy, "don't turn that until we're all out."

"I'm not stupid," she scorned and pushed Connor out of the way as she squatted next to the phone. She was a bit pale, though. Cindy, even paler, squatted next to her in support. Stan took giant steps back until he could observe both the tunnel and the chamber floor and the notch, like he could do anything if the Cryman attacked from any of those directions. Scream before getting eaten, Aaron supposed. Stan fished around in his pocket and pulled out a flashlight. "Here," he said, pitching it to Sawyer, who caught it with his free hand.

Sawyer nodded in approval. "You always prepared, ain't ya?"

Stan blushed a bit, the Boy Scout implications not lost on him, and how uncool that was. "Me, too," Sawyer said and he put down the bucket, fished around in his own pocket, and tossed something to Stan, who caught it one-handed.

A revolver. One of those Old West looking ones.

"Just in case," he said to Stan, who stared at it, round-eyed. Sawyer looked at the others. "Ready?" And without waiting for an answer, he picked up the bucket and ducked into the tunnel.

Looking at each other, Aaron and Gary picked up their own buckets and stumbled along behind, Connor following with the spool.

Chapter 30

It was still a tomb: dank and wet and smelling of death, the real death waiting for them. Sawyer paused, set down his bucket, clicked on the light, and shone it down the tunnel. "Lordy," he whispered as the beam got lost in the darkness.

Aaron chilled, stared at him. "Thought you were in here before," he whispered.

"Was," Sawyer kept the beam steady as he probed the distance. "When I was a kid," — Aaron flushed at the renewed insult — "but the Cryman wasn't awake then, and this wasn't so..." He paused. "Dark."

Aaron shivered. Sawyer didn't mean the absence of light; he meant a different kind of dark: alive, questing.

Hungry.

"You." Sawyer gestured the flashlight at Connor. "Play out the wire as we go. You two," gesture at Gary and Aaron, "stay close to me." Sawyer picked up his bucket and stepped forward.

Gary gave Connor a malevolent look and fell in behind Sawyer. Aaron took the next position in line and they headed into the hungry dark.

It was a stumbling, halting procession, once again made so by the closeness of the tunnel and the clay grabbing at their shoes, but also hampered by Sawyer having to duck the occasional rock protruding from the ceiling. The light danced ahead but the dark was actively fighting it, trying to swallow the beam whole and leave them blind. The sauna-like atmosphere brought back the heavy sweating, and even Gary had to wipe his eyes with a shirt sleeve. The buckets seemed lighter, though.

Fear made you stronger.

After what seemed like an hour, Sawyer pulled up short, Gary and Aaron and Connor piling into each other like the Three Stooges but without the requisite joking. Best to be quiet. "How much slack you got?" Sawyer whispered to Connor.

"About... ten feet," the whisper back.

"Then let's do it here," Sawyer said, placing his bucket in the middle of the floor.

"But," Connor protested, "we still got

some room!"

"You wanna pipe down?" Sawyer hissed. "Jesus, boy, you always shout? We need the slack to move the phone out of the entrance, right?"

"I'm not shouting," Connor half-shouted, which was about the lowest volume he could muster. "And I'm not sure we're deep enough," he said.

"Well, we ain't got much more wire, so this is as deep as she goes," Sawyer stepped out of the way. "Do what you gotta do."

Connor directed Gary and Aaron to place the other two buckets to form a triangle with the first one, fussing about half-inch intervals on either side until Sawyer looked ready to kill him.

"Okay, okay," Connor said, and waved them all back. Carefully, he extracted the plastic bag and, even more carefully, pulled one fuse at a time from it. He pushed a hole into the wax top of the first bucket with his thumb and then placed the fuse into it. "Whew," he said with some exaggeration and then grinned at their alarmed, flash-lit expressions. "Two more to go," he almost sang it and Aaron thought for sure Sawyer was going to punch the little dweeb. Like he'd blame him.

It took Connor even longer to place the other two fuses, and by the time he got the last one in a position that satisfied him, nervous sweat was pouring down the nerd's face.

Sawyer, noting that, asked with some

alarm, "You about to get us all killed?"

"No," Connor said with great and obvious relief, "Not now, anyway." Which was even more alarming and the three of them exchanged glances as Connor pulled a long strand of copper wire out of his jeans' pocket and linked the three fuses to it, taking the free end in one hand and the phone wire in the other. Frowning, he brushed the phone wire against his cheek, and then spat on it and held it up to his ear lobe. "No current that I can feel," he said, and quickly wrapped the exposed wire around the copper one. He stood up and stepped widely away. "It's ready," he said with reverence in his voice.

They all leaned forward, breathless. "Just one little twitch of the crank, and this thing will go," Connor added.

Aaron hastily stepped back, trying to put a little more space between him and the bomb in case Kathy's hand inadvertently brushed the crank.

Like a couple of feet would make any difference.

His heel came down on something soft and lumpy and, cautiously, he looked down. There wasn't enough light to see what it was because Sawyer was closely examining the wire connections as Connor assured their effectiveness, so Aaron probed with his fingers. A square of some kind, yielding, like cloth. Puzzled, he grabbed it and held it up, squinting in the feeble light. It looked like a wallet of some kind.

"What's that?" Gary said and, without waiting for an answer, snatched the square out of Aaron's hand.

"Hey!" Aaron yelped and grabbed back at it. "That's mine. I found it!"

They were both suddenly dazzled by light as Sawyer whipped the flashlight on them and hissed, "Quiet!"

Aaron backed off, annoyed at the triumphant look on Gary's face as he held the leather thing in the beam, examining it. Suddenly, Gary's eyes popped. "What the..." he said.

"What you got?" Sawyer asked, but Gary flipped it around to get a better look. He gasped.

"Grampaw!" he said. "This is Grampaw's wallet!"

Aaron gaped, taking in the scrollwork on the front (something like a bull or a steer) and a big key holder hanging from the bottom but with no keys attached. The wallet was grimy and dirt-covered and...

Bloody.

Gary, shocked as he realized the wallet's condition, yelped, "Grampaw!" He then looked down the tunnel, took a step forward and yelled as loud as he could, "Grampaw!"

"Quiet, you dumbass!" Sawyer yelled just as loud.

Too late.

The odor washed over them, the old wet

leather, the mold, the age. Mixed now with something else: the rusty smell of blood.

"Oh, no," Aaron breathed.

The odor paralyzed them as it strengthened. There was a thickening of the dark at the far end of the tunnel, a stirring.

Connor whimpered. Aaron couldn't because he was frozen, as was Gary. Not Sawyer. He snapped off the light, plunging them all into darkness. "Be real quiet, but let's go. Let's go now," he urgently whispered.

That broke the spell and Connor spun, gripping the spool and leaning into a sprint for the far-lit tunnel entrance, something Aaron thought a very good idea while bracing for his own pell-mell skedaddle, when Sawyer seized Connor by the back of the shirt and yanked him back. "Nobody run!" he hissed, "We do that, we're gonna pull the wires out or trip on 'em or something. And that thing," he jerked a thumb back down the tunnel, "is on us. We go together! You with me," and he hugged Connor to him. "You two" — Gary and Aaron —"together, making sure the wire don't get caught. Understand?"

They all looked at him. "Understand?" he insisted, and got nods of assent, at least from Aaron and, no doubt, from the others, too, because Sawyer was the only one making any sense right now and had their full attention. At least Aaron's.

"C'mon, then!' Sawyer whispered and he pulled Connor along, Aaron and Gary on their heels. "Watch the wire!" Sawyer reminded and Aaron looked down, squinting in the near total blackness to make sure he didn't catch it but, wow, look at this — Aaron saw the wire clearly against the floor — maybe fear gave you night vision as well as strength.

The entire tunnel was filled with the odor now and there was an audible shifting far behind them as something big hunkered along. Not in a hurry, not in pursuit, but as if it had been woken from a nap and was checking out the noise. So the Cryman didn't know they were in here.

Yet.

It was getting lighter as they approached the tunnel's entrance. Oh, God, thank you, sunlight! We're almost out of here!

Not yet.

"Grampaw's back there!" Gary whispered fiercely, grabbing Aaron's shoulder and almost causing him a heart attack because the big goof stepped right on top of the wire.

"So's the Cryman!" Aaron whispered back. "And watch where you're going!"

"But Grampaw's back there! I can't leave him!" and Gary stopped and turned, looking back down the tunnel. Aaron, horrified, watched as Gary took a step that way.

"What you doing, you idjit?" Sawyer was back on them, the near apoplectic Connor along in a headlock. "We gotta go! We gotta blow this place up!"

"We can't do that!" Gary snarled, losing

control of his whisper. "Grampaw's back there!"

Sawyer gawped at him. "Boy, you crazy? If he's back there, he's a Cryman meal!"

Gary's look darkened and the combat came into his eyes and he took a belligerent step towards Sawyer; proof, in Aaron's mind, that Gary was, indeed, crazy. Sawyer will snap his neck!

Preparing to do just that, Sawyer let go of Connor and leaned back into a wrestling stance. But Gary didn't launch. Instead, he swept up the wires at his feet and gave them a savage pull.

The wires whipped back to them in a big loop, piling unceremoniously at Aaron's feet and, obviously, no longer attached to the triggers. Sawyer could only stare at Gary, stunned.

"Oh, crap," Connor said.

Gary held the wires up triumphantly. "There ain't no Cryman!" he yelled. "And we ain't blowing up the tunnel while my Grampaw's up there hurt!"

No Cryman? Aaron was knocked speechless. First Kathy, now you, Gary? Well, let me assure you, there is a Cryman, and if you don't believe me, just wait a moment and I'll introduce the two of you. Aaron took a breath to say just that when someone else spoke:

"Gary?"

It was a quavery, old man's voice, soft and distant, somewhere back down the tunnel, coming from the middle of the odor vortex. Aaron recognized it from the puppet-head theater.

"Grampaw!" Gary called.

Bingo.

"That ain't your Grampaw!" Sawyer grabbed at Gary's shoulder, but Gary knocked his hand away fiercely.

"You keep your hillbilly hands off me!" he shouted and pushed Sawyer hard in the chest. Sawyer upended, smacking against the wall. Gary swept the flashlight out of Sawyer's hand and took two or three giant steps back down the tunnel. "I'm here, Grampaw! Where are you?" and he switched the light on.

The bomb was distantly illuminated, about thirty feet away, but one of the fuses was missing, probably pulled out when Gary grabbed the wires. Gasping, Aaron looked down at his feet to see if it was there and ready to blow should he step on it, but nothing. Gary played the beam past the buckets and down into the absorbing dark, nightmare layers that swirled and danced and spun into...

...a shape.

"Gary?" the shape quavered again.

"Grampaw!" Gary shouted, taking several more giant steps until he was next to the bombs, the light fixed on the far figure standing just past the edge of it. Aaron was stunned because the figure was a whole person, legs and body and arms and, yes, a head. So how could it be Grampaw?

Easy. It wasn't.

"No," he whispered

"Gawd damn," Sawyer, astonished, breathed somewhere behind Aaron's shoulder, conveying his own surprise at seeing what looked like a person down at the end of the tunnel.

"Oh, crap!" Connor repeated, louder this time as he realized he had almost committed Grampaw's murder.

"No," Aaron whispered again.

The figure wavered, unsteady, like an old man hurt, unable to keep balance and needing his grandson to come right down there and help him get home and to the hospital because I got drunk, yes, like I sometimes do and I don't know how I ended up in the Gulches, but hyeah I yam so come hep me, willja?

"Sure, Grampaw!" Gary called, pleased, happy, and took a running step down the tunnel towards the beckoning, sick and in need-of-an-ambulance Grampaw.

Aaron gasped, because Grampaw had not actually *said* anything about being drunk and hurt and in need of medical care. All that was conveyed in the tone and the stance of the Grampaw figure, and in the strange pictures forming in Aaron's head.

Magic. Black magic. Cryman magic.

"No!" Aaron screamed and launched at Gary, catching him in three leaps and tackling him hard.

"Oof!" Gary yelped as Aaron's momentum

carried them against the wall, crashing against it and to the floor. "Get off!" Gary yelled and kicked savagely at Aaron, who neutralized that by wrapping his arms and legs around the struggling kid. He screamed in Gary's ear, "It's not your Grampaw! It's the Cryman!"

"You idiot!" Gary screamed back. "There's no Cryman! Let go!" and he redoubled his efforts to break Aaron's grip.

With a strength he didn't know he had, Aaron wrenched the flashlight from Gary's hand and pointed the beam straight down the tunnel at the Grampaw thing standing there. "Look! Look!" he shrieked.

Grampaw was still there, still wavering, still insisting he needed help, but something changed. A ripple cast across Grampaw's center, like something had run up and down his torso, his stance shifting into a balance that was just wrong. The head tilted forward and the eyes suddenly glowed, like those of a cat caught in headlights. Grampaw smiled. "Gary," he said again, but not in the quavery, old man's weak voice, oh no, in a different voice altogether, one of graves and death and lost souls, a timbre that shattered light and good and heaven itself, the voice of death. The voice of evil.

Stunned, the two of them watched as the ripple that started somewhere in the middle of Grampaw roiled and cycloned and disappeared into itself. The Grampaw thing spun into a dark, borderless midnight and something else, huge, terrible, grew out of it. The Grampaw head rose as the shape rose, grinning wider and wider until the shark teeth took over. They convulsed and swallowed the Grampaw head.

"*aaAAAUH! aaAAAUH! aaAAAUH!*"

The Cryman reared back with each triumphant call, the shock of it tidal-waving down the tunnel like a living thing, tearing at Aaron and Gary as they lay there, terrified.

And screaming.

They weren't the only ones. Connor was screaming, too, sounding so much like a little girl that it would be hilarious, except all of them had become screaming little girls.

Except Sawyer.

"Move!" he roared. "Move!"

And he was on them, yanking Aaron and Gary to their feet and throwing them back towards the entrance. "Move!" he yelled again and there was something in his voice that jolted Aaron and electricity raced through him and, somehow, he vaulted the bombs and was on Gary's heels, Sawyer's hands on both of their backs and pushing hard and all the time yelling, "Move! Move!"

"*aaAAAUH! aaAAAUH! aaAAAUH!*"

Aaron ran, they all ran, like a herd of terror-stricken gazelles fleeing the lions, the dragon, the tiger, bearing down, shark teeth widening and the stench of decay and offal and blood, so much blood, breathing down on them. None of them fell, none of them stumbled; Sawyer kept them agile and flying with his, "Move! Move!" ahead of the "*aaAAAUH*! *aaAAAUH*! *aaAAAUH*!" of the Cryman and the thundering of its hoofs or claws or paws or feet or whatever that thing ran on, behind them.

And they were through the entrance and there was Stan, goggle-eyed, as Sawyer yelled "Move! Move!" at him and there was Kathy yelling, "What is it?" from where she crouched next to the phone...

"*aaAAAUH*! *aaAAAUH*! *aaAAAUH*!"

Both Kathy and Cindy collapsed into each other, screaming, the phone forgotten as the Sawyer blob yelled, "Move! Move!" at them and they were all, all, racing across the floor and jamming the notch, a mass of terrified kids struggling to get out.

Except Stan.

He was still at the turn, visible to all of them, tall and mouth open and shaken, but still there. "Run, you idiot!" Sawyer, from somewhere in the middle of the kid mass, yelled at him.

"*aaAAAUH*! *aaAAAUH*! *aaAAAUH*!"

Stan, his face ashen, stared down the tunnel entrance. The widening of his eyes and spasms that shook him told Aaron exactly what Stan was seeing:

A locomotive of shark teeth bearing down on him.

Stan raised the revolver, grasped it in two hands, and pointed it towards the entrance. *Bam*! Smoke wreathed his hand and he jolted from the recoil. *Bam!*

"Run!" Sawyer, untangled from the pile and standing straight up, screamed at Stan. "Don't shoot! Run!"

Stan did not hear him, weapon raised and aiming. *Bam!* And another. *Bam!*...

Ka-WHOOOOOM!

The ground dropped underneath Aaron and then slapped back, lifting him up and then throwing him aside as if he were nothing. A giant pulse of fire and dust and smoke engulfed Stan like a tornado, smashing him into the opposite wall. Earthquakes bounced all of them and there was a great roaring as the top of the ridge shivered and imploded, falling down as if all its supports had been kicked out.

"Stan!" Gary screamed from somewhere nearby, but Stan wasn't there anymore and then a great avalanche of dirt and rock and trees washed over Aaron and carried him along on a tumbling wave across the chamber floor and into the opposite wall, piling him up alongside the legs and arms and chests of other dirt-tidal-wave riders.

The avalanche stopped and the bucking of the floor subsided and the rumbles lessened and Aaron spat several pounds of red clay out of his mouth and lungs. There were other spittings and movements as disembodied limbs stirred and formed into Kathy and Cindy and Sawyer, pulling themselves out of the clay. The dirt next to Aaron whirlpooled and columned and Connor shot straight up from it, coughing and slapping at his clothes.

"You all right?" Aaron coughed in sympathy.

"Yeah," Connor mumbled and then straightened up and looked at where the ridge used to be. "Wow," he said, and then grinned at Aaron. "Told ya it'd work!"

Aaron, with Connor's help, got to his feet, and then they were helping Cindy and Kathy up and Kathy pushed Connor away as he got too insistent about brushing off her clothes.

"Give me a hand over here," Sawyer called and they turned and he was standing over a mound of dirt and crap on the other side of the pile and they went over and helped him dig at the feet and arms sticking out. Turned out to be Gary; they pulled him free and all of them took turns brushing him off until they, one by one, stepped back, staring at him.

"What?" Gary said, suspicious, "Did I lose my nose or something?"

"No," Sawyer said, "you're fine."

"Then, what?" Gary blinked, puzzled, but none of them would say it. He'd find out when he looked in a mirror.

And discovered his hair had turned completely white.

Chapter 31

They found Stan against the far wall under what looked like a half-ton of dirt and rocks. Unconscious and beaten up, it took a while to pull him out because they were afraid of doing more damage to him, blood pouring out of his nose and ears strong indications he was already damaged.

"Broken," Sawyer concluded as he tweaked Stan's off-centered nose.

Stan immediately came to, gasping in pain and struggling against them.

"Oh, Stan!" Cindy wailed, "You're alive!" and she fell on him, hugging and crying as Stan waved a hand at her.

"I can't hear anything," he croaked.

Connor, standing to the side, tapped his own ears vigorously. "Busted eardrums. Pressure wave will do that."

"What?" Stan shouted at him.

Connor leaned over Stan and kept up the ear tapping until he got it. Stan shook his head, wincing at what that did to his nose, and then patted his sister's back. "Let me up," he shouted.

They did, Cindy and Sawyer carefully helping because, wow, the kid was torn up. Half his clothes ripped off – fortunately, not in any embarrassing manner – sporting at least a million skin cuts and almost entirely red from the clay that had peppered him like a shotgun blast. Swaying and obviously in a lot of pain, he looked at them calmly and said, "Did we get it?"

Shouted more than spoken, of course, because he couldn't regulate the volume of his voice, but no one giggled or signaled him to quiet down. Instead, all of them turned and gazed at where the tunnel had been. A pile of rubble now, a surprising number of large boulders flung across it with a mass of clay and dirt twined between them and a lot of shattered trees tying it all together. No sign there had ever been a tunnel entrance here; no sign of anything, just rack and ruins.

"I'd say so," Sawyer murmured, looked back at Stan and made an exaggerated thumbs-up. Stan nodded, staring at Gary's white hair framed against the clay rubble. He didn't say or shout anything, only blinked, the understanding clear on his face.

They stood quietly, exchanging looks. No cheers, no handshakes or backslaps. No feeling of victory, only a sense that it was over. Auschwitz survivors, discovering the gate was open.

Gary picked his way to the closed entrance and stared at it. "Grampaw," he whispered at the rubble.

"He saved us," Aaron said.

Everyone looked at him, except Stan. "Who did?" Cindy asked. "Grampaw?"

Aaron shook his head and pointed at Stan, who raised eyebrows in query. "He did," Aaron said. "He shot one of the buckets."

"Yeah!" Connor enthused, "Must be! There's no other way those things went off."

"He didn't save us," Gary, squatted in front of the pile, spoke up bitterly, "He almost killed us. He definitely killed Grampaw," and he turned his newly white head belligerently at his brother.

"What?" Cindy was aghast. "What do you mean he killed Grampaw?"

Gary pointed at the rubble. "Grampaw was in there."

"What? What?" Cindy turned from one to the other like the play of a pinball machine, confused and uncomprehending and finally settled back on Gary. "What are you talking about?"

"Grampaw. Was. In. There!" Gary

emphasized each word, stabbing his fingers at the rubble in time with it.

"No, he wasn't," Aaron said, interrupting the horror rising to Cindy's face, "It wasn't Grampaw. Not even close."

Gary stood and whirled on him, his face screwing into itself like a kid about to cry, incongruous against his old man's hair. "It was so!"

Aaron remained calm. "You know it wasn't. You know what it was," he said, gaze fixed on Gary's hair because that was proof.

Gary pulsed, fists clenched, probably flushing but unnoticeable beneath the red clay powder all over him, and then, he cried.

Great tearing, animal sobs of loss and fear, and disbelief, burst from him, agonized and broken.

"Oh, Gary!" Cindy wailed and gathered her brother into comforting arms, the little mother making things better, as the horror washed through Gary and out in tears and wails.

"What's going on?" Stan, shocked, made helpless steps around a small perimeter he could not seem to cross and finally stopped and just stared, sealed off by silence but comprehending, in the figure of his broken brother and his white hair and the solace his sister was attempting, the grief.

"There can't be something like that, there can't!" Gary's wails summarized their horror, their disbelief, the realization that there was, indeed, something like that in this world.

The safety of God and angels and the remoteness of devils, mere shivery bedtime stories to keep kids safely tucked in beds and not wandering dark hallways, evaporated because the stories were true. And no angels had dropped from the heavens, flaming swords held high, to do battle with Lucifer's creature, the monster in the dark. Kids had to fight the monsters themselves. And there was no guarantee of victory.

Connor stood in complete bewilderment while Sawyer turned away, studying the ground. Kathy quietly stepped down from the rubble and put her hand on Aaron's shoulder.

"Let's go home," she said.

Somehow, they came up with a story before going separate ways: the gang was pine-sliding down the hill, Gramma, and Stan slammed into a bunch of trees. Gary was dirty and crying because it upset him so much. The white hair? Oh, newest fashion, it's okay. And that huge rumble off in the distance? Thunder.

Sawyer drove Connor home, Kathy and Aaron berating the little dweeb the whole time to keep his mouth shut, until he shut them up by saying, "Do you think I want anyone to know that I make bombs? *Sheesh*!" and he rolled his eyes and hopped out of the truck. He looked at Aaron, "You wanna come over tomorrow?" and the kid looked so eager and puppy-like that Aaron sighed and said, "Sure."

"So you got a boyfriend now," Kathy

observed as they clambered back in.

"Shut up," Aaron replied, but it wasn't his usual hot denial of some egregious insult; it was a genuine declaration that he was no longer subject to such ridicule. Kathy shut up. Sawyer looked at him and nodded, actual respect in his eyes.

They dropped him at the driveway, Kathy and Sawyer taking off together, but not before Sawyer said, "You did good," and shifted and pulled away.

Aaron watched them go and then went up the driveway to the outside hose and washed up, the cold water bracing and alive, so alive. When he figured he was somewhat human in appearance, he went into the house and down the hallway to the bedrooms. He tapped on the door. "Mom?" he said, then waited a moment. "Everything's all right now." He heard a caught sob, said a silent prayer of healing, and then turned away.

He spent the rest of the afternoon on the front lawn, some books, some comics scattered around him, and even a few old toys: Army men; a GI Joe abandoned to the bottom of the toy box months ago; Hot Wheels. They'd gradually lost their various charms, all except the comics and books, which he would never, ever, give up. Darrell had been gradually taking over Aaron's toys and should have enjoyed them for at least a couple more years before they made their final way to the trash. Instead, Aaron planned to keep them forever. He owed

Darrell an occasional, vicarious play with them.

He watched the road more than he played. He expected Sheriff Oakley to come roaring up any moment, Cody and Younger and the dogs and the National Guard hot on his heels. "Son!" he'd say, "What was that explosion?"

"Thunder, Sheriff."

"Like hell it was, son!" And dogs and deputies and soldiers would swarm the hills looking for the Chicom invasion while the Sheriff slapped him around, "Talk, son! Tell me where the Cong are holding your brother!" But Aaron says nothing. Never ever.

Ever.

No sheriff, no dogs, no Guard showed up. The desultory 18-wheeler and occasional pickup went by; the mailman, too, who waved cheerily and moved along. No one else.

Hmm.

Aaron put down a *Captain America* and moseyed down to the road and stood, gazing at the far ridge. Nothing looked different. And, as loud and destructive as the explosion had been, apparently, it didn't carry much past the Gulches. It might be weeks before anyone even noticed something had happened down there.

Or never ever, since all the kids who used to play there were either dead or broken.

Broken.

Aaron looked down at his hands, the clay etched deep into the cuts and abrasions. It would take weeks for the red lines to finally wash away. His torn-up hands would heal. Gary would, too. So would Stan. Well, maybe after he went to the hospital and got his nose and ears fixed.

Cindy.

Aaron frowned. She wasn't his girlfriend anymore; he knew that, and not because of his fussiness on the way to Aunt Mary's or her refusal to self-identify as Juliet. That was kid stuff. They were finished because of dead Darrell and Grampaw, deaf Stan and crying Gary. Any room their souls had for romance was overwhelmed by war. Ingrid Bergman and Humphrey Bogart kiss on the tarmac, but, four years later, they're strangers. War did that.

Aaron looked at the far ridge. "You did that," he said to the Cryman.

He waited for a response, but there was no, "*aaAAAUH!*" or flash of shark teeth in the tree line. All was still. No cows, no murderous bull, no rabbits moved.

Nothing moved.

Aaron blinked and stared at the lifeless pasture, the unmoving pine ridge, and then at the empty road. It was completely still out here, like a painting, but one that wavered in the frantic heat waves made by the run-over kids trying to get his attention. No birds called; none even flew by. No squirrels chittered or locusts buzzed.

It's too quiet.

Chilled, Aaron pivoted slowly and stared at Grampaw's house shimmering in the run-over kids. Silent. Nothing moved. No chickens chased around the yard. No grandchildren bounced around the house or called out to each other, no fussy Gramma threatening a caning if you didn't behave. It was like a graveyard over there.

A graveyard.

Aaron stepped down the berm and onto the side of the road, walking faster as he headed towards the Eckharts' driveway, downright running as he reached it. He stopped at the bottom, catching his breath but not from the run.

From terror.

"Cindy!" he called.

Silence.

"Cindy!" louder this time.

His echo. Nothing more.

Slowly, he mounted the driveway, Spidey sense tingling, every step a caution, his feet already primed to spin so he could run, screaming, for home. Grampaw's birddog, Lester, should have already crawled out from under the house, slobbery and shuffling and snuffling, to bay at him, and then wag its iron tail against his legs until he yelled, "Quit it!" and pushed the happy dog away, but no. No Lester.

Nothing.

He stood opposite the side porch, straining to see past the verbena and kudzu growing over it. The sun was off the other way, so the porch was murky and he could not make out any detail. He squinted. Something was not quite right with the geometry. He stepped forward and cupped hands around his eyes against the screen.

The kitchen door was gone. So was the kitchen.

Startled, Aaron rubbed his eyes and cupped again and, yes, the kitchen was gone. More than gone. A shambles. Slipping around, he mounted the porch in one leap, noting the screen door tossed across the backyard, and halted in the hole where the kitchen used to be. "Cindy!" he yelled.

His call echoed through the house and back to him, but then silence. He stared. Glass lay everywhere, as did fragments of dishes and cabinets. The kitchen table was in at least ten different pieces, some of them sticking out of the walls as though hurled from a catapult. The stove was upside down and bent in half, as if someone had crushed it over a knee.

"Cindy!" he screamed and stepped in and slid on something wet. He looked down.

Blood.

Somewhere, off above the ridge, he heard Darrell giggling.

Chapter 32

The Sheriff came. So did the dogs and the deputies and the Alabama State Police and, heck, maybe even the National Guard. Lots more uniforms than last time. They all trooped up, stared at the house, stared at each other, and then stared at Aaron sitting on the berm at the end of his driveway, his arms clasped around his knees and rocking back and forth, crying. Then the uniforms trooped into the house and did whatever sheriffs and deputies did in a house that had been savaged, ripped, destroyed, sacked, and plundered, blood everywhere, everywhere, but no bodies. None. Where could they be?

Aaron knew.

Dad stood with him, not angry — shocked. And fearful. Dad stared at the Eckhart house fearfully. Dad was, for the first time Aaron could remember, actually fearful.

That's rich.

Dad was the fear inspirer. The fear bringer. But this was something he had never encountered, not even when he stormed the beaches of Normandy and raged across Europe or blasted his tank through hordes of North Koreans and Chicoms. That was nothing. War was a horror he recognized.

This? This was something he could not even fathom.

Aaron could.

Sheriff Oakley circled Aaron, keeping a safe distance, his eyes fixed on Aaron as the pivot point. Occasionally, he broke the circle and made forays to the Eckharts' to ask or answer a question, then out to the yard to look at something, then to the pasture fence to stare up the ridge, but always came circling back. And always asked the same questions. And Aaron always gave the same answers:

"Boy, how'd you discover this?"

"I went over to play with Cindy and Gary and Stan. Found it like that."

"Did you hear anything?"

"No. It was silent. Not even locusts."

"How'd you get so torn up?"

"From earlier."

"Earlier?"

"Yes, sir. We all went up to the ridge this

morning."

"Thought I told you to stay away from there, son."

"You did, sir. But Cindy's Grampaw got drunk and disappeared and they were afraid he got lost up there somewhere, so they asked Connor and me to help look for him."

Which was a shade of the truth: enough to explain to the Sheriff and Cody and Younger and the dogs and the State Police and the US Air Force, when they all went up there to take a looksee, just how all those damned kids' footprints were all over the collapsed Gulches. Satisfied by Aaron's explanation, the uniforms could then concentrate on just how the Gulches collapsed like that, and maybe one or two of 'em — maybe even Sheriff Oakley himself — would wonder if a force pow'ful 'nough to dig its way out of a caved-in tunnel could, might just could, cave-in the entire back of a house and toss the kitchen around as if made of Lego.

Watcha think, Sheriff?

The Sheriff had no earthly idea. See, this wasn't a horror he could fathom, either.

But I did. And I tried to tell you, Sheriff, but you didn't believe me the first time.

Look what happened.

"Drunk, huh?" The Sheriff pushed his hat back and went faraway as the beginnings of a theory formed somewhere in his head, but one so wrong, it was almost laughable. A Sheriff had to deal with the real world, though, and, you know, sometimes, just sometimes, drunk people got all crazy and performed extraordinary feats of strength.

"Connor who?"

Aaron identified him and Sheriff Oakley dispatched a deputy and, ten minutes later, there was a shocked radio call and the Sheriff paled and left, and, a few radio calls later, some of the other deputies and State Troopers left, too, and the Sheriff came back and resumed his circling but did not ask any more questions, what he'd seen at Connor's house silencing him.

Aaron knew what he had seen. It more or less resembled the Eckharts'.

One trooper showed back up with Kathy and Sawyer in the back of his car; they both sat staring straight ahead throughout a conversation carried on nearby between Dad and Sheriff Oakley and an agreement reached; Kathy was released, but Sawyer wasn't, and Dad walked Kathy and Aaron up the driveway and shut them inside the house and took his shotgun and sat on the front porch, watching the distant troopers walk around puzzled and purposeless as night gathered.

"What'd you tell the cops?" Kathy's fierce whisper in his ear as they huddled in her bedroom. He told her. She nodded. "That's good."

What about her? "Nothing." What did Sawyer say? She looked at Aaron scornfully. "Sawyer never talks to cops."

So, they were safe. From Sheriff Oakley, at least.

Not the Cryman.

And not Dad.

"You two stay in the house. Don't even think about going outside," he'd yelled as he loaded the Browning. "There's some kind of motorcycle gang or a bunch of hippies after everybody around here, sacrificing them to the devil or something, and they'll get you, too!" He'd pointed his spear hand at them both, and Aaron struggled to keep from bursting into laughter.

Motorcycle gang? Bunch of hippies?

Wish it was, Dad.

But you did get that "sacrifice to Satan" part right.

Dad stared at Kathy, an ugly light in his eyes. "And if that Sawyer boy so much as looks in this direction, I am going to kill him. You hear?" A warlike sweep of the shotgun. "Wouldn't surprise me if he was part of this!" and Dad went outside, mounted the porch, a fearful sentinel.

At least you're right about Sawyer being a part of it, Dad.

"It should have worked," Aaron said.

Kathy said nothing, just hugged herself.

"There was five... seven of us. Sawyer said that was a magic number. We did what Aunt Mary said, went after it." He paused. "She lied to us."

"She doesn't lie," Kathy said.

He blinked at her. "How do you know?"

"She doesn't," but offered no further explanation.

"What are we going to do?" Aaron asked.

She offered no answer.

Night came.

Mom did not come out of her room, so Kathy and Aaron made peanut butter and banana sandwiches and ate them without appetite and stood in the picture window and watched the flashing lights across the road as cars and pickup trucks cruised up and down; the neighboring farmers and their families all taking a look at the murder house, slowing as they passed and craned their necks, and then looked over and saw Dad sitting there, grim, armed, protecting his family from the hippie drunk Grampaws.

Like that would do any good.

Kathy stared through the picture window at the back of Dad's head, just a silhouette of skull and shotgun barrel in the fallen light. "He won't shoot Sawyer," Aaron said.

She snorted, "Like Sawyer would let him."

Aaron, perversely, felt a sudden urge to defend Dad. "Let him?" He gaped at her. "Dad's been in two wars. Sawyer's just a kid. Dad could shoot him whenever he wanted."

"Sawyer's far from being a kid."

"You know what I mean. Dad's tough. Sawyer wouldn't stand a chance. Just because he's your boyfriend—"

"He's not my boyfriend."

Could have struck Aaron with a hammer. "What?" he rounded on her, mouth open. "What are you talking about? Did you guys break up or something?"

"He was never my boyfriend," her voice cold, her eyes locked on Dad's shadow.

"But..." he spluttered, "You're always running around with him! I saw you two kissing, for God's sake!"

"Did a lot more than that," she smirked and Aaron flushed.

Well, yeah, go figure.

"So how is he not your boyfriend, then?"

Kathy's face now glacial, her eyes bore into the back of Dad's head and Aaron wondered why Dad did not scream and leap to his feet to pull the two icicles out of his skull. She whirled on Aaron. "You don't understand a damn thing, do you?" And she flounced off towards the bedrooms. Her door slammed a second later.

Aaron blinked. Apparently not.

Chapter 33

Aaron sat in the window. No moon, the night pitch black, and Dad still on the porch, still armed, still on guard duty, but that didn't matter. Not at all. This was the Cryman's night. Any moment now, it'll show up and rip more heads from more bodies and take them all back to its brand spanking new home, freshly dug under the collapsed Gulches, and hang them on the walls. Teach the heads to sing Cryman songs, maybe stage bite fights.

Aaron wondered what special punishment the Cryman had in mind for him. After all, he'd walked its Thorny Path and then tried to bury it under tons of earth.

Which, in hindsight, had been a really

stupid plan, and he knew it was a stupid plan when first proposed, but you want to believe. You want to. You want magic numbers and friends to overcome evil, even an evil that *lived* under the earth, lived there. Probably thought the cave-in was a shower. Laughs and makes his puppet-head slaves eat a way out, as previously considered. Then it goes looking for the bombers, just as Aaron predicted.

Yep, Thorn Boy, sumpin' real good in store for you, beginning with a series of unspeakably revolting acts with Gar and Steve and Cory, then Darrell. Followed by Stan and Gary and Grampaw and Granma. Miss Dunphy.

Cindy.

Cold filled his veins. The Cryman will save Cindy for last.

She was probably still alive, tied up in the cave until the Cryman returned and tossed Aaron at her feet, then skinned her for a few hours to throw her, skinless, to the Gar head, which does unspeakable things to her as she screams and screams and screams, begging Aaron to save her. But he can't because the Cryman has tied him to the wall and ripped Aaron's eyelids off so he has to watch her torture. Then the Cryman slowly pulls Aaron's intestines out through a small hole in his stomach, one link at a time, eating them and laughing as the other heads, set up like an audience, also laugh and then, in turn, have their way with Cindy.

"No," he whispered to the night.

The locusts and crickets called to each other as if everything was normal but there was a mist hanging off the Spanish moss obscuring everything and he wouldn't see the Cryman until it was right in front of the window, its shark teeth wide and happy, its hairy arms reaching through and dragging him out to play. Death was inevitable, so just sit here quietly and wait, try to minimize damage to the house.

Not that he could. The Cryman had wrecked Cindy's house, so why would it spare Aaron's? It wanted to grab Kathy – and eventually, Sawyer, too – which required a bit of rummaging around. Dad, alerted, would run inside waving his shotgun around and Mom waving her Bible and then... head-puppets.

And the Cryman won't stop there. Cousins, uncles, fifth nephews twice-removed, Aaron's entire branch of the human race will end up as head-puppets. No mercy for anyone anywhere in his genealogy.

Mercy.

Aaron glanced up through the tree branches, but the mist was too thick. Not a star glowed. God hid His Face from him: Aaron had chosen a path too evil for the Father to forgive, so don't even think about asking for mercy now, you evil, evil child. You heretic. Blasphemer.

Walker of the Thorny Path.

But, God, I need your mercy because, God, nothing is going to defeat the Cryman but

You. Yourself. Just You.

Aaron scoured the upward reaches of sky and heaven, hopeful look on his face, straining against the mist for something: a sign, a comet, a celestial wink, anything to tell him that God had Forgiven and Will Rescue.

Nothing.

You're on your own, Thorn Boy.

Aaron took in a long, slow breath and watched the night thicken and dampen in preparation for the Cryman's entrance. These were Aaron's last hours on earth. So what will I miss? Won't get to start eighth grade in a couple of weeks. Because of absence, yuk yuk. Come to think of it, quite a few Damascus students will be absent, which should make for an exciting first day as all the other kids whispered and hunkered and looked askance and wondered what in the blue-blazing hell happened to Gar and Cory and Steve and Connor. And Aaron and his sister, and all of their families.

Drunk hippies, someone says.

He almost laughed at that but saw it as inevitable. Sheriff Oakley needed resolution for all the deaths and disappearances and damage, and a bunch of drug-crazed drunken hippies running around the countryside selecting young kids for their nightly blood orgies in honor of Satan fitted just nicely, especially with that Sharon Tate and the bloody "Pig" on her door. Country's going to hell, so Aaron fades into legend, becomes a ghost story.

And the Cryman will search for other kids with trouble in their soul, recruit someone else to the Thorny Path.

Aaron shivered and tallied more things he would never do: go to high school; drive a car; go to college; look through the Palomar Observatory telescope. Kiss a girl.

Well, he'd done that. And when Cindy got here, all skinned and screaming, he'd kiss her again.

Forever.

Something moved on the far corner of the lot.

Aaron froze, watching a black-on-black shadow float between a cluster of pine trees just behind the garage. Death approaches: his, Kathy's, Dad's, and Mom's, too. Maybe he should scream, bringing Dad from around the front of the house to see 'wot the hay-il's da matter wid yew, boy?' But, really, why? If tons of falling earth didn't faze the Cryman, what would a measly shotgun do?

Just keep quiet. Accept your fate. Maybe Mom and Dad and all the fifth cousins twice-removed will be spared.

In the morning, when Dad came off guard duty, he'd walk inside, bleary-eyed and muttering about drunk hippies, and then look up and see the torn screen in the den window and the blood around the sill and then rush into Kathy's room and see the same torn window and blood and then cry out, "My son! My daughter!" and Mom would rush out, the two of them collapsing into each other, their losses multiplied.

But at least you won't be head-puppets.

The shadow flowed to the back of the garage and stood there and Aaron idly wondered why the Cryman was being so discreet. Obviously, it had no concern about ripping houses apart even in broad daylight so, c'mon, make your move. Get this over with.

Hold on...

That shadow looked a little small, half the size of the Cryman. Did the avalanche smoosh it down or something? Like that meant anything: apparently, even a half-pint Cryman can tear the sides of houses open and play with stoves like they were Kenner Easy Bakes.

And wait... two shadows, one half the size of the half-sized Cryman, like a companion shadow clinging close to the first one.

Did the Cryman have a kid?

The shadows slipped down the side of the garage, stopping every foot or so to test the area before advancing a few more feet... taking an oblique path, but Aaron knew they were coming for him.

And then they didn't.

The shadows made a run at the washhouse and stood for a moment, somewhat blended together but still discernible as two separate entities. Aaron wondered what a Cryman kid was like: barracuda teeth instead of shark? Maybe wants to play baseball with the puppet-heads before eating them. Both shadows tiptoed past Aaron's window. As he watched, puzzled, the bigger shape resolved itself.

Not the Cryman.

"Sawyer!" Aaron yelped.

The shadow leaped like it had just been bitten and Sawyer was suddenly at the window, finger pressed to his lips and eyes wide with fright. "Pipe down!" he hissed.

The little shadow was still pressed at Sawyer's hip. It too, resolved itself and Aaron almost fell down. "Connor!" he squeaked.

"I said pipe down!"

"But... but..." Aaron spluttered. "Connor! My God! What happened?"

"He can't talk!" Sawyer looked like he wanted to pull Aaron through the window and strangle him into silence. "And you gonna get us caught!"

The implications of a silent Connor and an aroused Dad finally forced its way into Aaron's brain and he nervously checked behind him for the looming shotgun-wielding Protector of the Family. Lowering his tone, but not his confusion, Aaron whispered, "How is he with you?"

"He came to the house, found me. We came here."

All Aaron could think was, Connor knows where Sawyer lives? No one knew where Sawyer lived, not even Kathy. It was taken on faith that Sawyer lived in the woods with a tribe of wolves and hillbillies and iffn yew knows wots good fer ye, you don't look for him But King-of-the-Dweebs Connor knew where he was.

Aaron felt a bit lesser. "So what happened?" This to Sawyer.

"Tolja, he cain't talk, so I don't know." Sawyer, irritated. "Musta been bad, though," and he looked down at his shadow twin with a mix of fear and sympathy, and Aaron chilled as he took in Connor's matted hair and torn face, half his clothes gone, the ones remaining bloody, and his zombie eyes staring back at Aaron.

Yes, musta been bad.

"What are you doing here, then?" Aaron asked Sawyer.

"Come to see your sister," Sawyer whispered. "But you'll do."

Aaron couldn't believe it. "Are you trying to get killed or something? Dad's right out front with a shotgun and you wanna play kissy face?"

"Didn't come here for that. Your Dad's sound asleep. And, if you keep your voice down, he'll stay that way!"

Aaron tsked. So much for Dad's protection. "What do you want, then?"

"We gotta go back and see Aunt Mary."

"What?" Aaron was stunned. "Right now?"

"No," Sawyer said, "Too many cops around. Tomorrow night. Go on up to Ochs' Store. I'll be parked there waiting."

"Are you crazy? She got us into this mess!"

"And she'll get us out."

"Sure she will," Aaron snorted and looked to see if Dad was coming around the corner. "What's the next Magic Number? Thirteen?"

Sawyer was about to say something, but then Aaron heard the sound of the front door knob jiggling. Crap! "Dad's coming in!" he whispered frantically, "Go, just go!"

"Tell your sister!" Sawyer said, and he and zombie Connor were gone.

Aaron threw himself into the bed and rolled into the sheets, hoping Dad didn't hear the flurry of mattress springs or Sawyer and company racing through the woods like an elephant. Aaron forced his breath into the rhythm of someone fast asleep. Dad's heavy footsteps crossed the living room, and then the gun cabinet door creaked open. Dad was putting the shotgun up.

After what felt like three hours, Dad entered the den. And stood. Obviously, he was watching Aaron, maybe trying to figure out if he was asleep or not. Aaron made sure he gave that impression.

Apparently with success, because, after a moment or two, Dad turned and softly walked away. Aaron kept up the pretense, congratulating himself as Dad reached the end of the hallway...

And went into Kathy's bedroom.

Aaron went still. Oh, no. Her

interrogation was about to begin. Soon, Dad would know all.

Forget the Cryman. Dad will eat their intestines, instead.

He listened. He strained. For quite some time. But nothing... and, puzzled, fearful, worried, drifted off. To nightmares.

Chapter 34

"Sawyer wants us to meet him at the store tonight," Aaron whispered across the breakfast table. Kathy didn't look up from her cereal. Gave no indication that she'd even heard him. Frowning, Aaron measured Mom, framed against the kitchen window, busy with something under the running water, and tapped a finger on his bowl. "Did you hear me?"

"Stop that whispering!" Mom snapped. Aaron, startled, sat back, gaping. Mom half turned around, glaring at him from under un-brushed hair. "You'll wake your father!" And she was back at the sink.

Well, Jeez, Mom, what was more likely to do that, Aaron's whisper or your screeching?

Annoyed, he raised an eyebrow at Kathy and bulged his eyes but she gave no sign of life.

Zombie. Like Connor.

He examined Kathy, unsure if she'd broken under Dad's relentless questioning last night or not. Seemed not; Dad hadn't yet fallen on him like some fire-breathing dragon screaming about bombs and magic numbers and whatever else Kathy gave up. But maybe Dad was just too tired right now and preferred to rest up before strangling Aaron. If so, you'd think Kathy would warn him of what's coming.

But no. Zombie.

Aaron shook his head and pushed back, and ignored Mom's glare because Mom was so ineffectual these days she was reduced to a mere irritant and went into the living room. He slid up to the window and made a surreptitious surveillance of the Eckharts' place. Yep, a couple of sheriff's cars still over there, but no one moving around. Probably the deputies were sound asleep, like Dad. Couldn't blame 'em; there was nothing to stay awake for. The Cryman was done over there. It had business with Aaron, but cops didn't care about that until the house was peeled open and blood splashed everywhere. Cops were good for what happened after, not what happens before.

He turned on the TV, keeping the volume down so (a) Mom wouldn't screech about waking his father and (b) he wouldn't wake his father. He'd prefer to keep breathing for a little while longer, thank you very much. The morning news out of Dothan was on and they were talking about crop prices and Aaron wondered why they weren't covering the Eckharts' house. Maybe they already had, for the two or three minutes they'd take to tell everyone in lower Alabama about a bunch of drunk hippies running around the countryside breaking into houses and spiriting away whole families. You'd think that would garner at least ten minutes, maybe even the entire show, but nope. What did you expect? Walter Cronkite gave Sharon Tate and her "Pig" door maybe thirty seconds a night. Soon it will be twenty. Then five. Then none.

Maybe that's why no Cryman last night: it was waiting for the heat to die down.

Aaron chilled. When Cindy's and Connor's parents' disappearance became nothing more than a once-a-week five-second reminder, then the Cryman would come lumbering out of its new hole and find Aaron. By that time, everyone will have bought the drunk hippie-gang story, clucking their tongues and gossiping about it on the party line, with the conspicuous absence of Miss Dunphy, and wondering where all them damn hippies were hiding. There was a very good chance a couple of damn hippies in Enterprise and Dothan, which was about the total number of hippies in both places, will get thrown in jail, protests of innocence notwithstanding. Hippies lie, anyway. And the Cryman would be safe from discovery, spending its days watching puppet-head theater, its nights hunting for troubled souls.

Like Kathy's.

Aaron's lips pressed into a grim line. You know, maybe he'd gotten this all wrong. Kathy's soul was the troubled one. Not his. The more he thought about it, the more sense it made that *she'd* called the Cryman instead of him. Specifically, her carrying's-on with Sawyer had called it. Darrell had been eaten, his Cindy, too, and Connor was a zombie, just because Kathy liked to sneak out of the house and run around all night in Sawyer's crap truck. And he wasn't even her boyfriend.

Perhaps he should name her to the Cryman.

He sighed. We've already had this conversation, remember? You can't give your family to the Cryman, at least intentionally. The Cryman already took that liberty, anyway, having first snacked on Darrell, so no quotas need filling. So why didn't it go straight after Kathy in the first place, instead of using Aaron as a pit stop? If she was the scent, then the hunter should have followed it right to her bedroom window and stood outside, grinning its shark smile at her, instead of at Aaron and his telescope. It should have snapped her up and gone away, leaving the rest of them stunned and grieving at the bloody loss, but leaving them, just the same.

Perhaps it merely wakens at the scent. Then eats whatever is in the way.

Which was a whole other dynamic — the Cryman as juggernaut. Not Juggernaut, the X-Men enemy, who can be easily beaten once you get his helmet off. But the force of nature — once loosed — cut an inexorable path through wood and dale and everyone within a fifty-mile radius. Awake from its unholy slumber, it stalked and eviscerated and grinned and offered the Thorny Path to Aaron and any other troubled soul willing to walk it, building a legion of the damned that called out the names sending the golem on its missions.

All because Kathy crawled into Sawyer's truck.

He felt like running back into the kitchen, yanking the cereal bowl out of her hand, and dumping its contents all over her head while screaming, "See what you did? See?" She had put aside her paper dolls and playing tag and lying on the grass watching the clouds go by and put on a miniskirt and Susan Dey mascara and danced to the Cowsills and the Monkees and crawled into Sawyer's car, didn't ya? Had to embrace everything the devil offered, Jack Flash and Honky Tonk women and I'll lay your soul to waste.

And the Cryman stirred from its hole and went hunting.

It's not me. It wasn't me. It was never me.

Aaron didn't call it, had not invoked spell nor demon, didn't have an inkling of its existence enough to even think about calling it, yet the monster was on him, grinning its shark teeth and taking brother and girlfriend and friend (sort of), and asking for more. Name the ones you hate and become Nemesis, become vengeance, become... one of us. And Aaron did. And the Cryman laughed and ate the named and the innocent, growing stronger, pulling houses apart and gorging on the sweet, sweet flesh of the troubled as Aaron walked the Path scoured and torn until he rose from the bloody vines with his own shark teeth, his own giant arms, and a Hole of his own in the Gulches.

I did not call you. I do not want this.

But how do I stop?

Miserably, he stared at the TV. He couldn't stop, anymore than an avalanche can be turned or an earthquake softened. The Cryman must run its course, eat more souls, imprison heads. Aaron, carried on this tide, ripped and torn and left empty and eaten, the pain and agony of all his doings a constant companion, the heads of the named his constant reminder of the Path he chose.

Chose.

You could have gone the other path. You could have chosen the Dark one. But, no, no, the exultation of naming was a joy, wasn't it? Even the scouring of the thorns, the gasping pain of it, had a certain pleasure. An earned pain, like a wound on the battlefield. But you weren't the Allies breaking through the Siegfried Line, you were the Waffen SS marching lines of Jews into the showers, the

Cyklon B ready in your hand, smug, the self-righteous rage in your soul, a stink that wafted across graveyards and woke monsters.

Kathy may have called it, but Aaron kept it coming back.

A satellite picture on the screen showed a massive whirl of clouds spread out like a galaxy, superimposed on a map of the Gulf and the US, the arms reaching and reaching, hungry and unstoppable. "Camille," the weatherman called it.

"Cryman," Aaron corrected.

THE CRYMAN

Chapter 35

"This is really stupid," Aaron said.

Kathy and Sawyer didn't respond. How could they? This surreptitious rendezvous – guaranteed a Dad-beating when they made their way home, that is, if Dad was up from his day-long nap yet. Didn't even show for dinner – was one kind of stupid. Aaron and her slipping out of the house and up to Ochs as the sun set and then climbing into Sawyer's truck right next to Connor, who refused to give up his proximity to Sawyer, which really angered Kathy until she got a good look at the little dweeb and then, well. Riding out to see the Error Witch to get even more bad advice was another kind. Put the two together...

It was cloudy and the truck's cockeyed headlight made seeing almost impossible but, somehow, Sawyer found the track and pulled off and they were standing by the trail, Connor practically glued to him and Aaron examined the little jerk and, well. Couldn't blame him. Sawyer was about the only member of this group who had a fraction of a chance against the Cryman, should it come barreling out of the trees, and after what Connor had seen...

What had Connor seen? Dunno. He can't talk. Maybe was deaf, too, since he didn't respond at all to Kathy's cussing and Aaron's queries. Aaron wasn't even sure if he was fully conscious. "Lay off 'im, " Sawyer had ordered, and that was that.

Wind fussed at them, gusting here and there and swaying the devil trees into futile clutches at Aaron's shirt. The clouds ran hard before the wind, occasionally breaking open to reveal a star-lit and sliver-moon sky, a glimpse of redemption in the blackness before the clouds swallowed it. "Camille's coming," Sawyer said.

Cryman, Aaron corrected.

Demons moaned around Aunt Mary's house, her porch rocker oscillating on its own, perhaps some broken soul taking advantage of her absence. The red glow flowed out of every window and crack and, as they approached, Aaron made out a couple of figures standing either side of the door. Oh no, Aunt Mary's hellguards, slavering and craving human blood but no, they were small, about Aaron's size so, what, imps? Still deadly, but there was a familiarity about them... and one of them had white hair.

Aaron stopped dead in his tracks. "Cindy!" he yelped.

And Gary.

That stopped all of them, Sawyer and Kathy in consternation, Connor in zombie mode, Aaron too astonished to do anything more than stutter and spazz up and down the steps. "Cindy!"

What should he do? Should he run up and gather her into his arms and scream his relief and terror and wonder and comfort her and ask her what happened, what happened?

"What happened?" he managed, without the gathering in his arms, because he didn't know how to do that.

She was red-lit and wind-gusted and merely stared at him. Gary stood like a statue, offering nothing. That's because it was a stupid question. Aaron already knew the answer and shuffled and didn't know what to do with his hands. "Stan?" he asked softly.

Here Cindy reacted, turning to her brother and both of them reached hands in placation at each other, but didn't quite touch, and Cindy burst into tears and this Aaron understood and he was up and swept her into his arms and held her tight to him, her shudderings and sobs the release of terrors. "I'm sorry, I'm so sorry," he whispered over and over.

"He saved us," mourned into his shoulder. "We ran, but he stayed. We saw..." and her voice trailed back into the sobs.

Aaron looked over her at Gary, grim and solid, his hair a beacon in the night. "It got Grammaw," he said and Cindy's sobs renewed and Aaron stroked her hair because he did not know what else to do. "How did you get here?"

"We just came," Gary said, simply.

"But... how?" And he knew it was another stupid question. This was sanctuary, the only safe place in the whirlwind bearing down on them, the means and method unimportant if you knew where to go. Cindy knew where to go, and Gary was smart enough to listen.

"She's waiting," Gary said and gestured at the door. Cindy pulled back and nodded and the two of them melted, somehow, into the devil shadows on either side and watched... and Aaron felt a chill in the pit of his stomach because something was different.

Something about them was different.

Gary was subdued and internal, not offering a single insult. Cindy was expectant, like a soldier on the eve of battle. Aaron hesitated but Sawyer, with Connor in tow, mounted the steps and walked right in without knocking.

Aaron was sure trolls were jumping all over the idiots about now and he remained hesitant as Kathy followed, barely glancing at either Cindy or Gary. The trolls can have her next while Aaron stayed out here with them, whistling manfully until the demons were sated and then strolled back to the truck and figured out how to drive the three of them to, say, Mexico.

But the wind pushed and the rocker turned malevolently in his direction and Cindy pointed almost with violence at the door and said, "Go!"

He skipped inside, the door slamming shut behind him.

It was strangely quiet, almost peaceful, in here. The red light was not the hell-glow of demon eyes as he expected, but several shaded candles. Why Aunt Mary insisted on red glass covers for them, he could only guess. Made the occasional appearance of His Satanic Majesty more comfortable, he supposed. Or got her used to the Lake of Fire.

Which, given her appearance, is where she'd be heading off to any moment now. She was hunched at a rickety table, the top of it carved in runes and covered with wax candle stubs, burn marks, and suspicious stains. The grave-cloth draped over her head didn't hide the weariness on her face, the look of someone ready to just lie down and die. She was holding an open Bible and staring hard at it, which was truly creepy since her white orbs were just as blank and sightless as before, yet she muttered, as if reading it aloud.

Aaron strained to hear but the words

were odd, off rhythm. It took him a moment to realize she was speaking them backwards. Shivers ran up his spine.

"Aunt Mary," Sawyer spoke.

Her incantation heightened and became more rapid, the words indistinguishable but with a meter to them, a cast, and something swirled about her dark and hungry. Alarmed, Sawyer took a step back, dragging zombie Connor with him, and Kathy's eyes widened.

Aaron stood quietly. He read the intent of the chant: Aunt Mary sought strength. For what, he didn't know, and *how* he knew that he also didn't know but it was as clear to him as the hell light.

"Aunt Mary?" Sawyer, concerned, peered hard at the tranced witch. "Do you hear me?"

Her answer was to speak even louder and faster, her voice reaching a crescendo in a shriek rivaling what howled around the eaves. Sawyer and Kathy clapped hands to ears, Connor didn't — deaf or uncaring — but Aaron leaned forward eagerly, fascinated by her babble. The dark thing at Aunt Mary's shoulders lifted and flowed and was tall behind her, regarding them balefully. It wasn't a trick of the light or heightened imagination; something was there. Aaron regarded it with more interest than anything, although he understood how dangerous it was.

He wasn't the only one. "Auntie!" Sawyer dropped his hands into combat stance and stepped forward and reached for her...

...and everything went silent.

The wind, the chanting, all.

Sawyer snapped his arm back, frowning, the three of them looking about uneasily while Connor kept his coma stare straight ahead. It was like the Cone of Silence had come down, shutting out the rising storm, except they could hear each other. Aaron peered hard, but the dark thing was also gone. He understood that. Can't keep a demon once it's done with you.

"Auntie, are you all right?" Sawyer asked.

"I'm tired." It was a whisper from the grave, a claw against a tombstone, rasping and empty, what a skull would sound like.

"Do you want to rest, Aunt Mary?" Sawyer sounded concerned. "I can help you to the bed," and he moved to take her up.

Irritably, she waved a claw at him. "I rest by and by. What you doin' here?"

"We want your help again, Aunt Mary." Sawyer had stepped back out of claw range. "We in trouble."

"You are that." Aunt Mary's shroud bobbled at the Bible. "It walkin' hungry now. It walkin' this way."

"What?" Aaron spun, sure the Cryman was about to burst through the flimsy door, its shark teeth grinning and grinding for them, but Aunt Mary just laughed.

"Ain't come here, boy," she jeered, "It know me. It follow the Thorny Path. It follow you," and the claw pointed at him.

"Me?" Aaron stepped back. "I didn't call

it!" and he looked full at Kathy who frowned at him, not comprehending, but she was always a quick study and her eyes widened. "What? You think I did?"

"I *know* you did!" Aaron stormed. "You and him," he made a contemptuous gesture at Sawyer. "The two of you running around. You called it."

Kathy made a *twa*! sound of dismissal while Sawyer bobbed forward and said, "Boy, you crazy?"

Aaron was all set to explain exactly how the two of them, filling the air with the scent of defiance and trouble, had rooted the Cryman out of its hole, when Aunt Mary snorted, "Ain't them."

Aaron tilted at her. "Who, then? Who called it?"

She dismissed the question. "Ain't matter now. Only thing that matters," and the orbs bore into him, "is what you gonna do."

Aaron threw up hands in exasperation. "Do? Do?" A repetition of words that, in other circumstances, Aaron would find hilarious. "What's to do? We already tried blowing it up, like you said," and he glowered at her.

"Didn't tell you do that," Aunt Mary sniffed.

Aaron kept waving his hands about to demonstrate further exasperation. "You certainly did! You said go right at it!"

"From the dark path. Not this one," and she flung her hand across the table, something clattering against one of the candle stubs. Aaron looked, and horror seized him.

Thorns. Three of them.

"Dark path, you end alone but the Cryman sleep. You on this one," she gestured at the thorns, "so you go the whole way."

Aaron, utterly bewildered, stared at her. "I don't know what you mean."

"You call," and her orbs bore into him.

"Call?" he gasped. "Call what?"

"Call," she said again, and laid her hands down on the table, resting her chin on them. Her eyebulbs spun and leaked and focused on Connor. "Oh, child, child," she whispered and extended her grave-cloth arms, and Connor slipped away from Sawyer and stood in front of her, blinking for the first time tonight, and he stepped into her and she enveloped him. The cloth hid everything but Aaron heard Aunt Mary speaking... something. Something ancient. Calming.

A balm.

The cloth parted and there was Connor, head resting on Aunt Mary's shoulder, tears leaking down his face but silent still. He stepped back into Sawyer, tears flowing, eyes fixed on Aunt Mary, who laid her head back on her hands. In seconds, she was snoring.

Aaron, baffled, took a step forward to shake her awake but Sawyer intercepted. "Let's go," he said.

"But," Aaron said, "I don't know what she's talking about!"

"Doesn't matter," Sawyer pushed him towards the door, "It's all she's going to say."

"But what about Cindy?" And Gary, don't forget Gary.

Aaron tried to turn around but Sawyer pushed him again. "Great, just great!" Aaron shouted and stamped out of the door and stopped over the threshold and sought Cindy but she wasn't there. Neither was Gary. The porch was empty, the rocker the only thing moving but with the wind this time, not demon hands.

"Cindy!" he called. Nothing.

"Cindy! Come with us!" Still nothing, no call back of "Coming" or "Wait for us!" Just the wind.

Sawyer pushed him again and Aaron rattled down the dangerous steps and looked back at Sawyer and Kathy and Connor blocking his way back to Aunt Mary to demand she release Cindy and, yeah, Gary, too, and let both of them come away, but they won't budge, not at all. "I told you this was stupid!"

Kathy shook her head. "No, it wasn't. She said you can call it. So, call it."

"I can't just call it!" Aaron yelled at her. "It's not like a dog or something!"

Kathy folded her arms. "But it'll come to you, right? So, you call it like she said. And then Sawyer'll kill it."

Aaron threw up his hands. "How?"

"With this," Sawyer said, and pulled out another revolver, a big one like Wyatt Earp used to carry, hefting it in the red light. Geez, how many Old West guns did this guy have?

Aaron couldn't believe it. "That? With that? We dropped a whole cave on it and it still lived! That won't even scratch it."

"This is different."

"No, it's not!" Aaron stamped hard on the ground like a two-year-old, he was so frustrated. "Darrell shot it with a Luger and it ate the gun!" And Darrell, too, don't forget.

Sawyer flipped the gun over and opened the cylinder, reached in and pulled out a bullet. "These are different." At that moment, the murder clouds opened and the sliver moon cast a single beam at the thin, metal case Sawyer held upright. The tip gleamed like moonlight itself.

Silver.

"Where did you get that?" Aaron breathed.

"I made them."

"Them?"

"Yes, them." Sawyer dumped the cylinder into his hand and Aaron saw five more bullets there, four of them silver-tipped like the one in Sawyer's fingers.

Five. Silver. Bullets.

Five.

Aaron, stunned, looked at Sawyer. "How?"

"I know how to do this stuff," Sawyer replied, somewhat miffed, as he reloaded the gun with the silver bullets and the one normal one, which Aaron supposed was a throwaway, given their target.

Aaron remained unconvinced. Silver was expensive and Sawyer couldn't even afford a headlight. "Where'd you get the silver?" he challenged. Because, Sawyer, bullets colored with a silver crayon wouldn't stop the Cryman, magic number or no.

Sawyer said nothing, but turned to Kathy, who shrugged. "I took Dad's coin collection from the drawer."

Dad's coin collection. The one he grinned and slobbered over like Simon LeGree. Gold and silver coins, Kennedy half dollars.

The wind tore back at that moment and threw clouds over the moon and Aaron looked at her as though she was crazy. Apparently, he conveyed that quite clearly, even in the dark, because she turned a hard eye on him. "Dad owes me!" she hissed.

Which knocked Aaron back, wind or no. Owed her? What the heck did Dad owe her?

That's easy, the same thing he owed all of them: to be a good Dad. Which he had never been and never would be, so money was a just compensation.

Wasn't it?

Connor had slipped into one of the many guardian shadows surrounding Aunt Mary's door, but he stepped out of it and into a moonbeam that chose that minute to spotlight him. He stared hard at Aaron, the tears dry, but his eyes held a ferocious light. "Kill it," he whispered, the first time Aaron had ever heard him not at full volume, "You have to kill it."

They all gaped at him, then Aaron gasped in frustration. Well, yeah, Connor, what the heck do you think we've been trying to do? With your bombs, no less. He threw his hands up in surrender, "Alright, alright, fine, great, so now if the Cryman doesn't get us, Dad certainly will or, or," frustrated point at the sky, "this storm or something else. We're dead no matter what, so..." So, Aaron, so what? He chewed on it a moment. "So we might as well go out heroes."

"Now you're talkin'," Sawyer grinned and Kathy smirked approval as did Connor and, for a moment, a slight one, Aaron felt some pride. Some.

But then reality came back and Aaron stared at the gun. "I don't think it's going to work."

"Maybe," Sawyer conceded, "but what else we got?"

The clouds flew by, framing a forlorn sliver moon. The wind scrabbled at Aaron, a slap of cold he didn't expect and he shivered. The red light behind the door pulsed and gibbered and laughed and carried across the sky, singing before the storm.

What else, indeed, did they have?

"Here?" Aaron asked.

Sawyer shook his head. "No. The Cryman won't come here. Aunt Mary's too strong." He paused. "The sawdust pile."

"Now?"

Sawyer nodded, grim.

Aaron stared at him, then at the clouds roiling about the moon. He peered to either side of the porch hoping Cindy and even Gary stood there and he could urge them to come away, but no one. Off in the woods to the left, he swore he saw a little touch of white, like a Q-tip bobbing among the branches.

"Let's go," he said.

Chapter 36

"Uh oh," Sawyer said.

Aaron looked up. He'd spent the time since they left Aunt Mary's searching for answers in his lap. All he'd found there was the certainty of being gutted and made a head-puppet. "What?" he asked.

Sawyer was peering at the remnants of his driver's side mirror. "We got company," he said.

Aaron's breath caught. Oh no! The Cryman was chasing them down the road! But then red lights flashed inside the cab.

Cops.

"Just be cool," Sawyer said as he pulled the junk heap over to the shoulder, shaking all of them half to death in the process. Aaron and Kathy, anyway. Connor didn't react, had gone back into zombie mode.

The deputies ran to the truck yelling and shining gigantic flashlights all over the place and yanked all of them out, yelling even more, and yelling even louder when they stripped Sawyer of the pistol. Click! Click! Handcuffs, Sawyer tossed into the back of one car, Aaron and Kathy and Connor — sans handcuffs — into the back of another, commanded by the same fat deputy who'd gone with Stan and Gary and Gramma to the house after Darrell got eaten. The fat deputy yelled, too, but mostly about the company they kept.

"That boy just all trouble, all trash!" meaning Sawyer, a sentiment Aaron was inclined to second. "Wouldn't be surprised if he the one doin' all this!" A conclusion Aaron found hilariously inaccurate.

Aaron also concluded, with some accuracy, that there'd be no going to the sawdust pile now, no calling of the Cryman, no putting six rounds, five of them silver, into its shark teeth. The fat deputy probably wasn't going to allow that. Sheriff Oakley wouldn't allow it, either, and Dad, well, he'll probably save the Cryman future effort, eviscerating Aaron himself and turning him into a head-puppet. Along with Kathy. Especially when he finds out what his coin collection had become.

"Ain't you that preacher kid?" This directed at Connor, who, despite all the activity, remained zombie. The fat deputy's eyes widened as he paled and then spoke urgently into the car radio microphone in syllables Aaron couldn't make out. But he could guess: we got us some trouble here, boys.

The fat deputy drove down Damascus Road but, instead of turning left towards home, pulled into Ochs' Store and up to another cop car pointed across the road. Sheriff Oakley leaned against its bumper. "Thanks, Burditt," Oakley dismissed the fat deputy who, grumbling, let the three of them out, then drove away. Sheriff Oakley watched him go and then studied them by the feeble light glowing over the store entrance. Aaron saw Mrs. Ochs peer out of her living room window, frown, and then drop the curtain. No doubt, she was headed to the party line for a good hour of animated conversation about them kids under arrest, right now, right hyeah in my parking lot! Land's sake!

A gust of wind tore at the Sheriff and he grabbed his hat to keep it from sailing across the road. "Big storm coming," he said, peering at the ragged, angry clouds attacking the sliver moon.

"Camille," Aaron said. Cryman, he said to himself.

The Sheriff nodded. "That's the one. What are y'all doin' down at Aunt Mary's?"

Startled, Aaron blinked at him. "You know Aunt Mary?"

"Know most things around here, son.

Some I don't. Like, what you doin' with Sawyer at that voodoo woman's place."

And what can I tell you, Sheriff? That we sought Aunt Mary's advice about killing a monster, one you do not believe exists, one that's wreaking havoc across your county and stalks the Thorny Path with its eyes on me, waiting to be called. Based on her advice, we detonated buckets of illegal explosives, burying a Cryman you don't believe in for about oh, say, a second, an act propelling it into a massive killing spree. And then we stupidly sought her advice for the same problem a second time and all been headed to an inexplicable sawdust pile in the swamp so Sawyer could shoot it with illegal silver bullets when your Keystone cops waylaid us. A stupid plan, readily admitted, but, really, Sheriff, what else was there? Especially now that you and your idiot deputies had just put the kibosh on it... which may, or may not, be a good thing? And, oh yeah. Sheriff, Cindy and Gary are alive and hiding in the voodoo woods where they'll remain safe as long as Aunt Mary is alive, a very iffy proposition given her age and what hunted her.

Want me to explain all that?

"Just be cool," Sawyer had said. Aaron was. He said nothing.

The Sheriff grabbed at his hat again and frowned at the clouds. "Think I can guess," he said, "You went there to get some witchy charm, some kind of spell to protect you against everything that's happening. That was a waste of time. And money, if you gave her any. That's how she makes a living, doncha know. 'Cause ain't no charm or spell gonna help, although I think a little prayer would be good. That's because it ain't no ghost doing all this, no monster." He paused. "No Cryman, neither."

He put his full focus on zombie Connor. "It's some bad people, and you out here running around with that Sawyer boy is puttin' all ya'll at risk of running smack into those bad people. I know," the Sheriff raised a hand to stop Aaron's protest, "you been real hurt in all this. He" — finger point at Connor — "more than you. But this ain't helpin'. You gotta stay outta my way and let me catch these people."

"You can't catch them," Kathy said.

"What makes you say that, young lady?"

She shrugged, looking off. "Because they're long gone."

"You know something I should know?"

She was back on him, her look ferocious and intense and Aaron took a step sideways, wary. There was something in her eyes, a daring, a challenge, and the Sheriff read it and frowned but said nothing. Kathy blinked, then looked off. "No," but her tone said otherwise. She reached into her upper pocket and pulled out a cigarette.

The Sheriff regarded her. "You're too young to smoke," he said, but lit the cigarette for her with a pocket lighter. As the wind threw the smoke away, he added. "You're too young for everything."

Kathy cocked her head at that, but the look on her face was one of agreement, and Aaron was now thoroughly confused.

The Sheriff levered off the front of his car. "Sawyer gonna be gone for a while," he said to Kathy, "so I don't have to worry about him gettin' you into further trouble. And I think you might be more right than you know about them bad people being gone. Still, you shouldn't be out here at night anymore, not until we know for sure. So, don't be." He nodded at the car. "Get in, and I'll run you down the hill to your house." A pause. "Before I take this one" — another finger point at Connor — "to the hospital." Another pause as he placed a gentle hand on Connor's hand and guided him firmly to the car. "You in shock, son. Don't blame you, but we'll take care of you now." Gently, firmly, he placed the zombie into the back and held the door open expectantly.

"We'll just walk," Kathy said and flounced away with no further ceremony or word, not even bothering to look both ways before she crossed the road to the opposite berm and stomped down the hill.

"Suit yourself," the Sheriff called after. He pursed his lips, looked at Aaron, then looked up. "Storm'll be here soon. Best you hunker down until it's over," and nodded at him to follow Kathy.

Hesitating, Aaron considered the efficacy

of a ride over a hike, then Connor turned his head and stared intently at him. "Kill it," he mouthed, and turned back into a zombie. Hastily, Aaron sprinted across the road and towards Kathy's striding figure, dim in the Sheriff's headlights. He looked back at the Sheriff's silhouette still placed against the front of the car, where Aaron guessed he would stay until the two of them cleared the driveway a hundred yards farther on. Couldn't see Connor anymore. Thank God.

Stumbling over unseen rocks, Aaron caught up to her and gasped, "Dad's going to kill us."

She snorted. "Dad doesn't know we're out."

"What?" he blinked. "You think Dad doesn't know we were riding around with Sawyer?"

"No," she said, "'cause if he did, the Sheriff would have taken us straight home."

That made sense. "He'll know when we go back inside," Aaron pointed out. So we're dead, anyway.

"I'm not going back inside the house," she said, flatly.

"Huh?" Aaron almost fell across a big rock hidden in the grass. "What do you mean?"

"I'm not going back inside," she declared as they reached the top driveway and cut to the right, taking a beeline through the pine trees towards the house. Aaron looked around nervously. The gusty wind swayed the trees and their moss shrouds like a carnival funhouse, masking any movement beneath them. Perfect place for a Cryman ambush.

"How can you not go back inside?" Aaron protested as he scanned for shark teeth. "What are you gonna do, sleep on the lawn? With a hurricane coming?" Preposterous.

"I'm running away," she said, stopping on the edge of the driveway, just out of the porch light's reach.

What? "Running away?" Aaron spluttered, "How? Sawyer's in jail!"

"I'd never run away with him," she said, scornfully.

"But..." Aaron stared and he just didn't know what more to ask. Or say. A gust of wind tore through the upper branches, underscoring the absolute insanity of her stated intent.

"I need you to go into my closet and get the duffle bag that's stuffed back there. It's underneath a bunch of shoes, so you'll have to look for it, but it's there. Then bring it to me down at the sawdust pile. And don't get caught!" She jabbed a finger in his chest.

"But..." again, he was at a loss.

"Don't worry," she patted his arm, "I've got this all planned out. I'll be okay. I'll call you when I get where I'm going."

And his heart fell, just fell, an anvil dumped off a bridge. "Kathy!" he wailed, "Don't leave me!"

She caught her breath at that, her face sorrowful in the wavery light, but determined, too, and she pulled him to her, and there it was, the mother's love she'd provided all these years which was supposed to be Mom's job, but 99% of it she had reserved for Darrell, doling out an occasional spoonful Aaron's way but mostly, mostly, it had been Kathy's job. She'd been his rock, his comfort. And now...

"Aaron, I'm sorry, but I can't stay here one more night."

"But, why?" Which wasn't exactly what he wanted to ask. More like, 'why now?' With the Cryman killing them all, Darrell eaten, and a hurricane coming.

"Because Daddy's been raping me."

Chapter 37

"Where you been?" Dad's ugly voice flew out of the living room and slapped Aaron in the face as he cleared the kitchen door. Ordinarily, that would be enough to make him collapse in abject fear, but Aaron's nerves were seared beyond feeling. Beyond numbness. Because, ten minutes ago, Kathy, in quite graphic detail, had explained exactly what Dad had been doing to her for the past year. At least three nights a week. At least.

"Outside," Aaron toned. "Watching the hurricane."

Squeak of leather as Dad adjusted his chair. "Should watch it on TV," the disembodied voice floated around the corner and slapped him again. "You can see the rain bands on the radar." True delight in his voice. Dad liked weather. Storms, especially.

Of course. They wreaked havoc and destroyed lives. Just like he did.

"Where's your sister?" Another voice slap in a tone Aaron always interpreted, until ten minutes ago, as Dad's need to control everyone in the house. But, now, he knew it was calculation — where were certain people at certain times, and how difficult will it be to access certain people at later points of the evening?

"Outside watching, too."

"*Hmph*," a non-committal grunt and a further squeaking of leather as he settled, instant proof that Dad was, indeed, unaware they'd snuck out after dinner.

Aaron's turn for a question. "Where's Mom?"

"Sleeping."

Okay, everyone is accounted for: Mom is in the throes of another 12-15 hour coma, tossing and turning and occasionally whimpering, "Darrell!" before going quiet again; Dad, sated from last night's 'interrogation' – gawd, Aaron, how could you have been so stupid? – and rested from an all-day sleep, comfortably settled into his chair and entranced by rain bands. Probably had a beer and a bag of pig skins within reach. Dad is gonna spend the next few hours right there, then head into Kathy's room for another midnight interrogation.

Boy, are you gonna be surprised.

Aaron quietly slipped through the den, staying out of shadow and reflection view because he didn't want to be sidelined by a Dad request for another beer or some potato chips. Which would mean he'd have to see Dad. He didn't want to see Dad at all.

Because Aaron would kill him.

It was a thought so certain, so sure, that Aaron didn't even question it. If Dad demanded Aaron bring him something to stuff into his pig snout mouth, then Aaron, instead of fulfilling said request, would take the shotgun out of the gun cabinet, walk into the living room, and fire right into Dad's fat, dumb evil butt lolling piglike in that chair.

Well, not his butt; that'd be difficult since he was sitting on it. His chest. Without hesitation. Or, get the .38 out of the silverware drawer and empty it into Dad's stomach and then stand there, cold, dispassionate, as Dad gasped and wailed and stared at Aaron with incomprehension and confusion until Aaron spat, "For Kathy!" into his dying face.

Which will no doubt initiate some consequences.

Aaron's arrest, first of all, Sheriff Oakley slapping on the cuffs, shocked, uncomprehending because Aaron, cool, would not say a word, not one, about why, tossed into the back of the car alongside shocked Connor, who'd say, "You killed the wrong monster."

Maybe to you, Connor.

They'd throw Aaron in prison, where he wouldn't do very well, and eat gruel and break rocks, a big ball-and-chain stapled to his ankle, until the day they marched him off to the electric chair, frying him without hesitation because he had done the worst thing a son could ever do: murder his father. People will buy tickets to see that one.

Second, Mom loses everything. Everything. She'd always been remote, a specter and more so recently, but this would be a trauma too much, and she would simply disappear. No one would ever know what happened to her. Least of all Aaron.

Third, and worst of all, everyone would know what Dad had done to Kathy.

Not that Aaron would tell. He'd be cool. Even after days of relentless questioning and slapping around and having his fingernails pulled out, he'd stay cool. He'd go to the chair cool, silent, stoic. But, things have a way of coming out. They always do. Like when Aaron took a couple of extra comics from the drug store without paying for them and was all wrapped up with delight examining them in the backseat until Dad asked where he got those.

Probably the first time in history a kid got beaten half to death with a *Captain America*.

Let's say Kathy, in some futile effort to get the governor's pardon, whispered the terrible, terrible things she endured from Dad, and Governor Wallace, shocked, called the death chamber and dramatically proclaimed, "Release Aaron! He's a hero!" The warden would ask why and the governor would explain, and then there's Kathy, shamed. Marked. For the rest of her life. She'd have to go around masked.

So, while shooting the bastard would give Aaron an immense feeling of satisfaction, best not. Best to avoid Dad altogether. Just help Kathy to get away.

Aaron got past the door without a Dad command for refreshments and tiptoed into Kathy's room. Need to keep quiet so Dad's black heart doesn't trigger and he'd get to thinkin' and a pickin' and a grinnin' like the hillbilly he was, and then he'd lower the recliner and stalk into the bedroom, snuffling, questing, where's my daughter? Heh heh heh... Aaron could almost hear that evil laugh and his chest throbbed and his fingers itched for the shotgun and he stopped and breathed deeply. Get control. Just help Kathy to get away.

He pulled her closet light string and, quietly, moved shoes and dolls and fallen clothes around until the duffel revealed itself. One of Dad's old ones from Dubya Dubya Two, no doubt taken from the pile of duffels carelessly tossed in the back of the shed. The faded stencil was still readable: Name, Rank, and Serial Number, back when Dad was a hero.

Not a monster.

Carefully, Aaron dragged it out of the closet, ensuring he didn't knock anything over and bring Dad in here... heh heh heh.

Man, this thing is heavy.

"I've got some food cans in there," she'd told him, "and some coats and shoes." Food cans. What, did she intend to do, live in the woods? Live by the railroad tracks? Aaron set the duffel next to the chest of drawers and shook his head. Seemed like this running away idea was half-baked.

But it was better than enduring Dad.

Cautiously, Aaron peered out of the room and down the hall towards the back door. Okay, sneak down there without alerting Dad, slip outside and run down to the pile, hand over the duffel, a quick hug, and Kathy was down the creek trail, gone. Where? "Best you don't know," she'd answered, an indication that she had addressed the logistics of this crazy scheme at some length already, and Aaron shouldn't worry about it.

Except, this will no doubt initiate some consequences.

First, Dad, at some point in the evening, discovers his daughter-lover had gone. That will probably initiate a bad mood, and a Dad bad mood needs immediate venting on the closest available target. Guess who? Getting fingernails pulled out would be the least of Aaron's tortures. No matter how much he truthfully screamed that he knew nothing of Kathy's whereabouts, Aaron will end up armless, legless, and kidneyless.

Second, Mom would probably discern, through all the bellowing and rage, why Kathy had run off: her own daughter was supplementing, if not completely taking over, Mom's wifely duties. Now, what will that do to her? Send her to the shotgun, or turn her into a permanent specter? Aaron could only imagine.

Third, and most importantly, he will never see his sister again.

Aaron had been holding on to a somewhat forlorn hope that, in time, Kathy would resume her motherly duties as the two of them drifted back into the camaraderie and joy they had shared, before Kathy discovered boys. The loss of Darrell, the assaults on friends and neighbors and world views by the appearance of the Cryman, the arrest of Sawyer, all of that should eventually repair the breaches, heal the wounds, bring them together. But if she was hunched under a tarp next to some fire and eating hobo stew out of a tin can, then there's no healing.

I will be alone.

No Cindy, no friends, no sister. Schoolmates watching him with shocked and ridiculing eyes in class and the hallway, cafeteria tables emptying as he sat down. Dad and Mom refusing him entry into the house, throwing a sandwich out of the window for his dinner. Bereft, sorrowed, solitary. All because Dad was a monster.

Monster.

He blinked, pulled his head back into the room and stared at the duffel. Maybe, Kathy, you don't have to run away, live beside railroad tracks, and eat hobo stew. Maybe you can stay here, safe, unbothered, unafraid. Because, Kathy, there's another path.

The Thorny Path.

Quietly, Aaron stepped over the duffel and to the window, opened it, and dropped outside.

Chapter 38

Before Aaron had cleared the back of the wash house, fierce winds made of fists and stinging rain lashed and slammed him against the wall. Wow. Some storm. Dad must be doing a gleeful dance in front of the TV screen.

Aaron pressed against the building, trying to use the slight overhang to keep the rain off, but no go — it was driving sideways, a machine gun of water needles. He ducked his head and braced for a mad, blind run down the trail when, just as suddenly as it appeared, the rain stopped.

One band through. More to follow.

Aaron looked up. The sliver moon danced among torn and rotten black clouds that spun into wisps, then melded into a single mass, fragmented and climbed, cloudy fingers reaching for it and glowing with its light and their own internal frictions, all framed by sky. Uncertain, Aaron took a step off the wall...

...and saw the trail down to the pile. Clearly.

He blinked, more puzzled than scared. Was the sliver moon that bright? He thrust an arm into its light to see and no, it wasn't; his hand was barely discernible. He turned back to the trail, which was glowing. Actually glowing.

Unnaturally glowing.

It waved bone fingers at him, beckoned, urged him to walk this way, walk the death light, find your sister on this path.

This Path of Thorns.

Aaron gasped and slammed back against the washhouse, afraid. This was not good, not good at all. Angels did not light the trail, devils did, and any place devils wanted him to go was bad, very bad. Hesitating, he looked back at the house and the open window and thought, perhaps, maybe, I should abandon this silly venture, crawl back inside and hide in the closet, let things fall the way they will.

"Go," Aunt Mary whispered in his ear.

He started and pushed off and ran towards the corpse-lit trail, unwilling but compelled, a moth to the death lights, the wind whipping past his ears like gibbering demons, the path smooth and spongy, a comfort, nothing tearing at his body, no spiked thorns shredding his flesh; and he flew, flew, the storm boiling around him with ghouls and vampires riding its currents and sweeping the way before him as he ran the death trail, the graveyard road, his soul a feast for worms, forever. He hit the downslope as dead hands pointed the way, Darrell and Stan and Grampaw urging him faster, faster! This is the Thorny Path! This is your destiny!

And then it was gone.

Aaron froze, the blackness closing on him, buffeted by wind-tossed limbs and fallen vines draped in Spanish moss, the road no longer smooth beneath his feet but tilted and rocky, wet red clay and sharp stones. There was a rush of wolf wind and he was again lashed by the storm. Another band. But, this time, he had no protection, and the cold rain slapped and beat him and he knew he had been tricked. He was lost, helpless, and the Cryman reached for him in the dark. Then, the rain stopped, and the sliver moon came out...

...and he stood at the edge of the Magic Sawdust Pile.

It was quiet, as if no killer storm raged above. Something fluttered on the other side of the pile and Aaron's breath stopped. The Cryman!

"Aaron?"

Relief flooded through him and he almost fell to his knees as Kathy emerged from around the side, squinting and trying to make him out against the woods. "Here," he said, and stepped out.

She jumped and then laughed, "You scared me!" running over and giving him a quick hug. "I thought you were a coyote." Pause. "Or Dad."

"He's watching TV." A gesture upwards. "Watching this."

She frowned at the tearing clouds. "It's pretty bad. I'm soaked through. I should get going before it gets any worse." She looked around. "Where's the bag?"

"Kathy..."

"Is it back here?" and she pushed past him and rummaged around the underbrush.

"I didn't bring it."

There was a sudden, shocked, pause before she whirled on him and released another storm. "You IDIOT!" she shrieked, "You dumbbell! I NEED that!" and she shoved him and he fell back, hitting his tailbone hard on a rock. "*Oww*!"

She loomed over him, face a devil mask. "I told you! I told you! I've got to have it! It's got Dad's coin collection and food and everything I need to get away from here! I HAVE TO GET AWAY!"

He blinked up at her. "I thought the coins were silver bullets now."

She was on him, pounding at his head with her fists. "Not all of them, you idiot! I kept most of them for me because I've GOT to get away!' over and over as she beat at his forehead, unable to reach his eyes and nose behind his crossed arms.

Man, was she strong! "Stop!" he yelled. To no effect.

"You're supposed to help me! You're my brother! You're supposed to HELP!" More fists, more shrieks and Aaron rolled, throwing her off and scrambled to his feet and up the side of the pile in record time.

"Stop hitting me!" he cried.

She looked up at him, the sliver moon concentrated on her face. Stricken, wild-eyed, panicked, she fell to her knees and tears, half rage, half frustration, poured. "I'm not going back home!"

Aaron sat down but thought it wise to remain out of reach, "You don't have to."

"Well, then, you do!" she pointed a fierce finger at him, "You go back right now and get my bag!" said, with emphatic finger stabs.

"I mean, you don't have to run away. You can stay here, and you'll be safe. Because I've got a better idea."

She crossed her arms, suspicious. "What?"

"The Cryman."

She stared at him, unsure what she had heard. "What?"

"I'm going to call the Cryman." He paused, watching as the God of the sliver moon hid His Holy Face away in murder clouds, in holy disgust, in scorn. "On Dad."

She was silent, watching him. "That..." she said.

He leaned forward, anticipating, sure her face would break into joy and relief and she would dance up the side of the pile and hug him and thank him and say she was so sorry about the way she'd distanced herself these past months but it was Dad's fault and please call the Cryman, have it eat Dad, and make me free.

"...is the STUPIDEST THING I EVER HEARD!" and she was up the pile, all right, but not dancing, certainly not in joy, as her maniacal harpy claws reached for his throat.

"*Ack*!" he dodged out of the way, upending and tangling in his own feet and sliding down the other side of the pile.

"You idiot!" grabbing huge gobs of wet sawdust from the top of the pile and hurling it down on his head. The gobs were big enough to hurt. "There is no Cryman!"

"*Ow*!" he said as the fourth or fifth gob pelted him. Then, "What? What? How can you say that? You were just there, just there! At Aunt Mary's! You told me to call it! Sawyer was going to shoot it and you told me to call the Cryman..."

A joke.

It was all a gigantic, side-splitting, ridiculous joke to her. Everything was. This whole time, she'd been laughing at him and his tales of shark-toothed monsters. She had told him to call it so she could prove he was stupid, laugh at him and Sawyer as they stood there beside the pile looking foolish when no Cryman appeared, then she would scorn both of them into going back and getting her bag and they would do so, sheepish and stung, and she'd be away, away from Dad and Sawyer and Aaron and Alabama, forever.

She'd used them. She'd used him.

"But," he said, "Darrell. And Stan. And Gar."

"That's those stupid hippies, the ones who killed Sharon Tate!"

But... "You went to the Gulches with us. You saw it."

"I didn't see anything but your stupid friend blowing up some dumb tunnel!" And she glared at him, wind-whipped hair flying about her like Medusa, fists clenched. And he understood.

How could she believe in a Cryman when she faced a real monster every day and every night?

Dad.

"You go back right now and get my bag. Right NOW!" and she stomped her foot into the pile, slightly funny because she almost pitched forward as her foot sank in. "And stop talking about that stupid Cryman. THERE IS NO CRYMAN!"

"What the HELL is all this yelling?" roared out from the top of the trail.

Dad.

Aaron, on the other side of the pile and out of Dad's sight, froze. Kathy, on top of the pile and well within Dad's sight, paled, brighter than the sliver moon, her eyes almost rolling back into her head from sheer fright. She turned and faced the real monster.

"Just what in the HELL are you doing out here? In this weather?" Dad yelled, word cudgels driving the breath and resolve right out of Kathy. Paralyzed, her back to Aaron, eyes fixed on Dad, her chance to get away gone, now gone. Caught, at the mercy of the beast. She needed help. Her brother's help, the help she had counted on to make her safe, free her from this horror.

So, help.

Aaron scrambled out of the pile and stepped around where he could see Dad, who turned his murder gaze away from Kathy and straight at him. "What the... you get your stupid ass up that trail and into the house, boy!"

"No," Aaron said.

The wind tore at them and the clouds spun and the moon rolled and flexed and it was a night made for terror, but the expression on Dad's face — eyes popped out, his jaw dropped in sheer astonishment — almost made Aaron laugh. Almost.

"Boy!" Dad snarled. "Don't you sass me!"

In for a penny...

"We're not going back to the house," Aaron said. "Not with you."

A cloud whirled past the moon and everything went black, but then it was gone and funnels of light poured down, spotlighting

Dad, who took giant steps into the clearing and right up to Aaron. "Boy!" He hissed. "You better get yourself back up to that house right now before you go in an ambulance!"

This was the point during past similar encounters, when Aaron quailed and cried and, ducking a series of blows, scampered up to the house to await the further beatings necessary to punish such temerity. But, not tonight.

Not ever again.

Kathy needed his help.

Aaron stood taller, did not yield, became a rock. Dad, not used to this, stopped short, the confusion racing across his face. "I know what you did," Aaron said.

Dad blinked. "What?"

"I know what you're doing." And Aaron looked up at the stricken, frightened Kathy, and then back at Dad.

Dad furrowed his brow, glanced up at Kathy, then his face cleared. He took a step back, wary, and pointed a finger at her. "What kind of lies she been telling you?"

What the... lies? Lies? What girl lies about something like that? It's like Sharon Tate lying about being murdered, when all the evidence is right there in her ripped body. What kind of a completely evil bastard could call his daughter a liar...

A shock wave ran through Aaron and he knew, right then, that it wasn't Kathy who'd called the Cryman. Oh no. Not her. Not Aaron or Sawyer, either. Not even Darrell. Another scent had wafted over the fields and ridgelines and into the Gulches, the odor of rot and corruption and sulfur a savor to the red-eyed demons of lust and evil, the green stink a call, loud and pealing, waking the beast, the trouble a perfume to it:

Dad's.

Dad called it.

"'Cause that girl is a WHORE!" Dad's finger was a spear point, stabbing at Kathy, and she screamed in agony and sorrow and collapsed, whimpering, on top of the pile. "She out running around with them boys and showing herself! You don't think I don't know?" He glared at Kathy, eyes of lust and evil, and then back at Aaron, eyes of rage and blood. "And if I gotta check her every once in a while and see if she's still intact, that's my duty!" He raised a finger to the boiling sky. "My right as a father!"

Dad's face twisted into judgment, into self-regard and approval, and he turned it full on Aaron. "And you ain't got any right to interfere!" He reached down and lifted Aaron by his shirt. "Now, you get your ass back to the house!" And he flung Aaron aside.

Aaron landed hard on some rocks, the air driving out of him. "*Oof!*"

Dad watched him fall, then looked up at Kathy curled on the pile, still whimpering. "As for you," he said. And grinned. And began climbing.

Aaron struggled, trying to get his breath

back, looking around wildly for something he could use as a weapon, a tree branch, a board, a bazooka, anything, but there was nothing in reach. Gasping, he crawled over and seized Dad's foot, yanking as hard as he could.

"Let go!" Dad roared and kicked savagely, driving a boot into Aaron's chest and knocking him over, facing the trail...

...which glowed, sparkled, running with the death lights. And, standing at the top, Aunt Mary, her eyes whiter than the full moon, her claw finger extended, pointing at Dad. "Call," she said.

Aaron did. "Dad."

It wasn't Aaron's voice. It was something primeval, rising from times before the world was formed, when forces of pure fury shrieked and battered each other into swirls of proto-galaxy and half-formed stars, all seeking primacy, who would rule, who would wield the very stuff of the universe. It was an ancient call, an invocation, an appeal to darkness and light, justice and war, to troubles born and carried since the world was seas and half-light.

And was answered.

"*AaaAAuh! AaaAAuh! AaaAAuh!*"

Dad, halfway up the pile, turned, his mouth agape, his prey forgotten. "What the HELL was that?"

Thoom! Thoom! Thoom!

The sound was of something huge and terrible breaking through trees, its retribution shaking the ground, something now more monstrous than it ever was, more certain, following the savor, the scent, oh-so delicious, getting closer, getting louder.

Dad slid down the pile and stood, staring in the distance as trees cracked and fell.

Thoom! Thoom! THOOM!

A mass, a giant black shape, shouldered its way through swamp and vine, and stomped into the clearing. And stood, swaying.

And smiled.

Dad dropped back against the pile, his arms spasming for purchase, his eyes bulging with terror at the shark teeth looming over him. The heads were arrayed along the Cryman's waist and chest, all of them lit from within, their eyes glowing with hellfire, all chuckling and gnashing their teeth: Stan and Gar, Grampaw and Gramma, Mrs. Dunphy...

Darrell.

"Oh, smells so good!" The Gar head giggled.

"Like Baaar B Cue!" Cody and Steven, in chorus.

"Thanks for dinner, Aaron!" Mr. Connor's Dad, staring at him, gleeful.

And Darrell.

"Da-a-a-a-dy!" the Darrell-head cried. "I've missed you!"

Dad screamed. Piercing shrieks of sheer, pure horror. Kathy screamed, pure and high in disbelief, because there was no Cryman, was no... and this was just not happening, not happening at all, because there was no monster in the woods with laughing heads around its waist. Only Dad in her room at night. That's all.

No, Kathy, there are lots of monsters. That are pleased to meet you. Hope you guessed its name.

Aaron smiled. And watched.

The Cryman reached out with a giant, hairy arm and pulled Dad up above its head. Dad yanked at the giant hairy paw locked around his throat, gasping and choking. The nearest heads tore at his flailing legs, ripping out great chunks of flesh. Blood, black in the sliver moon, shot across the clearing.

"*Gaaaa!*" Dad tried to scream but couldn't. His bowls loosened and the air filled with the smell of sewer and death. The Cryman extended its free paw and Aaron saw a long, ragged talon emerge from the center. The Cryman flipped the paw around and drove the talon into the bottom of Dad's stomach...

And Aaron screamed, in great, white-hot pain as thousands of thorns suddenly whirled about him like a razor-sharp tornado, stabbing and coursing his skin from the top of his head to the bottom of his feet, shredding him, gouging every inch of him.

The air filled with screams.

Not Dad's. He was well beyond screaming as the Cryman slowly pulled the jagged claw straight up Dad's stomach, taking its time, delighting in every spasm of Dad's reaction, the heads jeering and begging for more. It pulled the claw out at the base of Dad's throat and cocked its huge, hairy head, staring at Dad's pain dance.

Then put its shark teeth against the long, gaping wound, and ate.

The thorns slashed and cut and drove Aaron harder against the ground, but he could still see as the Cryman slurped and sucked at Dad's innards like someone eating an orange until only bloody shreds were left, what remained of the ghastly pulp stuck to Dad's flapping skin. The Cryman licked its lips and lowered the carcass so the puppet-heads could eagerly lick it, then flung the empty skin at Aaron.

It floated, more than fell, at Aaron's feet. It was an empty, gutted thing, a paper sack, what was left of a deer after hunters cleaned it. Then the eyes lit. "This is your fault," Dad said.

Aaron screamed louder. The thorns became thicker, buzzing like millions of hornets, seeking any bit of his intact skin left, and Kathy screamed and the Cryman tilted its head back in triumph, raised arms to the malevolent, pulsing clouds, and exulted. "*AaaAAuh! AaaAAuh! AaaAAuh!*"

And was gone.

Then the clouds closed in and the wind howled and the storm was on them.

Chapter 39

"Ready?"

Mom did not even turn her head when she asked it. She remained fixed on the garage door, closed and locked in front of the car. It wasn't even a question, more a point of reference. Whether you're ready or not, we are leaving.

"Yes," Kathy said, unnecessarily, from the front seat.

Aaron merely grunted, careful not to disturb the stitches across his cheeks and jaw and brow and face. And the rest of his body. What happens when you're caught in the open during the biggest storm to ever hit the Gulf Coast.

"How'd your sister avoid getting all cut up, then?" Sheriff Oakley, next to Aaron's hospital bed, had asked.

"She dove into the sawdust pile." I didn't make it, Sheriff. Storm was on me before I knew it. Yes, Sheriff, I'm lucky to be alive. No, Sheriff, I didn't see Dad out there anywhere looking for us. I don't know where he got to.

Sheriff didn't push it.

Weeks in bed. Aaron watched out of the window every day and every night, but nothing moved out there. No shark teeth. No puppet-head theater.

No need. The Cryman was sated now.

Sawyer came by once. Said Aunt Mary's shack, and Aunt Mary, were gone. Must have been the storm.

Yeah, the storm.

Sawyer never came back.

Connor came by once. He didn't enter the room, simply stood in the doorway regarding him. Then smiled, gave him a thumbs-up, and walked away. And never came back.

Cindy and Gary never showed. Just as well.

Kathy was in a coma for about a week and, when she awoke, was unable to speak. Or unwilling, Aaron never knew. Later, in a low, colorless voice, she told the Sheriff that the pile had, indeed, saved her and no, no, didn't see Dad. Not at all. But she did not speak to Aaron. Ever. He caught her staring at him from time to time. Looking at the scars. Then looking away.

He had a permanent tattoo of scars, coursed and gouged and unhealed, because, when you walk the Thorny Path, you carry the reminders. He wondered what the kids at his new school would call him. Mercator. Sketch. Road Map. Something like that. But then, in the middle of their sneers, they would look into his eyes. And stop giggling. And walk away.

He was going to be very lonely. As if he had chosen the dark path.

All paths lead to the same end, he supposed.

The house was sold, their stuff packed and on its way up north to Mom's parents. She wasn't a specter anymore. She had become whole again, like a phoenix rising from the ashes. Fire in her eye and she was determined to take them all far, far away from this place of reminders. She looked at Kathy with compassion. She looked at Aaron with concern.

Needn't worry, Mom. I will be all right.

I walk the Thorny Path.

She put the car in reverse and they backed down to the road and drove away.